Painted Blind

Annette V Hart

Annette Hart.

x 🐤

22/4/25

Dedication

To all my family for their continued encouragement and support, especially my husband and editor extraordinaire, Rob Hart.

Acknowledgements

A big thank you goes to my husband, Rob Hart, for his help with editing my story and saving my sanity, particularly in relation to the dreaded comma. I also welcomed the help of Kristen Chavez via her useful website ARTiculate Editing.

The cover image, which seemed just perfect for my book, was created by CentralTAlliance and obtained via iStockphoto.com. I also had the help of my daughters, Katy and Jenny, whose advice stopped me from procrastinating over decisions about the cover for far too long.

"Love looks not with the eyes, but with the mind,
And therefore is winged Cupid painted blind."
(*A Midsummer Night's Dream*, Act 1 Scene 1)

William Shakespeare

Prologue

While he walked across the worn stone flags of the great hall, his leather shoes padding gently, the small boy was concentrating very hard on two things: his feet and his hands. Ed ignored the happy crowds around him, wearing their most sumptuous finery for this prestigious occasion and watching his sedate, measured progress with amusement. His audience were a colourful blur as Ed focused solely on where the lofty vaulted ceiling met the far wall, the object of his quest lying beneath it. The sun streamed through the arched window centred in that wall, bathing everyone in a glorious golden light. Peeking out from under his dark, unruly hair from time-to-time to orientate himself, the boy checked that the direction in which he was carefully travelling was the correct one.

Putting one foot slowly and methodically in front of the other, his mouth forming the words of a silent prayer that he would not falter, Ed made his cautious way towards an enormous and ornately carved oak crib beneath the window. His eyebrows were drawn together in a frown of concentration. Otherwise engaged, he did not notice the indulgent smiles his meticulousness aroused from his parents.

In his hands, the young boy held a plump red velvet cushion trimmed with gold braid. He was trying hard to keep it horizontal and steady as he walked, not wishing to drop, and therefore ruin, the delicate necklace which was the personal gift he was presenting to the new baby.

When he reached the crib, Ed hesitantly raised the cushion to the Queen whilst trying to bend on one knee, wobbled, then shifted awkwardly to maintain his balance. The Queen laughed in delight, her broad smile crinkling the corners of her eyes and illuminating her otherwise plain face, clapping her hands together before taking the present from him. Ed sighed with relief; he had played his part in the proceedings today without mishap.

"Your son's growing into an exceptional young prince – he's a real credit to you, Irwin," Queen Averil said to the extremely tall and broad man by her side who completely overshadowed her.

He was her most honoured guest today: the King of Torland, their neighbour and High King of The Alliance.

Averil held up the dainty gold chain with a beautiful butterfly pendant that the boy had chosen with the help of his mother, who was sitting on the other side of King Irwin and beaming encouragement at her son. The shape of the butterfly was traced in gold and filled with slithers of a dark orange garnet that glinted in the bright sunlight dancing down from the high windows.

"It's the perfect gift for my gorgeous little princess," continued Averil, her voice filled with adoration for her new daughter while her eyes were irrevocably drawn back towards the baby.

"And a continuing symbol of the friendship

between our countries… and our families," added Irwin, smiling contentedly.

The young Prince, meanwhile, stood up, dusted down his tunic and rose on tiptoe to peer into the crib. He could only just discern the slight six-week-old baby surrounded by a mass of satin pillows, silky sheets and soft blankets. The tiny pink face was scrunched up in a scowl, wrinkling her brow, her head crowned with tufts of fine black fluff, looking as if she was irritated by all the unusual noise and movement around her. He thought she was probably deciding whether now would be a good time to cry.

He also wondered what all the fuss was about.

ACT 1

Chapter 1

Guthway 1274, in transit to Torland

Nell sighed deeply. She peered out of the wagon at the last vestiges of the lush pastures Guthway was famous for. Meadows rolled past in a bright green haze. Soon they would be travelling through the vineyards that graced the lower slopes of the mountains, row upon row of ancient tiered vines, before heading higher up to the rocky pass that cut through them. In less than a day, they would be crossing the border, passing from her homeland to the neighbouring land of Torland, and into the unknown. Although she was the eldest daughter and heir to the King of Guthway, this was the first time Nell had left her country, as tradition dictated, and she felt very nervous.

Not that leaving the places she knew and loved bothered her. It would be exciting seeing new towns, entering unfamiliar buildings and meeting different people. She welcomed the cosmopolitan atmosphere that Nell presumed she would encounter at the court of the High King. No, it was how she was bound to be treated that concerned her. As a royal heiress, Nell realised that she would be perceived as a spectacular prize. She had seen it before, even amongst the nobles and ministers of her own country: a gleam and a calculation in their eyes that had only increased with her age and marriageability. People would not be interested in her for herself and her own abilities, just the throne and therefore the power she represented. And it all came with an inordinate amount of suffocating attention to her every word, every action. In public, Nell always felt like a shell of her real self, no more than a fancy costume supposed to perform in a particular way. She found such events draining and was pleased Guthwayan custom had sheltered her from public duty for so long. But that was now changing; she wondered how she would cope.

For once, the fact that Nell had a commonplace appearance would not matter; men would desire her, or rather her status, whatever she looked like. The sparkle of the crown, real or metaphorical, would outshine her ordinary face. Her mother had been more fanciful, perhaps in an attempt to cheer her after some playmate's unkind words, describing Nell's plain brown hair as the soft colour of doe skin and her hazel eyes as being dabbed with flecks of amber and jade. Nell knew her sister, Rae, was the prettier daughter, taking after their father, with her chestnut locks, large burnt umber eyes and fashionably pale skin. Nell spent too much time in the sun enjoying outside activities, her lightly tanned skin dotted with delicate freckles across her nose, for which her nurse and tutors had often berated her. Always tall, exercise had kept her lean and willowy, and only in recent years had she developed the fuller, softer feminine curves which prevented her looking boyish.

However, both sisters paled into insignificance next to their radiant cousin.

Nell let out another long sigh when she glanced across at the young woman who sat opposite her and who was accompanying her on this journey. It was very different for her cousin, Elly. Although also of royal blood, Elly's father being the King's brother, she would not be seen purely as a symbol of her country and rich pickings for anyone who gained her father's trust. Elly would be regarded as a person in her own right.

Furthermore, she was beautiful. With long wavy tresses the colour of ripe corn, periwinkle blue eyes, a clear strawberries-and-cream complexion, and a buxom figure that strained against the constrictive fabric of her gown, Elly was the image of an archetypal princess, the perfect match for any prince or king. Additionally, she knew how attractive her physical charms were, and she would use them to her advantage as she gently flirted, winding men around her finger, always getting exactly what she wanted. She would love to have all the attention accorded a princess and certainly would not mind people ogling at her face and clothes, seeing the crown whenever they viewed her, scrutinising her every move.

That was when a plot formulated in Nell's mind.

Nell and Elly were both twenty-one, and neither had been abroad before. As Guthwayan custom dictated, since the age of twelve, they had been closeted away for most of each year in a court of their own with other daughters of the nobility, a kind of finishing school. Residing in a large castle in the heart of the countryside, they were taught all that was demanded from noblewomen: reading and conversation, drawing, dancing and music but, most importantly, running an estate. While they learnt in theory about other countries, it was traditionally believed that the nobility should learn, first and foremost, about everything to do with their own country. It was seen as even more important for royalty to develop a strong bond and understanding with their own people and the land that created them. Only now, at twenty-one, was Nell afforded the opportunity to visit another court to finish her education.

Growing up, when Nell and her sister returned home to Roxleburg on trips, her father had always made sure it was strictly time for their family and kept strangers at bay. He wished to make the most of their time alone together, especially when visiting their palace by the sea in Shirborne, a welcome and private holiday retreat. However, in the past few years, the King had involved her more in matters of state, discussing events as they happened, perceiving it as part of her training to be a future monarch. She was particularly included in those incidents that dealt directly with their boundaries, like the increasing troubles along their northern and eastern borders. Even so, she was never allowed to meet foreign dignitaries, her father greedily protecting his relationship with her.

Today, on this lovely late spring morning, they were travelling for the first time to Erlwick, in Torland, to live for a few years at the court of the High King. It was a chance to finally spend time mixing with different nobility from across The Alliance and to discover about other countries, alongside learning the ways of the most fashionable society as befitted young women of their status.

Presently, as they rattled through the countryside on their six-day journey, Elly chatted excitedly about the city and castle they were going to, the setting for their lives over the next few years, but especially about the characters they might meet.

"I've heard they have enormous markets where you can buy things from across The Alliance. They have really strong links with Angonna; hence you can buy silks in all sorts of colours. I just adore the sensation of silk against my skin."

"Don't forget the velvets, satins and damasks, my lady," added her maid, Daisy.

"Oh, the feasts and dances at the castle will be glorious – so colourful – a real spectacle for the eyes, as well as a treat for our mouths and feet," continued Elly without acknowledging Daisy's contribution. "They say it is a fascinating building which at times can be filled with nobles from every country. I shall finally get to meet some handsome and fashionable lords."

Nell hadn't particularly noticed Elly having a disregard for her own countrymen before, but her comment jolted Nell's meditations, as she suspected her father had an ulterior motive in their elongated residence abroad. The King of Guthway was a strong military leader and would wish to see the same security for the future of his country. She was positive he would be hoping that at least one of them would form a suitable match, a good alliance to aid that security, before they returned home. Nell groaned inwardly; it was yet another expectation heaped upon her, a part she was reluctant to play.

Not that Nell had ever had any interest in boys, or men, that way. Unlike her cousin Elly, who always seemed to be dallying with some member of the court and playing, as Nell perceived it, at being in love or broken hearted. Men adored her; entranced by her countenance, they happily did whatever she asked. Even Rae, three years younger than herself, had had a few superficial romances.

All the men Nell knew, from serving lads and stable hands through to lords and earls, she had grown up with, and those she liked best she regarded more as brothers. Only once was her curiosity aroused by a man enough for her to want to know more about him, or desire to spend more time with him. A person who, met only once, had grown into the perfect male in her imagination. A figure nobody else could possibly compare with, probably not even the man himself.

When she was twelve, Nell had been swaying inverted from an apple tree in a very unladylike fashion, as was her custom, in the old orchard just beyond the castle walls. Her governess would have admonished her for such behaviour while her father would have laughed in encouragement.

Some particularly special visitors had arrived from Torland, and since Nell was soon to leave for her new home in the countryside, once again closeted away from society, she was not allowed to meet them. She had been confined to her own rooms. Disgruntled and bored, especially to be stuck inside in such good weather, she had managed to sneak out undetected to one of her favourite haunts. Nell had climbed a tree which she found particularly good for such activities, swung herself backwards and forwards from a branch at a height that would have made her governess blanch, then finished finely balanced in the crook of her knees and upside down. Closing her eyes, she breathed in the slightly sickly-sweet scent of overripe apples while enjoying the unseasonal warmth of the mid-autumn sun on her skin, storing memories of her beloved home to take away with her.

A slight noise suddenly alerted her to the fact that she had company. Opening her eyes, she was surprised to find herself meeting the amused stare of a young man, albeit the wrong way up. Instantly, she blushed in consternation but tried to keep her own gaze steady, covering her panic at being discovered, and by such a handsome stranger. Nell speculated he must be a few years older than herself; even so, he was very tall. He had led a rather elegant chestnut horse amongst the trees, treating it to a few windfalls. His confident handling of the stallion, alongside his rather scruffy travelling clothes, made her conjecture that he must be a stable lad who had arrived with their visitors.

"Hello," he said politely. "Are you stuck? Can I help you down?"

She immediately readjusted her view of him after hearing his educated, metered voice. Maybe he was a squire.

"No… I can cope," was all she could manage in reply, flustered.

Gracefully, Nell swung around the branch in a complete circle before dropping neatly to the ground. She tried to straighten her gown surreptitiously while watching him continue to pat and whisper soothingly to the horse. He struck her as gentle and kind, considering the way he treated the animal with such fondness, but she realised he must also be strong, despite his youth, in order to control it. She wondered who he was then reddened again as he gazed back at her, aware that he was also studying her inquisitively.

"What's your name?" he asked simply.

For a few seconds, Nell could not answer. If anyone found out from him that she had been in the orchard, she would be in big trouble for breaking such an important rule; an appropriately large punishment would ensue. She did not want to lie, but self-preservation kicked in, and she gave him her new maid's name instead of her own, trusting to the fact no visitors would be meeting either of them.

"My name is… Hope," came her hesitant reply. "I live here, but I'm not supposed to be outside the castle today. Please don't tell on me!"

"I won't," he grinned. "It'll be our secret."

She had grimaced at her half-truth and wondered if his smile, which she reckoned made his face even more attractive, was because he had seen right through her. Now on the ground, she balanced awkwardly on one leg like a crane. Despite her discomfort, Nell suddenly found that she wanted to tarry and talk to him, share his company for a bit longer. She wondered what she should say or do to facilitate that.

Finally, the horse whinnied, attracting her attention and giving her an idea.

She asked, edging slowly forward, "May I stroke the horse?"

"Of course you can. I saw the orchard on our ride up and thought I'd bring him here for a treat before stabling him. He's rather partial to an apple."

"He's magnificent!" she exclaimed, and the young man glowed with pleasure at her praise.

Nell softly brushed the horse's neck, her fingers straying into the long main. Busy studying the animal's head, caressing absently, she was shocked when her fingertips suddenly met the young man's where he held the reigns. Jumping back, embarrassed, she suspected that he was amused at her naive reaction, perhaps even proud that he could garner such a response, if only in a youngster like herself, while the stallion whinnied again at her abrupt movement.

"I must go… before I'm missed," Nell stuttered, her cheeks burning and heart thumping.

She pivoted on her toes and ran back up towards the castle wall, only delaying for one last backwards glimpse. He was still observing her and gave her a cheery wave goodbye.

The young man had obviously kept her secret because no one had reprimanded Nell for leaving her rooms. She was very grateful to him, and he had risen even further in her estimation. Although she did not see him again, the unusual sensations his voice and his touch had aroused lingered with her over the years, the memory growing in importance and intensity as she left childhood behind. When her friends in the country talked about boys they liked, his was the face she saw in her adolescent dreams, and those were the feelings she remembered.

As Nell recollected that scene, she realised that no one from outside Guthway had seen either of the girls for a very long time. What's more, they had grown and changed within those years; no one would know which of them was really the Princess. They could swap places, and she would be free of both the restrictions and expectations that suffocated her. With little time to ponder any problems associated with her plan, Nell couldn't currently see any reasons against it. She made her decision impulsively.

"Listen, Elly, I've had a brilliant idea… and it'll be to your advantage," explained Nell, her voice fast and excited, her eyes bright. "When we get to Erlwick, I want you to pretend to be me, Princess Helen, and I'll be you, Lady Eleanor. No one knows us there yet, so we should be able to get away with it. It'll be fun – a joke, a bit of a laugh. We can retain our shorter family names, Elly and Nell, as that will stop us getting confused and answering to the wrong name. Either name could be short for our given names anyway."

When Nell faltered for a moment in her fast flow of words, Elly just gaped at her silently in astonishment, wondering why her cousin would possibly want to do such a thing, casting away all the benefits of her rank, and at such a significant time.

Swiftly, breathlessly, and before Elly could speak, Nell continued, "I don't anticipate that we need to change clothes and luggage or anything – yours are much more fashionable than mine anyway, and exactly what they would associate with a princess. You just need to accept my coronet to wear while we're there."

Without waiting for a response of agreement from Elly, Nell leant across the wagon and placed the golden circlet on her cousin's head, calculating that it might help her envisage the advantages of such a swap. Her supposition was correct; Elly instantly twinkled with pleasure at the vision of wearing this piece of royal paraphernalia. She removed it, twisted it about in her hands, her fingers caressing the floral etchings, before restoring it back on to her own head. The coronet had sparked its magic, offering all sorts of images to her of what being a princess, for a short while at least, might mean. Leaving Elly musing, Nell referred to the other two girls sitting beside them.

"We'll retain our own maids of course, but they're the only people who need to know our secret."

Nell smiled at the two young servants, and taking a hand of each girl in one of her own, she asked, "Will you swear to keep our secret safe, not tell anyone about our swap?"

"We promise, Your Highness," they swore in unison.

"Good. If any letters come for me, Daisy," she said to Elly's maid, "you can receive them and pass them on later, and we can do the same in return if we get anything for Elly. The system can work in reverse if I want to write to my father or sister."

Nell ceased for a minute, a brief doubt shadowing her face as she studied her startled, and still silent, cousin.

"Will you do it?" Nell requested more quietly, soberly.

Elly was still considering the proposition, her hand almost constantly fluttering around the coronet. Yet Nell already knew in her heart of hearts that Elly would be keen to do it, to savour the prestige of having top royal status, to be admired for both her beauty and her position. She would not agonise about any repercussions, just delight in the pleasures of this opportunity. Nell loved her cousin dearly, one of her playmates throughout her childhood, but she was under no illusions about her character; Elly had a vain streak and had always been slightly jealous of Nell's position. Guiltily, Nell also recognised that she was using that vanity to her own advantage now.

"Yes, of course I'll do it," laughed Elly suddenly, releasing a stream of words and reflections, "because it'll be fun. And, if you don't mind me saying so, I'll be excellent at playing the part of a princess. I'll go shopping and dancing and will always look gorgeous, of course. Will I get extra servants or a bigger room? And I wonder how long we can prolong the charade for? For a few days at least, I hope… but a week or more would be amazing. I do hope I'll get to go to a real banquet and dance first as you." Elly clapped her hands together excitedly. "I'll have to get a new outfit for that, and I have wonderful ideas of how to do my hair… Oh, do you think the High King will dance with me? I hear he's young, strong and very handsome. Oh, Daisy," she said, now turning to her maid, "your sister's seen some of the nobles at court, hasn't she, and told you all about them?"

"Yes, my lady," chortled Daisy, "my sister travels to the markets often and has glimpsed many of the attractive, virile noblemen and royals from The Alliance. She says there's a lot worth drooling over. And there's plenty of presentable, young men who work at the castle too, Hope, for you and me," she giggled and winked as she nudged Nell's maid.

Hope blushed, painfully embarrassed at Daisy's suggestiveness. Trying to hide her face, her reaction to the comments, she peered out of the wagon at the blurred roadside rushing passed. Excessively shy, she had always found it hard mixing with people and, in particular, knew little about how to talk to boys, let alone men. She had been happy while the Princess was cloistered away from court life, requiring little interaction with strangers or the opposite sex. Now, here she was, travelling with the Princess to a much grander castle than their own where she would be expected to assist her mistress in public more, even serve her at table in the great hall and mingle with the likes of lofty squires as a result. It was a great honour, but her stomach ached, knotted with anxiety, making her feel slightly queasy. She curled her fingers into tight balls, trying to resist resuming her childhood nervous habit of biting her nails, gnawing a little at her lip instead.

"Oh, my!" exclaimed Elly, sitting bolt upright and her eyes widening as a sudden thought came to her, "What shall I say if the King's there to greet you? I mean me!"

"Of course he will be there to greet us. Just relax and be yourself… Everybody adores you anyway," wheedled Nell, not wanting Elly to get scared and change her mind now Nell had begun to taste freedom. "The hardest bit to remember will be your initial conversation with him. After that, everything should fall into place. You will have to talk before me and introduce us formally – then remember to ask them all to use our short names, and we won't get muddled. It'll work!" insisted Nell, her fingers tightly crossed behind her back and praying her words were true.

So, having sworn Elly and their maids to secrecy over their plans, Nell sat back smiling and began to enjoy the view during their ride through the Guthway Pass and into Torland. Over the next few days, she contemplated what she could do with her increased freedom, relishing various tableaux of her riding, reading or travelling alone in her imagination, while the wagon drove on at a more leisurely pace towards the city of Erlwick where the High King's court was based.

Chapter 2

Late morning and Erlwick was already very busy, full of people milling about their own affairs and too intent on them to heed those of others. No one took much notice of the well-dressed figure hurrying through the streets in one of the less salubrious parts of the city. Such men sometimes had business to do in this area, the sort of activities about which it was usually best not to ask. Alone and on foot, the man was obviously well-to-do, his hooded, rich velvet cloak held tight about him and his face hidden in shadow, but he guessed nobody would take any interest in his exploits around here. Still, he wanted to be assured that he was safe, unseen. Squinting up and down the road, he slipped surreptitiously into a squalid coaching inn, the sign so cracked and the paint so peeled that its name could no longer be read. Although not new to either the area or the establishment, he was hoping not to be recognised during this particular errand today.

He looked cautiously around the room, trying not to attract attention with any overt gestures. The bar was occupied enough with an early lunchtime flurry of customers for his entrance to avoid being remarked upon, the chatter sufficient to cover his conversation. Smiling grimly, he saw that his acquaintance was already here, waiting for him in one of the small enclosed cubby-holes set aside for more private dining at the furthest corner of the room. As he sat down, he was pleased to be enveloped in the dingy gloom that would help to conceal both their presence and their actions.

His companion, wearing a long grubby cloak around his shoulders which covered a worn and dirty leather sur-coat, poured him a flagon of ale from a pewter jug which was already on the table. He pushed it towards the nobleman. The man, however, ignored it after one disdainful glance at the quality of the beer within, the few scant bubbles on its murky surface rapidly dissipating to leave a lifeless, pallid liquid.

"I'm not staying long – I've got other important things to do today," he said dismissively in a muted but firm voice.

The other man shrugged indifferently.

"More for me," he muttered and knocked back the remnants of his own tankard in one long draught.

"Do you have the item I require?" the nobleman asked curtly, dispensing with small talk.

"Yes, Your Highness," replied the other man in a low, gruff voice, wiping some beer off his chin with the back of his hand, "for the price we agreed. Obtaining such a… thing… and without raising questions is tricky… but I managed it."

He was about to embellish the story of his mission, enlarging his part in the performance, when the lord raised his hand, a firm gesture commanding silence.

Delving beneath his cloak and withdrawing a smart velvet pouch, the nobleman took out a handful of gold muncs, counted them into a pile, which he then pushed across the tabletop with his leather-gloved hand.

The other man now wiped his hand on his breeches before snatching the coins greedily, whisking them hastily into his own pocket without bothering to examine the amount. Then, with little movement apparent above the table, he passed an object underneath to the nobleman opposite him.

"It's the best quality there is!" exclaimed the dubious character with obvious satisfaction at his work.

Glimpsing down discreetly, the lord rolled the slight glass bottle over in his hand. The smooth oval body fitted snugly in his palm, the glass so dark it was difficult to tell what colour it, or the deadly liquid it contained, was. He smirked smugly to himself, pleased with his purchase, a new light gleaming in his eyes.

Now he could put his own drama in to play whenever he saw fit.

Chapter 3

Erlwick sprawled over a wide area of land. In the heart of Torland, this city was also the political and cultural centre of The Alliance, a group of countries who had joined together many decades ago to give themselves stronger protection against the more volatile and ever encroaching northern regions. Over the years, farms and homesteads had gradually grown closer together until, joined with other cottages, houses, shops and inns, they created the ramshackle suburbs that spread outside the city walls. Studying the passing streets, Nell knew that Guthway had nowhere nearly as vast as this.

The main city itself sat on the junction of several broad roads running from different points of the compass and across the River Berbeck. Small hills circled the outer walls of Erlwick, and on each one rose a fort, securing a wary watch over the surrounding countryside. Inside the city walls and on the other side of the river, a further long, low hill made a platform for the castle.

Even from a distance, Nell could tell the castle was a huge, magnificent structure. Torland was the biggest and most powerful of the countries in The

Alliance, hence its King holding the position of the High King with the authority to hold a High Court where important meetings and fateful decisions could be made. Therefore, it was also where many members of the nobility and royalty from throughout The Alliance congregated from time to time, making it the social hub of their union too.

Nell was proud of her own home in Roxleburg but realised it could not compare to this castle. As they rode down from one of the surrounding hills opposite it, the grey stone of its numerous buildings seemed to gleam a pale blue. While the outer curtain wall of the castle was a simple circle, inside the wall the keep was a jumbled complex of many layered buildings and towers, constructed and expanded over hundreds of years. Copious square turrets and cylindrical pinnacles rose into the sky, some roofed in a dark grey slate, others tiled in a white marble that shone with a soft lustre in the mellowing late afternoon sun. In contrast, the vivid greens of hedges and trees, alongside pinpricks of colour, indicated terraced gardens beneath the fortress. When they got closer, Nell could see a myriad of balconies, colonnades, stairs and elegant archways crossing and linking sections of the castle on every level. She shook her head in amazement. It would take her ages to learn her way around the labyrinth of her temporary home.

Then she beamed encouragingly at Hope, her young and timid maid, who was staring horrified at the building and had obviously harboured similar thoughts to herself.

"Don't fret, Hope! I believe you and Daisy get a small room to share next to ours so you're close at hand to help us. We can find our way about the castle together," suggested Nell reassuringly. "I'll need weeks to get used to it too."

Erlwick itself was an important, thriving trading post. At mid-afternoon, the streets were very busy with people working in front of their shops and homes, others buying or selling goods, and merchants travelling through to the market square. A few people stopped to gawp at them fleetingly as their wagon rode by, curiosity piqued by their royal status, signified by the coronet Elly was now wearing and the mini flag of Guthway fluttering on the canvas roof. Then, just as briskly, they slipped back to their work, more concerned with earning their livelihood.

Both the city wall and the moated outer curtain wall of the castle were heavily fortified and guarded, offering peace and security to all those within their confines. Not that the city walls had seen action in many decades. Soldiers patrolled between the towers spaced along the walls, and archers were placed at regular intervals behind the crenulations. Five or six large gates with portcullises stood open where roads entered the city, but Nell could only see one at the moment, across a drawbridge, which led into the castle itself.

Nell surveyed the scene from the wagon a touch nervously as they crossed the wide River Berbeck which ran through the centre of the city. It bubbled and swirled noisily beneath the bridge, rushing headlong out of the city and down towards the sea, many miles away. However, the bridge was strong, high and wide, built from the same grey stone as the castle; a firm wall spanned either side with a row of tall and elegant arches extending along the top. She smiled at a couple of laughing young lads, oblivious to their passing, who perched precariously atop the wall and dangled string into the water, hoping to catch a fish for their supper.

The water filling the moat was much stiller and deeper than the river but was clear of algae and covered in creamy-white lilies, brushed pale pink on the inside of their up-turned cups amongst the large flat pads. Every so often, the surface rippled as a silvery fish broke through, while other shadows of a variety of sizes flickered more mysteriously in the murky depths.

Passing through the gatehouse, a trumpet blew shrilly somewhere above them, a fanfare to herald their arrival, making Nell jump and breaking her quiet observations, bringing her back to reality.

The wagon bumped in a sweeping curve across the cobbled bailey and halted before a wide flight of worn steps that led to a stone terrace fronting the main door to the keep. A group, mainly of men from different ranks of society, emerged onto the terrace as Elly and Nell climbed down from the wagon and, lifting the skirts of their woollen travelling gowns a little, began to mount the steps.

Nell made sure she placed herself a pace or two behind Elly in deference, their personal maids following further behind with some of their smaller luggage. She could not help smiling to herself as, peering discreetly from under her lowered lashes, she caught the already admiring glances thrown in Elly's direction from the many young men assembled ahead of them.

One handsome, assured man stood taller than the rest amongst this youthful group, very upright and slightly to the fore. With a modest golden crown on his dark brown head, Nell deduced this must be the High King, Edward. Now twenty-five, he had been crowned just a few years ago following the early death of his father. She knew a heavy responsibility lay on his less experienced shoulders. Nell also knew her own father rated the attitude and abilities of this young king very highly, that many other nobles did too. Her father had returned from the coronation enthused with news of how he had spent time with Edward, discussing politics, in tourney fights, playing cards or the old strategic game of Sige. In fact, her father had travelled to Torland a few times since for both business and pleasure; a great warrior himself, he enjoyed a good tournament.

Sometimes, though, Nell had felt a little uncomfortable with the way her father studied her speculatively when he talked about the High King, as if he had great hopes. However, Nell reckoned she knew better; such a king could have the pick of The Alliance and beyond for a bride, so why would he be interested in a modest neighbour? What's more, their countries were already friends who traded freely; what benefit would there be in such a deal for him? She knew that royal marriages were all about political expediency. Nell wished her father had more confidence in her own ability to rule, allow her the freedom to grow into the role of monarch on her own and without seeking a consort.

Nell was currently very conscious of Edward's serious dark brown eyes contemplating them as they approached, but he smiled warmly, brightening his face and lending it a hint of mischief, as both women dropped into a formal curtsy before him, the skirts of their gowns and travelling cloaks billowing out in pools of fabric around them. Although the King's green sur-coat and tunic were shot through with gold thread, his attire was fairly simple, arousing Nell's approval, excepting a gold studded leather belt slung low around his waist where his hand rested. Bare-headed other than the simple coronet, he stood lean, muscular and at least half a foot taller than the cheerful young man with an attractive smile who was now positioned at his side. She had seen them swap laughing comments as the two women walked up the steps towards them, and Nell self-consciously wondered what they had said, whether it was about her or Elly. Instinctively, her hands went to straighten her skirts in a gesture of attempted control.

A sharp movement to the rear of the group caught her attention, and she saw another young man skulking aloofly from the rest of the cast, lurking in the wings yet itching to play his part, dressed in the black costume of the villain of the piece. Equally as handsome as the King, Nell deemed that his features were completely ruined by his sullen scowl. Despite his darker hair, almost jet-black, something in his face bore a likeness to the King, and Nell conjectured that this was Edward's younger brother, Prince Warwick.

Nell looked away rapidly as his cool and speculative pale blue eyes settled on her with a piercing glare. Instantly she felt uncomfortable, as if he was burrowing into her brain like a parasite and calculating her thoughts, that he would quickly uncover their ruse, expose her as a fraud and identify all her secrets. She didn't like the intrusive sensation and needed to shield her eyes and mind from him.

Becoming aware that the King was speaking, Nell focused her own contemplation back to observing him with relief. She realised there was something familiar in the line of his face and the friendly eyes, so much warmer than Warwick's. With a jolt, Nell suddenly recognised the young man she had met, and fantasised about, in the orchard all those years ago and had so recently been remembering. Except that, today, he had morphed into the powerful, confident leader before her. He had not been the servant or squire she had suspected; he had been a prince. This revelation aroused her interest further in the King who took time out of a busy schedule to feed a horse and who protected a servant, alongside the renewed stirrings of other long-buried, fledgling emotions.

Then, as Edward leant forward to raise Elly to her feet first and all his attention was bent on her, Nell pondered, 'The plan's working.'

Yet that thought was not without a surprising twinge of both regret and guilt at their subterfuge.

"Welcome to Torland, Princess Helen. We are delighted to have you and your cousin, the Lady Eleanor, to dwell at our court here in Erlwick. You must consider the castle as your home for the duration of your stay," said Edward, speaking in rich, measured tones, deeper than usual for his age, a confident voice already used to command.

Almost musical, Nell found she enjoyed listening to him, realised she had leant forward to hear him better.

"Please don't hesitate to ask for anything you need," he continued. "Your father, King Robert, is a great friend and a warrior of renown. He honours us with your presence."

Imperceptibly, Nell nudged the awestruck Elly to answer.

"Thank you, Your Majesty, we will endeavour to follow your wishes." Elly spoke in her lilting voice, and all eyes were now drawn to her. "And, please, we would rather be addressed less formally as this is to be our home. My name is shortened to Elly, my cousin's to Nell."

'Good response,' reflected Nell, impressed for once with her cousin's initiative, followed by a stab of irritation that Elly's voice complemented Edward's deeper tones so beautifully.

While Edward studied Elly, his eyes lingering over her glorious golden hair and unmistakably taking in her graceful neck and curved figure, a brief flicker of perplexion shadowed his brow. Visibly shaking off his confused meditations, whatever they might be, he now focused his attention on Nell. He put forward his hand once again to raise her from the ground. His grasp was warm and robust as it closed around her own fingers. There was nothing unusual in his hold, however pleasant it might be, yet the physical contact sent an unexpected shudder through her body. Nell immediately tensed, putting extra pressure in her grip, as she tried to hold herself steady for the second time in his presence. She was worried that she might have given herself away, but chivalrously, Edward gave no indication that he had discerned anything amiss with her reaction.

"Lady Eleanor… I mean Nell," he said, smiling at his self-correction, "your father too, Prince Harold, was a brilliant and accomplished commander, and his memory is respected here. You must also treat my castle as if it is your own home."

"Thank you, Your Majesty," said Nell, reciprocating his smile and noting that, up close, his eyes resembled the colour of chestnut shells.

"Please, I also wish that you will both just call me Ed – I like my companions to treat me as an equal, and I am hoping we will become good friends," the King grinned engagingly, his gaze including Elly in his remark.

"My great friend, Crown Prince Kaspar of Angonna, will escort you, Nell, into the castle and hopefully give you every assistance," he added with a twinkle. "Ask him as many questions as you like, enough to vex him."

"Ha!" snorted the Prince, the cheerful young man poised at the King's side, meeting Nell's eyes with a laugh from his own lively and intelligent brown ones. "I'm happy to chat to anyone for hours on end. And I don't get easily bamboozled by female company."

Ed, meanwhile, had reverted all his attention to Elly. Purposefully placing her hand on his arm, he began to walk her into the keep as he continued to talk.

"We have lain on a little light refreshment for you both to have now, after such a long journey, in the courtyard behind the great hall. My squire, Marshall, will show your maids to your rooms to sort out your luggage and possessions. In a short while, we'll direct you that way, too, so that you may prepare yourselves for this evening. There will be a banquet tonight in celebration of your arrival… That is, if you're not too tired? Please forgive our haste in putting on a party, but we are thrilled to have new female company again. We delight in gathering friends together at any opportunity."

"Oh, no! I'm not too tired, and I always love the chance for some dancing!" exclaimed Elly excitedly.

"And I suspect that you are a really wonderful dancer – you move so gracefully," Ed admired charmingly.

Nell rolled her eyes, viewing from a distance as the pair continued to flirt lightly while they talked. Even the King was not immune to Elly's charms and beautiful melodic voice. No one questioned whether she was the Princess. Nell was surprised to detect a pinch of disappointment at that result.

"Come, Nell, join us for a drink. I believe there will be some of the cook's fabled shortbread which simply melts in your mouth. You know, we have been starved of the engaging company of ladies of your rank for quite some time," said Kaspar, appearing at her side, his raven hair bouncing in loose curls as he leant forward to gallantly kiss her hand. "Too long," he added with a mock shake of the head, "too long!"

"How long have you been so famished?" asked Nell, amused.

"Ooh… At least a couple of weeks!" he laughed in reply. "The last princess left in quite a hurry, or she would have been here to meet you too. As a result, we don't have many nobles currently visiting from abroad. Sadly, you're not seeing us at our most cosmopolitan. I, of course, don't count because I'm almost part of the furniture here. In fact, my family bemoan that I never visit home."

"And we can't seem to get rid of him, however hard we try," quipped another young noble close behind.

"But, Ralph, you know the castle would be a much duller place without my presence," rejoined Kaspar.

Ralph snorted derisively.

"Besides, my father has a bevy of sons to install in my place. I doubt they miss me one bit," Kaspar remarked, grinning.

"I'm sure that's not true," laughed Nell. Then, suddenly curious, "Why did the Princess leave?" she queried.

"I'm sorry to say, she was rather disgruntled about something," whispered Kaspar, conspiratorially. "Events here didn't pan out quite as she'd hoped. I promise it wasn't my fault. I've been on my best behaviour for ages," he added, his eyes rolling in the direction of the King.

Nell laughed. Detecting how her face glowed and eyes sparkled in merriment, her whole countenance lifted in amusement, Kaspar beamed back at her.

"I guess a proposal wasn't forthcoming then," chuckled Nell, immediately recognising the connotations of the situation.

"Ouch, you're quick!" groaned Kaspar, dramatically clutching at his heart as if stung by an arrow. "We'll have to watch ourselves around you, or we'll be giving away too many of our deepest, darkest secrets. Still... one scene ends and another begins," and he nodded towards Ed and Elly, close in conversation.

Then Kaspar proffered his arm towards her.

For a minute, she hesitated to put her hand on his arm, and Kaspar spoke to her with piercing and thoughtful insight.

"Don't panic – I'm not proposing either!" he laughed. "Friendship is all I'm offering, so you're pretty safe with me. Actually, I'm already spoken for," and Kaspar gestured across to a girl, a couple of years younger than Nell, who was walking into the castle ahead of the main group. "I've been betrothed to Ed's sister, Princess Allys, for ten years." Again, he laughed joyfully, this time at good memories. "In fact, since about the time she trailed around after her brother and me for one entire summer. Wherever we went, she followed, getting in our way and spoiling our – perhaps rather dangerous – games. In the end, we gave up trying to lose her and let her join in with our fun instead. It was easier that way."

Decisively taking his extended arm, Nell examined Allys as she entered the castle doorway before them. The girl had wheeled around briefly and smiled whimsically at her, almost as if she had known she was the topic of their conversation. Her hair was worn loose in long burnt umber waves that matched Ed's, but her eyes were similar in colour to Warwick's. Although, in Allys, they were somehow infinitely warmer.

"I believe Angonna is several countries south-west of Torland," chatted Nell. "Geography isn't my strongest subject, but my fa… my country does a lot of trade with yours."

"Yes, we swap a lot of your wine, cheese and fruits for our minerals and spices. We produce a good yard of silk…"

Suddenly, Kaspar broke off when Nell and he had to pull up short, but too late to avoid careering into the back of Warwick. They gaped at each other in astonishment. The Prince glared around at them with an icy glint as if they were in the wrong, daring them to say anything contradictory, yet it was Warwick who had deliberately stepped in front of them so closely that they nearly knocked him over.

"Such carelessness!" spat Warwick arrogantly. "I hope my hose aren't ruined – they're expensive and some of my best."

"You are unscathed! I'm more concerned for our guest," snapped Kaspar.

"Our guest?" exclaimed Warwick in surprise.

"I'm fine," mumbled Nell, wincing slightly at her stubbed toe.

Letting Warwick walk in front of them, shaking his head dramatically and muttering as he went, Nell whispered to Kaspar, "Well, at least if I walk in with you, I won't have to partner him. I've only been here ten minutes, and he already gives me the creeps!"

"Um, he has that effect on most people. I rather imagine he fosters it with all his black attire and even darker brooding glances. Ignoring him whenever possible works quite well for me."

Then, with a sigh, Kaspar added, "And – although I dread to say it – making him disappear in a puff of smoke would be even better!"

While the nobles went on into the keep first, Hope shouldered a lightweight travelling bag ready to be shown where to go and then dithered, miserably watching proceedings. Their arrival had confirmed all of her fears when she viewed the large group of lords waiting for them. She had presumed the young men towards the back of the ensemble were the squires and saw them chatting and laughing, presumably about them. Instantly she had blushed, her redness and embarrassment only deepening as Daisy began to throw flirtatious glances back at the men. Hope had an irrational desire to close her eyes in an attempt to avoid communication with anyone else, wishing a trap door would open up beneath her, swallowing her into the shadowy depths below the stage, and thus solving all her problems.

One of the young squires, rangy and muscular with sleek blond hair and deep blue eyes, detached himself from the others and came over to the two maids.

"Welcome to Erlwick and Torland," Marshall said, smiling warmly. "I will escort you to your suite of rooms," he continued, gracefully bending to pick up a couple of large bags from their luggage. "If you have any trouble finding your way about or, indeed, if there is anything else you need, please don't hesitate to ask. We shall probably be seeing a lot of each other as I am Marshall, the King's squire, and our rooms are directly below yours."

"Ooh, I will certainly make sure we ask for whatever we might need," laughed Daisy with a suggestive wink, making Hope cringe and look away.

As she followed the squire into the building, Hope stared down miserably at her feet and, therefore, completely missed Marshall's appraising and sympathetic glance. He cast his eyes over her cheeks, crimson with embarrassment, bright against her pale, freckled skin and clashing with the few wisps of copper-red hair that escaped from beneath her headscarf. Compassionate in nature and detecting how ill at ease she was with both her companion and new surroundings, Marshall felt sorry for her and wondered how he might ease her transition to court.

Chapter 4

Groaning, Hope lowered two huge pails of steaming, hot water to the floor. She was struggling to carry them up to Nell's room for her mistress's bath. It was such a long way from the kitchens and required climbing several flights of stairs. Pausing for breath before the next set, she stretched to ease her aching back, wondering if there was an easier way to get hot water to the different bedrooms.

"Let me help you," said a soft, low voice behind her.

Jumping, she spun around, her face reddening yet again and hating herself for that uncontrollable reaction.

It was the King's squire. Without pausing for a reply, he grasped the bucket handles, picking them up as easily as if each weighed no more than a glass of milk. He was already continuing up the steps, anticipating Hope would follow, before she could utter a word.

"I meant what I said earlier," Marshall reminded her, having no problem at talking through his exertion. "If you need any help, just ask. We're like one big family here, and we're bound to see a lot of each other with the

King and your mistress socialising together. The castle's massive – it can be a bit daunting and confusing learning your way around to start with. So, when Ed leaves for supper, I'll come and find you to show you the way to the servery. I'll teach you all the short cuts too. And don't fret, we won't bite – we're not that scary really. If you want to be left alone, we will do exactly that."

"Thank you," whispered Hope.

Following, she peered out from under her lashes at Marshall. She was terrified at interacting with this high-ranking squire, probably a noble in his own right, but Hope realised she had to try and work through that fear in order to respond to the hand of friendship offered to her by this kind and handsome man.

Nell let out a long sigh of relief. So far, everything was going to plan. Standing on the quirkily curved and pillared balcony between her room and Elly's, looking over Erlwick and the River Berbeck below, Nell breathed in deeply. The rising warm air gently fanned her skin. Smelling the faint traces of fragrant flowers from the gardens below, she felt immensely free for the first time in years. She smiled at that satisfying idea.

Elly certainly gave the impression as enjoying her part in their charade. She had already bathed, changed and gone down early to supper, planning to chat and mingle with everyone she could before they went in for the meal, making the most of her role as guest of honour.

Instead of following her cousin, Nell had spent some time sorting out the things she had brought with her from Guthway with Hope. Then, having chanced upon a book she particularly liked, Nell had retreated to the balcony and read for a while. The book still lay on the small marble table tucked into a bend in the wall. She had had plenty of time for a leisurely soak in the rose-scented water Hope had prepared for her before throwing on a thick, warm dressing-robe over her silk chemise. Stepping back out onto the balcony, Nell had intended to enjoy another chapter of her book in the dying light of the day before she finished dressing, but she had been drawn, instead, to the beautiful view in front of her.

While she dawdled, watching the gradually deepening pinks and oranges of the sunset, small golden pinpricks of light would suddenly surface hither and thither, as if by magic, in the houses below. Then Nell heard footfalls somewhere nearby. Modestly pulling the robe closer about her, she turned to face King Edward as he emerged, as if from nowhere himself, beside her. Wearing brighter colours than earlier that day and in more exquisite fabrics, he carried himself with easy authority and looked every bit a monarch. Yet the strong aura of power and control broke when he grinned at her confusion about his sudden appearance.

"There's a narrow, winding staircase tucked away in an alcove just around the corner of the balcony. You'll find there's lots of little nooks and crannies like that in this castle," Ed explained, gesturing casually behind him. "It leads straight to the balcony below which happens to be mine and my brother's. I just figured that I'd grab advantage of the useful short cut to pop up and see if either you or the Princess were still around and ready to go down to supper. I hope I didn't alarm you."

He faltered for an instant, scanning her up and down, taking in with one sweeping glance the book on the table and her state of unreadiness. Feeling his perusal, one eyebrow raised questioningly, Nell flushed at the unexpected close scrutiny.

"But I see you are set upon being fashionably late – or perhaps just on time – rather than early," he said with a touch of irony.

Thoroughly disconcerted, Nell tried to smile as she spoke, "I decided not to rush. Elly has already gone ahead, but I'm sure you can catch up with her if you wish."

Instead of following after Elly as she assumed, Ed came over and sat down, precariously balancing his long frame on the edge of the ornate balcony, giving her a moment of anxiety for his safety. He picked up her book and nonchalantly flipped over a few pages.

"No, I'm not in a hurry, so I might as well tarry here now – for you – while you finish getting yourself ready." Then he added, with a glimmer of amusement, "Unless you're actually planning on being ages? In which case, I might just give up and head downstairs to find something to eat anyway. After all, I am quite peckish."

"Ha!" Nell laughed with more than a hint of self-deprecation, "I'm usually pretty speedy. I'm not too bothered with how I look and dress… but I expect you've guessed that already."

"No," said Ed reflectively whilst studying her with an unnerving intensity, "I haven't decided on anything about you yet. I try not to jump to snap judgements about people."

"Well, then," Nell continued, flustered and self-conscious, "I'll be back shortly," and she dived for the relative cover of her room, urgently signalling for Hope to bring her gown.

Although not as brightly coloured or ostentatiously fashionable as the clothes worn by her cousin, Nell's gowns were still exquisitely cut and expensively made as befitting someone of her status. Tonight, she chose to wear a dark claret brocade gown, laced tightly to the waist and with beautiful intricate gold thread detailing around the hem, the low off-the-shoulder neckline and the cuffs of the long, drooping, open-cut sleeves. She removed the necklace she wore almost every day under her clothing, a pretty Welcoming present in the shape of a butterfly and, rummaging through her silver jewellery box, chose instead a simple set of five cabochon garnets that shone smoothly like fresh beads of blood against her skin.

"Here, let me do that," said a quiet voice behind her.

Startled into speechlessness, realising Ed had entered the room and speculating how long he had been there, Nell simply passed him the necklace. Pulling aside her hair, she let him fasten the catch around her throat. His slight touch was warm and gentle but aroused goosebumps along her skin. Nell was perturbed at these uncontrollable physical responses to this man she barely knew; she found herself blushing yet again and felt her heart suddenly pounding in her chest. She wondered if he had noticed but hoped he had not.

"Wear your hair down," Ed added. "It suits you better like that, softens your face. And I believe it's quite the thing to do... Not that I really know about fashion, it's what I'm reliably told."

Still lost for words, unused to having a man, let alone a king, comment on her appearance, Nell just did as he requested. Giving her long tresses a brisk but firm brush through, she declared herself ready to leave.

Nodding at her in satisfaction, recognising but not commenting on the attractive flush to her sculptured cheekbones, Ed remarked, "Yes, that was pretty fast – almost as quick as my sister, and she definitely takes some beating."

With her hand fluttering nervously on his arm, they left the room and headed down a broad corridor. A myriad of doors, passages and stairs led off in all directions, and Nell stared at them with a mixture of curiosity, puzzlement and despair.

"How am I ever going to find my way around here?" she mused.

"I imagine you will learn your way about sooner than you envision, and you've got plenty of time to hunt around. At least it's fairly straightforward between your room and the great hall. When we get there, I'll be escorting the Princess in, of course, but you don't need to fear about being sat with my brother," he added with a grin, making Nell wonder if Kaspar had shared their conversation with him, suspecting that, as friends, they probably had, "as he almost always skulks in late. Kaspar will be with my sister, so I've arranged for an old friend of mine Albert, the Earl of Langford, to partner you. Having seen the pile of books in your bedroom, I'm presuming the two of you should get on like a house on fire – he's always borrowing books from my library. Ah, right on cue! Al!" Ed called across to a young man who was emerging from a passageway further ahead and to their left.

Al stopped and smiled as he paused for them to catch up with him, observing their approach. His sandy hair might have suggested a plain countenance, but rather, his face was open, friendly and intelligent with alert clear grey eyes that sparkled with humour.

"Have you seen Warwick?" Ed asked Al, a flicker of apprehension furrowing his brow as he reflected on his brother.

Al winced, disliking being the bearer of bad news.

"I think I saw his back proceeding in the opposite direction to everyone else," he sighed. "I'm afraid he's going to pull his usual dramatic stunt of a spectacular and angry, late arrival."

Ed continued to frown as he deliberated about his problematic brother. Then he shook off his worries, physically, and turned to face his friend.

"Al, may I introduce you to Lady Eleanor – Nell – who will be you partner at table tonight?" he said.

"Of course," Al replied and, addressing Nell, bowed elegantly to her. "I apologise for not being here earlier for your arrival, but I can now rescue you from the King and his abysmal conversation."

"Me? Never! Watch out, Nell! I presume Al will bend your ears by asking an interminable number of questions about your country," joked Ed with his own graceful bow before heading off in search of Elly.

"What does he expect?" exclaimed Al, raising his eyebrows. "I've never been to Guthway even though you are our next-door neighbour. Come, Nell, I am going to ask you lots of questions – if you are happy to answer them – beginning with… have you brought any interesting books with you?"

"That's an easy one to answer – plenty. And I'm happy to share them," Nell replied. "You should see the amazing library in our palace by the sea."

"Now, I've definitely heard of the Pearl Palace – it's said to shimmer on the horizon for all the ships to see like the sugar centrepiece at a banquet."

"Yes, that's the one!" laughed Nell. "And it is as beautiful as everyone says, but it's certainly more solid than a confection."

"Please, I'd like you to describe it to me as we walk," Al asked, waving his hand in the direction Ed had just taken.

Nell was delighted to have such a genial companion as they went into supper, and all of her qualms about spending her first night in this big castle amongst strangers were lost.

They sat towards one end of the raised dais at the top of the great hall, and Nell was comfortable there, able to relax and observe everyone from a discreet distance, while Hope hovered behind to serve her and Al, darting in and out of a half open curtain from time-to-time that led to the busy servery beyond.

Nell felt all of her vexations about her position were well founded as, throughout the evening, during both the meal and the dancing afterwards, she observed her cousin Elly draw an inordinate amount of attention and flattery from almost every male in the room. Even Warwick appeared enchanted with her. He had materialised midway through the meal in an overly theatrical entrance, slamming open the hall doors, pacing slowly and deliberately across the room, making a fuss about his sword and drink to the servants while he noisily pulled out his chair. Once sitting on the opposite side of Elly to Ed, he was keen to interrupt her conversation with the King and constantly drew her attention to himself. In reaction, Ed was particularly eager to continue talking with Elly, vying with his brother to garner her interest in him and regularly returned to dance with her after the feast. Nell was pleased that she was not on the receiving end of such persistent attention; she would find it suffocating.

However, she did not avoid all gallantries that night. The King had been right in saying there were few high-ranking ladies at court and, presently, only Nell and Elly from abroad. So, however plain she would be judged next to her cousin, she was still in demand as a dancing partner and could not escape that interest for long.

Al, of course, led her out onto the floor, following Ed and Elly, for the first dance, apologising profusely in advance for any ungainliness on his behalf. He was, however, a very accomplished and considerate partner. Nell didn't mind dancing with Al, but several other partners came after him of varying degrees of ability and grace.

When she finally got a break later, Nell found herself sitting at a table next to Princess Allys.

"You're a better dancer than me," confided Allys. "Your footwork is light, skilful and regular."

"Thank you," said Nell. "It's kind of you to say so, but it's all down to a great dance master… and probably as much to do with the time I spend in the tiltyard."

"The tiltyard?" Allys exclaimed in surprise, but she smiled all the same. "You are an unusual lady! Well, I tend to get rather carried away with the music, lost in the emotions of it," added Allys. "I become a bit enthusiastic, wild and definitely unladylike. I often get berated for it."

"Who berates you?" asked Nell. "I reckon it's good to feel the rhythm of the music, let yourself be free. I wish I could be like that more often – I've always had to be aware of who's watching me." She sighed a little. "And what's so good about being ladylike all the time? That's certainly no good for riding or protecting yourself and others."

Allys gaped at Nell in astonishment, and then both women burst out laughing. She may have been a few years younger than herself but, in Ed's sister, Nell had found a kindred spirit. Their joint laughter instantly opened a door between them. They sat for a while, Nell asking questions about various courtiers and nobles, Allys providing her with all the gossip. Allys proved quite a good mimic and could do a particularly good impression of the King's glum first minister, Caldwell, astonishing considering how much older, bent and ashen faced he appeared. When they saw Ed and Kaspar approaching, though, both women immediately sat upright, trying to look prim, proper and innocent.

"I hope Allys isn't leading you astray?" queried Ed as he flopped down on the bench next to Nell.

"What makes you think she's leading me astray and not the other way around? I thought you were reserving judgement on me?" asked Nell, straight-faced, and Allys giggled beside her.

"Then perhaps we should whisk you away from each other to prevent any further mischief," stated Ed, firmly grasping Nell's hand and hauling her on to her feet, making her gasp in surprise and cling to him in support.

He clasped her waist close to him as he swept her around the room. It was just her luck that they were playing music for a more intimate dance, and Ed had no qualms in holding her tight for it; she was not used to being clasped so firmly by a man, being given more deference at home. Yet she found his strength, confidence and authority gave her a strange sensation of warmth and security; enjoying it, she relaxed and followed his lead.

"You lied to me, Nell!"

His sudden comment caught her off guard. Immediately tensing, her feet faltered, but Ed continued to hold her firmly, keeping her upright. Nell held her breath as she waited for his denouncement, presuming her deception had already been found out. Although fairly tall herself, she still had to gaze up to see his face, trying to read the verdict behind the guarded expression. There was no sign of anger or sternness, just a small twitch of his lips.

"When we met before, Nell," Ed now explained with only a slight hint of reproof, "you told me your name was Hope… but that's your maid's name."

With understanding dawning, Nell let out a long breath of relief; Ed had also remembered their previous encounter in the orchard. He deemed her deception was only the name she had given him and not her status. Relaxing once more, Nell grinned back at him.

"I did not know who you were. I suspected that you might be a squire, at most, otherwise I would not have lied to a prince, of course," she said with pretend decorum. "And I also conjectured that you might tell on me, as I was somewhere that I should not have been."

"I'm sorry that I'm not a squire, only a king," Ed teased. "But maybe I can forgive you, as you were only twelve at the time," he added, his smile increasing, "and a quaint, gawky, skinny thing as I recall, not at all like a lady – an easy mistake for me to make."

"No, not like Elly… even then, she was always pristine and beautifully attired. I don't reckon she's ever been up a tree!" Nell retorted drily, although a sharp twist of hurt cramped her stomach at his careless words.

Was that really his vision of her? Quaint and gawky?

As they whirled around the room, they passed another couple. The nobleman gave a curt and barely civil nod towards the King. Such discourtesy was unheard of, and Nell could not help but look askance at Ed.

He grimaced.

"An unhappy foreign ambassador…" was all he was willing to say in explanation.

The bronze scit dropped for Nell.

"Ah, the Princess who left early!" exclaimed Nell.

"News – or rather gossip – travels fast around the court," he muttered in disgust.

"Always," laughed Nell. "But you needn't fret about Elly and me in that same regard. We are both here to expand our horizons, have some fun, and not close them down in marriage yet."

"Thank goodness for that! I'd appreciate the chance to unwind a bit and have some fun myself. That last episode got a bit tense and involved. My ministers just had to stick their oars in, adding a lot of pressure, by proclaiming that it was a good match for the country and that it was my duty to provide heirs, never mind whether I liked her at all or not. Caldwell in particular mentions it whenever I see him. You would conclude that I was sixty-five – not twenty-five – the way he continually declares that I'm 'not getting any younger'! He anticipates that

Torland is doomed if I don't get married within the year, and I swear his expression increases in gloominess month by month."

Ed regarded her meditatively whilst his clasp around her waist and his footsteps never faltered.

"Is that how you really feel about marriage?" he asked. "That you'll be trapped? Not a chance to share your life with a fitting partner? Maybe even a friend?"

Nell squirmed a little under his gaze.

"It's different for men and women!" she retorted. "Unlike you, I'll get hardly any say – if any – in the choice of a marriage partner."

Heeding her discomfort, Ed changed tack, "Elly certainly appears to be producing wonders already."

Nell regarded him questioningly.

"She's certainly been working a miracle on my brother," Ed added admiringly.

He reeled Nell around slightly to change her view and nodded across the floor in the direction of a dancing couple Nell had not yet spotted. Peering towards them, she realised that the couple were causing quite a stir. They looked stunning together, Elly's blonde waves against Warwick's black locks. Yet that was not what was causing the greatest interest.

"I haven't seen Warwick dancing for several years. And I swear he's almost smiling! It lightens my heart to see him happy for once," added Ed, contemplating the couple reflectively. "I can see Elly is going to create some excitement at court."

Chapter 5

Nell settled swiftly into the routines of life at Erlwick Castle, but she was also fast to utilise the many amenities available to her. She was a frequent visitor to the expansive library, often meeting Al there and discussing books together, but she also had other interests.

Her father was a great warrior, hence Nell, as eldest child and heir to his throne, had been schooled in swordplay, archery and horse riding from an early age. She wished to continue her practise; therefore, as soon as she had found her feet, Nell sought out the Master-at-Arms for his services, only to discover he was an old friend and sparring partner of her father's. He, of course, immediately recognised who she was, and Nell had to ask for his discretion.

"I will not offer what I know freely to anyone, but if he asks a direct question of me, I cannot lie to His Majesty," he said.

"That is fair enough," accepted Nell.

Ed, passing the tiltyard one day, was surprised to hear Nell's gasps and grunts of exertion. Stopping behind a creepered column, feet away from Hope perched on a bench, he observed silently for a while as Nell battled with the Master across the yard. Her hair plaited tightly, dressed in plain, masculine breeches and tunic, with a leather sur-coat for basic protection, whirling and fighting with yells of effort, he considered how she represented the complete antithesis of her cousin. He had passed Elly minutes before discussing new clothes with a seamstress. So he found this woman, Nell, intriguingly different from most of the other noblewomen he had ever met and wondered where her passion and strength came from.

As Ed contemplated her, he recognised and admired her skill with a light double-edged sword and appreciated the rosy bloom the exercise gave to her complexion. Maybe not as obviously pretty as her cousin Elly, he mused that Nell had a good strong bone structure and deep-set, almond shaped eyes that made her attractive in a different way. Furthermore, all this exercise explained the firmness and suppleness in her limbs which he had been distinctly aware of when they had danced together. He also noticed that there was something familiar in the way she handled her sword; a memory stirred in the depths of his brain, but for the moment, he could not quite put his finger on who Nell reminded him of. Ed loitered a minute more, puzzling, and then he slipped quietly away, winking at Hope with a finger to his lips as he passed nearby, and without Nell discerning that he had been there at all.

Hope, meanwhile, had been absorbed in her own thoughts, sewing untouched in her lap, and had not registered the King had been there until he left. Suddenly aware that she had been staring beyond Nell to a group of squires, she was horrified at herself, realising that she had been watching Marshall closely, entranced by his elegant swordplay. Then, to her acute embarrassment, he had glanced up, caught her eye and, like the King, winked at her, grinning hugely. Instantly, she coloured up.

Nell certainly seized advantage of just being a lady and the greater freedom it gave her to wonder around the city or travel into the countryside, sometimes with only Hope or Ed's squire, Marshall, to accompany her. Often, she sought out the company of Princess Allys for her excursions, someone as likely to enjoy a picnic in the woods or a walk through the markets as herself. She particularly delighted in taking a back seat at any big social event, enjoying the opportunity to observe other people or experiencing the activities from amongst the lower orders of nobility, sure she was making a greater variety of friends. Furthermore, the occasional view of Ed surrounded by his black-robed ministers, like hovering crows ready to swoop and feast on a carcass, or sidelined in delicate, tangled discussions with ambassadors made her shudder with relief.

Elly, too, was relishing the trappings of her new position, the veneration and attention it accorded her. She played fully the role of an indulged princess by buying new clothes and jewellery. She appeared to enjoy spending time with many of the younger and more fashionable nobles at court, not just the King and his brother, and delighted in being at the forefront of entertaining the other occasional royal visitors from The Alliance.

One summer evening, after a long, hot and muggy day, Nell could not get to sleep. She tossed and turned in her bed, but despite being tired after a busy day, she was too warm to doze even a little. She threw off all her sheets but continued to feel hot and sticky, beads of sweat moistening her skin and her chemise clinging uncomfortably to her body. Moving to a seat near the window, she hoped for a breath of fresh air, but the night was still and very close. Giving up her attempt to sleep, Nell decided to make her way to the kitchens to see if she could find some fresh, cold milk.

She crept down the back stair Ed had shown her on her first night here and was about to slip passed the King's door when she realised it stood open. Startled for a second, she stopped in the doorway, and the slight movement must have alerted Ed to her presence. Sitting by an alcove window, he turned and smiled softly.

"Come in, Nell. I see that I'm not the only person who can't sleep tonight, and I would appreciate some company."

She moved slowly, self-consciously, forward. Ed still sat in his hose and open shirt, but shoeless, his bare feet rested on the window ledge. There was something beguiling about his half-dressed state; although, it also increased Nell's awareness of her own. Then her eye was caught by an unfinished game of Sige positioned on the table beside him. Fascinated, she could not resist sizing up the game in action.

"Do you play?" asked Ed, detecting her interest. "Al left a while ago – we never got to finish the match."

"Yes, I do," Nell answered simply, gradually dropping on to the seat Al must have vacated as she studied the current game, evaluating all the pieces presently in play and their positions.

Then she moved a delicately carved yew wood horse to the path around the edge of the beautifully and intricately inlaid circular board.

Leaning forward to assess her move and ponder what he should do next, Ed grinned.

"Have some cider," he suggested. "It's currently cool and fresh but will rapidly warm up at this temperature. It needs to be drunk soon."

He passed her a green glass beaker which she took, swallowing a large mouthful to soothe her dry throat and savouring the sharp tang of apple. She discerned a slight sheen of sweat lingering on his skin, expected that she probably looked the same. Ed bent across the table to move his ebony archer and then paused for her turn. His shirt hung open, and she couldn't help her eyes sliding over his muscular chest and the slight covering of curled, dark hair. Disconcerted but also recognising that she appreciated the view, Nell dragged her eyes away to concentrate on the Sige board mapped out in a variety of delicate wooden veneers. Quietly, swapping occasional comments on the play, they companionably continued the match.

After an hour, a sudden flash of light, followed by a crash of thunder and the patter of rain, brought some relief to the heat of the night. Nell rushed across the short distance to the window and leaned out to breathe in the fresher air and the smell of the wetting earth beneath them. She listened to the big blobs of hard rain falling around them, caught a few in her hand, relishing the dampness, and observed the stonework soak them up hungrily in irregular, fuzzy circles.

"I think we might finally manage to get some sleep now," remarked Ed, amused, as she leant further against the window ledge, her chemise clamped tight between her body and the stonework, with one arm outstretched and laughing with joy at the change in the weather. "I suggest we both at least try. But I have enjoyed your company and our game tonight, so feel free to drop by on another evening if you're suffering from sleeplessness again. If my door's open, I'm awake and available for a chat."

Nell gave a sidelong peek at the rumpled bed. Although young and cosseted, she was not so innocent that she did not know how noblemen sometimes gained company, and what for.

"You mean, if you have no pretty bedfellow to entertain you?" she asked archly, gaining boldness from their improving camaraderie.

Ed just snorted, "Well, if that was the case, my door would be shut!"

Yet he followed his comment with a hard stare, making her redden.

"Actually, I don't often indulge in such physical urges – a hard ride or a tough bout in the tiltyard usually does the trick – especially close to home. That way often leads to too many complications."

Intrigued, and before she could hinder herself, she asked, "No discreet mistress?"

He spluttered into his beaker of cider at her daring questioning.

"As I said, that way can lead to problems."

Moving across to a desk, Ed fiddled with something on it as he considered his words.

"I did have one once, but she…" Fleetingly, a frown crossed his brow, and he spoke more hesitantly than usual. "It didn't work out… Pain and trouble on both sides… therefore… I want to avoid that happening again."

Then, worried she had overstepped the mark, Nell bit her lip as she peered at him from beneath her long lashes. The King had resumed his seat, stretched out and appeared relaxed, so he could not have been annoyed by her very personal probing.

"As you have opened up such intimate subjects, what about you?" asked Ed, studying her with his head on one side and a slight twitch to the corners of his mouth. "You have told me that you don't plan to marry soon, but has there been anyone special in your past?"

She supposed his inquiry was only fair considering hers, but Nell wondered how much she could safely mention. Their friendship certainly had gained strength in leaps and bounds.

"Only a dashing, young squire who transformed into someone else!" she said lightly, trying to sound tongue-in-cheek.

Ed guffawed.

From then on, Nell often found herself with Ed in the evening, playing a game of Sige or cards. Sometimes it would just be the two of them, especially if it was very late, but often they would be joined by Al, Kaspar or even Allys. Another younger member of Torland nobility might occasionally be present, like Ralph, their squires in attendance.

Noticeably, Warwick never joined them or spent time with his brother.

Nell liked being part of this sociable and stimulating company, as they often also casually discussed matters of state or culture. She was pleased that they had welcomed her so readily into their group of friends, and that they seemed to accept her ideas and comments as equally important as anyone else's, whatever her status might be.

Nevertheless, a little part of her began to experience guilt at how she was deceiving them, however innocently it had originated. Moreover, she was not quite sure how she could finish the deception without evoking disappointment and reproach.

Chapter 6

Alongside continuing her lessons in swordplay and archery, Nell was insistent on wanting to learn how to ride fast, cross-country and under pressure, as men did in hunting, battle or flight. She was determined that she would be ready for anything that may one day be needed of her back home in Guthway.

Nell recognised that her country's defences were weakening and that there might come a time when they failed altogether. Situated on the outskirts of The Alliance, their enemies sometimes pressed hard on their borders, seeing the lush and fertile country as rich pickings. They had already made inroads into the valleys to the east; Hope's family being one of several noble families who had fallen victim to their incursions, their lands seized and homes destroyed in a previous generation, sometimes reducing them to penury. Even if she was a woman, Nell knew she wanted to be at the forefront of any defence, a strong leader of her people. Sighing, she also understood that her father had doubts it would be enough and that was why he might be searching for a strong coalition for her through marriage. Could she persuade him otherwise with her own actions?

Burgess, the Master-at-Arms, occasionally accompanied her for rides into the countryside, teaching her not only to gallop hard but to do it while avoiding obstacles. Often, they would ride through the local forest, using these tactics as if on a stag hunt. Nell really enjoyed these days, dressed in men's clothes, exhilarated by the speed and the challenge as they ducked under branches, jumped fallen trees or swerved around rocks, trunks and shrubs.

When they pulled to a halt on yet another sweltering summer's day, taking a minute to catch their breath, they heard the unmistakable sound of another horse and rider fast approaching. They held their horses motionless in a clearing, waiting to see the newcomer, whether it was a friend or foe. Burgess had one hand on his sword hilt, alert to any danger.

Abruptly, Ed broke through the surrounding shrubs on his magnificent chestnut stallion, intent on his own gallop. He hurtled forwards, but then catching sight of them, he swerved to a halt beside Nell.

Burgess's grip on his weapon relaxed.

"Aah, good morning – or, should I say, good afternoon – Nell," Ed said, holding his reins in check and breathing hard.

"Good afternoon, Your Majesty," Nell replied primly, back straight.

"I think it's going to be another very hot day. Burgess, you may resume your other duties – I will escort the Lady Eleanor safely back to the castle," insisted Ed.

The Master nodded in affirmation then, bowing courteously to both of them, wheeled around and rode back towards Erlwick.

"You say you will escort me home," pointed out Nell, "but I haven't yet finished my ride for the day. I was on my way out, not back."

"Then we will continue your outing first and return when you are ready," said Ed.

"If you can keep up with me," teased Nell, suddenly playful, commanding her horse into a gallop and vanishing into the trees.

Frowning pensively for a minute at her recklessness, Ed then broke out into a smile, deciding to dally a few more minutes before giving chase, allowing her a good head start.

Nell did not glance back to check if the King was following. She wondered if he would and, if he did, how far she could get before he caught up with her. According to all reports, Ed was an excellent horseman. Determined to put distance between them, she embarked on the path of least resistance, following deer tracks through the trees. Eventually, she brought her horse to a standstill and listened for sounds that he might be following her. She could hear nothing.

Nell continued on, daring to go further than she had ever been before. She ignored the nagging thought that she might not be able to find her way back, putting herself in danger. Instead, she advanced on deeper through the forest and up into the hills towards the tors the country was named after. It was another half an hour before she stopped again.

Leaving the trees behind her, she had come out into an expanse of low but hilly meadow encircled by the forest, before the trees ultimately petered out onto the moors beyond. A river ran through the clearing, a waterfall tumbling into a large dark pool at one end before continuing on its gushing journey into the forest at the other.

Nell peered down into the cool, glistening water. The heat of the day was at its fullest, her skin baking from the rays of the sun and her clothes sticking to her body with sweat, so the deep black water looked enticing, beckoning her in. Hesitating, she glanced around her again. There was no sign of the King, or anyone else for that matter, and all was quiet excepting the lazy buzz of insects and the occasional cheerful chirping of birds. Nell was confident that she was completely alone. Taking off the tunic, leather sur-coat and boots she was wearing for her ride, she leapt into the pool in just a long silk shirt and breeches. Suddenly hit by the cold water, she gasped, but this was a welcome relief from the hot day. With goosebumps materialising along her arms, she swam across the roughly circular area of cool, fresh water. The peaty pool was so murky, her body seemed to dissipate eerily within inches of the surface, the bottom completely obscured. Rolling onto her back, she floated for a while, staring up at the cloudless azure sky, before swimming over to the waterfall to feel the touch of the fine spray raining on her face.

Behind her, Nell heard a splash. Treading water, she spun around but could see nobody. Then a dark, shark-like shadow beneath the surface moved swiftly towards her, and in a fountain of spray, Ed rose in front of her like a dolphin vaulting out of the ocean.

"That's better!" exclaimed Ed, shaking the water from his hair, spraying her in goblets.

"Ugh! I presumed I'd lost you!" Nell gurgled, mortified at him finding her here, like this.

"I just gave you a head start to give my tracking skills some practise," laughed Ed. "We need to give you lessons in evasion and avoiding leaving a trail if you're bent on this sort of activity. Although, I suppose I shouldn't really be encouraging you to go off on your own. We're fairly safe enough around the city, but… who knows what dodgy characters and ruffians might be in the hills, spying out for an unwary traveller."

"Quite! One seems to have found me," muttered Nell through clenched teeth.

He laughed again and pushed off backwards lazily, his arms extending in long and relaxed strokes through the water, swimming across the pool and returning before speaking again. Nell watched, admiring his form and elegant movement.

"If you've cooled down enough to leave the water, I have some food in my saddlebag. I was given plenty, so I have ample to share in a picnic with you."

He swam leisurely to the bank, his length making his strokes appear effortless, and heaved himself up onto a group of rocks that tumbled into the water. Nell followed him. She wavered at the edge; it had been easy enough to jump in, but the bank was steeper than she had realised. She was also acutely aware of her lack of clothing, the shirt rendered semi-transparent by the water and clinging to her arms and breasts. Ed leant down across the rocks to offer her a hand, his wet shirt sleeves dripping on her, sticking to his taut muscles and highlighting her own predicament.

Raising his eyebrows as she continued to hesitate, then understanding dawning, he offered a suggestion, "I'll try not to look in your direction until you've dried out a bit."

Taking his hand as he directed his face away, she let him pull her up and then flopped beside him on the grass in the baking sun. Self-consciously, she rolled over, her back to him, fully aware that, however gallant he may be, he could not have helped but see more than propriety allowed. Nell blanched as she envisaged him perusing her on his arrival at the pool, inspecting her through the transparent clothing as she floated in the water. However, perceiving his eyes on her back now and feeling the silk clinging to her skin, she also detected a strange stirring in her own body and new sensations of pleasure at these thoughts.

"Well, that certainly was a refreshing dip! Perfect for this weather. I expect it won't take us too long to dry out in this blazing sun," said Ed.

He was right; her shirt was already drying.

Ed then delved into his bag and brought out a meat pie which he proceeded to cut into slices with a knife from his belt, a couple of apples, a huge chunk of fruit cake and a flask of wine.

"You're a good swimmer, Nell – strong and lithe. I don't know many girls who can, but I guess that explains your complexion – you look as if you spend a lot of time outside. Unlike Elly – she's as pale as milk," he reflected, lying back down on the grass.

Nell blushed furiously, her stomach twisting painfully at the comparison with her cousin and the implied criticism. She suddenly felt very trivial, pathetic. She bent her head guardedly, raising a hand self-consciously to hide her cheek and tucking her knees up protectively towards her chest, warding off the metaphysical blow.

"I couldn't bear to spend all my time stuck inside a building the way she does," Nell whispered defensively. "Elly only rides when she needs to join a hunt or picnic as part of a social gathering."

Ed rolled over onto his stomach towards her and put a hand on her arm, suddenly aware of the discomfort he had caused her, reaching out compassionately to this young woman who, brought up under close control, was probably still naive when it came to communication and relationships.

"Nell, I wasn't being critical… It just tells me a little more about you – the real you – and what you like to do. And, I must say, it adds a whole lot more questions too!" Ed sighed, a frown across his brow, "Elly certainly seems to have a lot in common with Warwick. He spends rather too much time mooching around the castle for my liking. Except, he does practise a lot in the tiltyard and the archery range… as you might have noticed with all the time you spend there yourself."

Ed grinned at Nell while her cheeks reddened again.

Then his face brightened a little, "Warwick does appear to have made some new friends recently, meeting up with them outside the castle. And he certainly strikes as utterly enchanted with your cousin. Elly and he are getting along marvellously. I'm hoping this signifies a change for him… a change for the better.

"Now, tell me, Nell – when and where did you learn to swim?"

Nell laughed at his sudden change of tack and tried to calculate how much she could safely tell him truthfully.

"Well, we've always spent our summers on the coast at the Pearl Palace, as it's so much cooler by the sea. The Palace has its own cove, only reached by a steep staircase from the building or via the sea. You can probably deduce that I spent a lot of time on the beach, digging in the sand, exploring the rock pools and climbing the cliffs as a child. It's not surprising that I learnt to swim there, too, buoyed amongst the salty waves."

Relaxing, Nell uncurled and, sufficiently dry, rolled towards Ed.

"Wow – you've been given enough food for a company of soldiers! Where were you stashing it all?" she chuckled, reaching for some pie.

They spent a further couple of leisurely and enjoyable hours eating, chatting and daring to have a further swim before they thoroughly dried out again, the King gallantly continuing to avert his eyes when necessary, before Ed suggested that they should be heading back to the castle.

"If we're both away for much longer, they might send out an armed guard as a search party. I will soon be missed by some minister or other, that's for sure, and concern will be raised for my safety… and possibly your virtue when they realise you're alone with me! As you have already hit upon, I have form in that direction. Unfortunately, I cannot ever be totally free, and I have to account for my whereabouts most of the time," he muttered, "but a small piece of freedom like this, now and again, does me the world of good. Thanks for this afternoon, Nell."

Nell looked at him in surprise. For the first time, she recognised a similarity between his plight and her own; that realisation added to the growing guilt she felt at her own behaviour towards her new friends.

Chapter 7

On their return to the castle, Nell noticed that the servants were bustling around the gardens, arms loaded with torches, flowers and bunting, and she finally remembered it was Midsummer; a special feast and ball was to be held at the castle tonight. As the light would tarry and the warmth of the day would carry on well into the night, there was to be music, singing, acrobats and clowns exhibiting throughout the evening and into the early hours of the morning, all over the castle. Every area of the building would be utilised, spilling out to the courtyards and gardens. Nonetheless, the main dancing would still be staged in the great hall.

Not just the nobles of the land but many dignitaries from all the cities of Torland were to attend. Nell knew every room of the castle had been filled with extra guests, having offered her help in making sure that everything was ready for them. The memory brought a pang of disappointment for her cousin's sake. Elly would have loved this party, but earlier in the week, she had received a message that her mother was ill and requested her presence at home. Dutifully, if more than a little regretfully, Elly had retreated to Guthway for a couple of weeks with a carefully constructed cover story disguising the truth. Tonight, Nell's presence would be craved as one of the highest-ranking females at court however she might feel about it.

When she returned from her ride, Nell felt hot and dirty despite her earlier swim, but Hope had already prepared a bath for her brimming with rose essence and petals. Aware that Elly would not be there, Nell suddenly felt keen to make the best of herself tonight, whatever her physical short comings might be. She was not sure if her pleasurable afternoon spent with Ed had something to do with it, but she was now certain that she enjoyed spending time with him, relished his occasional compliments and was cut to the quick by any imagined criticism.

As Nell plunged into her bath, letting her hair swirl around in the water, she continued to think of Ed and her realisation that he could feel tied to his role as king just as she felt trapped in her role of heir presumptive, meaning he also missed the freedom she was currently enjoying. Unlike her, he rarely had a chance to escape his responsibilities, finding opportunities to release the pressures of his difficult and important role.

Sitting up again, breathing in deeply the intense, sweet scent rising from the water, she viewed Hope efficiently tidying around the room and wondered how well her timid maid was settling in at the castle. After all, Hope had also left the family and friends she was close to behind in Guthway when she had accompanied Nell to Torland.

"Hope," said Nell gently, "it's a special evening for everyone tonight which means, when I go down to supper, you can join the festivities around the castle too. Don't hide in this room. Go out and try to make some new friends."

61

"Oh no, Ma'am!" gasped Hope in horror, "I couldn't!"

Nell inwardly sighed as she observed the girl's terrified face but did not want to push her further.

Hope helped her into a chemise of the lightest silk followed by a gown of a very sheer and delicate satin, designed to alleviate the worst of the summer heat. The silk was of the palest lilac, and the satin a purple reminiscent of the fragrant lavenders in the gardens below. A delicate silver thread was woven around the hemmed edges of the dress like a dewy daisy chain. Today, the cuffs of her gown draped open, dangling almost to the floor, while the sleeves of the chemise clung closely like a filmy, glimmering second skin. A matching lace and silver thread belt skimmed her hips.

While Hope brushed out her hair, Nell rifled through her jewellery box. She put aside her butterfly necklace, choosing instead a string of silver filigree flowers dotted with shimmering, milky pearls and opalescent moonstones. She found matching jewelled daisy pins which Hope twisted into her hair, hanging both loose and in small braids around her shoulders.

Satisfied with the results of her ministrations as evidenced by the mirror yet suddenly experiencing nerves, Nell tarried, having agreed that Ed would come to collect her on his way to the great hall. Would he notice and would he comment?

Waiting on her balcony to enjoy what cool breeze she could find, Nell anticipated the footfalls on the stairs before they came, making her heart thud. She swivelled about as Ed stepped out of the alcove. Briefly, he paused, scrutinising her, and Nell reciprocated his stare, for once blatantly admiring the figure he created. He wore a longer length tunic of russet silk over a cream silk shirt. His sur-coat and hose were of a darker brown, the coat sleeves cut open almost from the shoulder in the current courtly fashion. It was lightly quilted in a zigzagged pattern of diamonds with gold thread.

Nell caught her breath. She reflected on how handsome he looked; authoritative yet still warm and kind, a trait that sadly could so often be missing from high ranking noblemen.

The King stepped towards her and, taking her hand, gently kissed it.

"With Elly absent, I am retrieving you from Al – you are to be my partner tonight," said Ed, "and you will do me a great honour by sitting next to me at supper. I apologise in advance if doing so causes you any embarrassment or discomfort. I know how some people can find such prominence under public scrutiny quite daunting on occasions like this. But… I don't reckon I could have a better partner – Nell, you look radiant tonight!"

In response to his words, Nell grew pinker. She dropped a very courtly curtsy to hide her self-consciousness, and a hint of guilt, before speaking.

"I am proud to be your partner tonight and only hope I can justify your confidence in me."

She wondered if he could hear her heart drumming.

With a nod towards her maid, Ed continued, "It is going to be a very long and busy evening. Let us have one quiet drink here before we go down to meet our guests… in memory of our freedom this afternoon."

Hope brought over two silver goblets of wine, and they drank as they sat together companionably on the balcony. Below them, the terraces were already filling with people, milling amongst the extra torches and lanterns which were lit in serried rows to illuminate the walkways and meeting places of the castle tonight. Ed leaned close, their shoulders touching, to point out dignitaries and nobles he spotted, telling her what he knew about them. Nell savoured that slight physical contact and the waft of sandalwood that drifted off him.

"There's Caldwell, as serious as ever – I wish I could see him enjoy himself for once, relax and forget affairs of state. He has a family, but we never see any of them," Ed chatted. "Aah, can you pick out the mayor of Ostlebridge? He's adopted an Angonnan style of dress – I don't know if it's to impress Kaspar. If it is, then that wouldn't be much good, as Kaspar doesn't often wear it himself in Torland. He complains that it makes him appear fat – all those swathes of material – so, if you ever do see him in it, don't forget to mention how he looks like he's put on weight. Oh, there's Lord Paxton… I wondered if he is a relative of yours because he resembles your father."

Nell scanned the faces below her in confusion, searching for someone who looked like King Robert but without any luck.

Ed turned towards her, an eyebrow raised and an inquisitive twitch lifting the corner of his mouth.

"He's right below us, Nell, in front of the steps by the terraces."

She blinked, recognising her mistake; the man Ed was talking about was the spitting image of her uncle, Prince Harold. She rapidly swallowed a large gulp of wine.

Despite that slip, Nell felt very content as she walked down to supper, her hand resting on Ed's arm, this time without any tremor. For once, she didn't mind being observed throughout the meal or being the first to proceed to the floor for the dancing. She smiled blissfully back into the King's dark brown eyes as they whirled around the room and out into the courtyard behind the great hall, which was magical as it twinkled with strings of lanterns for the occasion. But Nell also made sure she acted correctly and courteously, dancing with many other nobles and some of the visiting dignitaries.

Then, in need of a rest and some cool air, Nell asked Al, her current escort, if they could stroll out onto one of the many terraces where the various entertainments were being laid on tonight. She searched around her as they collected some fruit punch before walking out. She could not see Ed, but that was not surprising, as the whole castle was extremely full and very busy. They stopped when they reached the terraces and sat for a break on a carved wooden bench. Appreciating the breeze as it wafted her skin, Nell gazed happily and curiously at the people milling along the terraces and gardens beneath them. She smiled in delight when she caught sight of Hope, who had ventured forth with Daisy after all.

Hope was feeling extremely self-conscious amongst the crowds circulating the castle grounds, despite the surreptitious goblet of Nell's wine she had swallowed swiftly for courage. Daisy had persuaded her to change into her best gown for the evening, made from a fine blue wool that complemented her eyes, and to let her hair hang loose and uncovered. Yet, with the gown much lower cut than she was used to, she felt exposed and vulnerable. Hope hesitantly followed Daisy, continually wishing she had stayed in her room, particularly when the other maid commenced flirting loudly with several young men from the town.

Uncomfortable, she began to slowly edge away from Daisy, sidling into the crowd until, not concentrating on where she was going, she bumped into someone standing close behind her.

"Oh!" she squealed in consternation as that person lightly grabbed her arm, steadying her.

Terrified, she swivelled around and found herself face-to-face with Marshall.

"Would you like to dance with me, Hope?" he asked quietly, ignoring her discomposure while admiring the bright copper highlights that shone in her red hair under the torch light, displayed in all its magnificence for the first time.

Hope faltered, petrified like a tiny, frightened mouse caught in the gaze of a playful cat. She felt scared, foolish even, to be approached by Marshall in front of all these important people and considered that he might be joking with her. Yet a new small voice in her head egged her on to say yes.

"Go on, Hope, he doesn't bite!"

"Well not much, anyway!"

"He's not a bad dancer... Go for it, Hope!" cajoled some of the other squires grouped nearby as she continued to hesitate.

"Watch your toes!"

Reluctantly, she folded, allowing Marshall to lead her towards one of the small areas where music was playing for those outside to dance.

Watching them complete a dance together and then embark on a second, Nell was grinning broadly with pleasure.

Suddenly, above the music and dancing, Nell heard raised, irate voices near where she sat, and her attention was immediately drawn back to another group of people in front of and directly below her. She gasped as she recognised the King's voice followed by the sharp ring of steel on steel. Nell gaped at Al, horrified and temporarily frozen, before they both hastily moved further down the terraces to find out exactly what was going on.

"Stop!" shouted Al, as he clambered down through the crowds to join Kaspar, who had also been nearby, and then the two of them quickly placed themselves between the arguing royal brothers.

Staring at the scene, Nell saw Ed and Warwick opposing each other, both brandishing swords and faces contorted in fury. Behind Warwick, some rough and tough looking young men struggled, pinioned by the stronger castle guard.

"Not here!" hissed Kaspar. "Let's shift this argument inside, away from public scrutiny."

Between him and Al, they somehow bundled the two brothers up the terraces and into a nearby room, closely followed by Nell. As they moved, Ed called to the guard to eject the prisoners.

"Get them out of my castle!" he shouted in uncharacteristic anger.

"Put the weapons down," Kaspar insisted when they reached the empty room, shutting the door firmly behind him.

Both brothers reluctantly placed their swords aside.

"How dare you raise a sword at me!" asserted Ed, his voice rumbling deep and low, his temper barely held in check.

"I have nothing. Even the friends I have you snatch away from me. I hate you!" yelled Warwick across the room like an adolescent, his face almost purple with rage.

Nell remained shocked but transfixed by the door, unable to move, her heart pounding as before but this time with fear.

"Those men… are your… friends?" queried Ed in disgust. "They came here to steal from my guests and instigate brawls, yet you call them your friends!"

"Yes, my friends – people I have chosen! You have had them arrested or thrown out because you are jealous," snarled Warwick, his face now ugly in its contortions, "and, once again, I am left with nothing. I have nothing of my own."

"You have so much!" insisted Ed firmly. "You have lands, properties and people of your own. You even have a role in my ministerial council. There are plenty of nobles who would be your friends if you just gave them half a chance. Several of your old companions still admire your prowess in the field, would gladly get to know you again."

Ed was almost pleading now in his wish to do well by his brother, to help him.

"But I have no real power! Nothing is decided by me!" spat Warwick, not really listening in his fury.

Ed, realisation dawning, looked horrified.

"Is that what this is all about… because I am king and not you?"

"Yes, it's what it's always been about – the luck that you had of being born first. You have all the power, and what do you do with it? Nothing! You could avenge our mother's death, get The Alliance to wage war on the North and regain our lands there. But you don't! You sit around here playing at being king, the big chief and magnanimous host, preventing me from doing what I want to do."

With his final parting volley, Warwick grabbed his sword and swung out of the room, still wearing a face like thunder and storming past Nell as she shrank nervously away from him.

Speechless, Ed spun away. He stood by the window, not looking out, his head drooping in despair.

"We'll go and find him – try to calm him down," said Kaspar.

He and Al left with an acknowledging hand gesture from Ed.

Slowly, cautiously, Nell stepped towards him and placed a hand gently on Ed's arm, wanting to offer comfort and support; she gave it a reassuring squeeze. Fleetingly, she surmised that he was ignoring her, would rather she was not there, but then he exhaled heavily and laid his hand over hers, squeezed it in return.

He coughed slightly to clear his throat.

"I don't know what to do about him, Nell, I really don't! He never used to be this way. Once, he was a great young man, a good companion, but now… well, you've seen… so angry…"

Ed faltered for a short time; he seemed to be thinking deeply before continuing.

"As he got older, Warwick started blaming my father for the death of my mother. She loved my father greatly and didn't want to be parted from him. So, when he went to war, my mother accompanied him, joining the other women, the camp followers. My brother maintains that my father should have insisted that she remain at home, but it wouldn't have done any good. My mother wouldn't have listened – she always did exactly as she wished, would have found a way to follow her husband on her own. Her independence and fierceness of spirit was one of the things my father loved about her – he wouldn't have changed her for the world.

"Then, during one long and ferocious battle, troop positions changed, and the poorly protected camp was overrun by the enemy. It was a blood bath – many of the women and children were massacred… including my mother."

Ed ceased momentarily and swallowed hard.

"Fortunately, my sister, Allys, who was also there and just a baby at the time, somehow survived hidden in blankets. It could have been a lot worse for my family.

But that's what Warwick means about seeking revenge and waging war. And he's right – I haven't and neither did my father. It wasn't deemed either politic or winnable at the time. And, for my father, there was us to take in to consideration too. Once our borders were settled, it was always judged more important to hold them firm, keep our people safe. Warwick doesn't understand that these decisions aren't made and discharged by just one man or for the happiness of one family, however powerful that person or family is. I don't imagine my father would have wished for anything better than to attack his enemies. In fact, it plagued him, festered inside him like poison for the rest of his life and led to his early death."

Both stood, hands still resting together, pondering his words.

"I'm not sure if there's anything I can do or say that'll help," Nell eventually responded, having mulled over all that he had said, "except in that he's wrong to blame you for everything. It was never your fault. And you're a good king, everyone knows that. Ed, you have helped hold this country and The Alliance firm. As a result, we've all prospered because of you and your father. You have nothing to be ashamed of. I suppose, whatever he's going through right now, all we can do is be patient and be here for Warwick. Although that won't be easy if he's throwing abuse around at everyone who knows him."

"Thanks, Nell… You're right. I reckon I should leave my brother to Kaspar and Al and get back to my guests. I'm not sure if I could be civil to Warwick presently anyway."

He attempted to shake off his mood and smiled down at Nell.

"Come… I don't want to brood on it anymore, and tonight is supposed to be a celebration. I should be putting my best foot forward amongst my guests. And I shouldn't waste any more time away from the dance floor when I have a beautiful young woman on my arm."

Astonished, Nell realised Ed was talking about her, but she willingly went back to the great hall and to the dancing with him, hoping she could distract him enough from his problems with his brother to allow him to concentrate on his guests. He certainly held her tightly around the waist as if her company was reassuring to him.

However, a little while later, she saw Kaspar and Al catch up with Ed, shaking their heads. They had not been able to find Warwick.

Chapter 8

From Midsummer on, they saw much less of Warwick which was, in itself, a relief. When they did see him, he was sullen, morose and silent. He no longer attended the regular council meetings with the other nobles and ministers. Both brothers took great care not to cross each other's paths if they could help it. Nell had little to do with Warwick either. He seemed to disregard her as of no consequence, while she, in response, was angry with his behaviour towards Ed and could not trust herself to be civil.

However, in one area, the brothers vied in direct competition against one another; with her mother feeling much better, Elly had returned to Erlwick at her vivacious best. Ed and Warwick were adversaries for her attention, one determined to duet with her more than the other. It caused Nell a pang of disappointment after the time she and the King had spent together, and the development of sentiments she had reckoned to have detected between them, to find Ed still enamoured with Elly. Although, she supposed she should not be surprised with Elly's beauty and the added spice of rivalry with his brother. Nell certainly noticed her cousin was always in the company of either of the two men. She was often seen walking around the castle with Warwick and even, on occasion, riding out with Ed.

One afternoon, Nell came across Elly on their balcony cradling a delicate pink rose in her hands, its petals beginning to unfurl from bud. Dreaming herself, Elly jumped guiltily as Nell approached, her cheeks reddening.

"Don't be cross with me, Nell," whispered Elly. "I've met somebody special, someone very important here. I know we only planned to have fun, but... he means a lot to me and I fancy he cares for me too."

"No, Elly," said Nell, compassionately, "I'm not cross with you. You can't help who you fall in love with and when that might happen. I'd just ask you to keep quiet about our personal ruse for a little bit longer if you can, only sharing that information when you're sure of his intentions towards you. If he does love you, you are very fortunate to find that special someone. I'm happy for you."

Nell did not ask who gave Elly the rose. She suddenly found herself scared of what the answer might be. Like her cousin, she had come to Erlwick determined merely to have fun only to find herself falling for the King. She could not blame Elly for doing the same thing. But suppose they were in love with the same man? Nell presumed she would have no chance in competing against her cousin for love. Moreover, whatever the outcome for Elly, Nell felt sure it was time to tell the truth about who she really was; the only problem would be when to do so.

As the weeks passed by, one summer month rolling into another, Nell continued with her round of riding lessons, swordplay and archery. Sometimes she was joined whilst out riding by Ed, who seemed to have acquired an interest in her progress since their riding excursion together, occasionally bringing Marshall and other squires in attendance for their own improvement. She often sat with Al in the library or joined Allys for shopping trips into town and, in the evening, she continued to meet some of her friends in Ed's room for a game or just a chat. This was a peaceful and happy time she would never forget.

Aware that she might encounter some anger or disappointment by revealing herself, Nell prevaricated about telling the truth despite her resolution to do so, not wishing to spoil this enjoyable period of her life. There were, however, guilty moments that punctuated her bubble like the occasions when her friends shared confidences with her. Or she would spot Ed hurrying off to a council meeting, usually leaving behind some much more pleasurable activity and flanked by sour-faced ministers, who all appeared more miserable than those in Guthway. She certainly did not miss that particular part of court life.

Frequently, she would attend court or state occasions, from hunts and games to banquets and balls, as befitted the visiting dignitary, ambassador or noble. Nell would remind herself that, even if she was playing a different role from usual at these events, she still represented her country and wanted to perform to the best of her ability. She would leave the flirting and dancing to Elly, instead trying to size up the politics, friendships and trade of each country through gentle chit-chat.

"What do you think of my cousin, Faraz?" asked Kaspar, grinning, on one such occasion when an ambassador had arrived from Angonna.

They were travelling along the River Berbeck in a barge for a picnic at a local beauty spot.

"Do you want the honest answer?" Nell rejoined, keeping her face totally straight, as she sat next to Kaspar after spending a difficult half an hour on the riverbank trying to talk to Faraz.

"Perhaps not," Kaspar sighed, "I can only offer my apologies and suggest that he is the odd-one-out amongst us. Every family has one, be he a clown or a black sheep. Faraz is ours, Warwick is Ed's, so who is yours?"

"Maybe it's me!" laughed Nell. "I must say that I'm glad Faraz is in Ed's boat and not ours," she added. "He's nearly capsized it on more than one occasion."

They both chuckled, continuing to watch Faraz struggling to balance in the ridiculously foppish clothing he was wearing, totally unsuitable for their outing, while ordering about his servants and glaring imperiously at the passing ducks.

Suddenly serious, seeing an opportunity, Nell decided to take the plunge.

"Kaspar… I have a confession which may mean that I am the black sheep of my family," Nell wavered, biting her lip with anxiety.

Kaspar stared at her intrigued.

"Go on, Nell, you can't suggest dark deeds then stop and say no more."

Nell focused on her feet where she shuffled them nervously in the bottom of the boat.

"I'm worried about what you'll think of me."

"Go on," he urged, one eyebrow raised inquisitively, wondering what could have made Nell so cagey.

"My cousin and I… well… we played a silly game… At least, it seems silly now… now we've got to know you all… become friends… and I am ashamed of it." She drew a deep breath to steady her voice before continuing, plunging in more decidedly, "Elly and I swapped identities. I am actually Princess Helen. I wanted a chance to enjoy more freedom and this, ostensibly, was a good way to do it. I'm sorry, Kaspar... sorry for deceiving you."

Immediately, Kaspar clasped her hand in his, saying, "Thank you for admitting the truth, Nell. That means a lot to me. Don't agonise about the past – it may have been a silly idea but you can make it right now. Tell the others – especially Ed, if you haven't told him already – as soon as you can. We have more understanding than you might suspect, being in similar situations ourselves. In a few months' time, we'll all be laughing at your ruse, but it is best if you come clean yourself."

"I will, Kaspar! I'm just waiting for the right moment."

Nell was relieved; one confession down, many more to go.

It was late summer and, just a day after her chat with Kaspar in the boat, Nell discovered that there were preparations in progress for a longer than usual hunt. It was to occur over two days with the hunting party dwelling overnight at the royal lodge in the hills. Hope had gone on in advance with other servants to organise a picnic and prepare the lodge for supper and sleeping arrangements.

Nell was excited at the prospect, never having been on such an extended hunt before, thrilled with the idea of them all camping out together at the lodge, and it would be a great opportunity to put in to practise her new riding skills. For once, they were to have a full royal contingent with both Allys and Warwick joining Ed for the event, the brothers temporarily putting aside any quarrel.

The party set off mid-morning after a ceremonial blessing of the hunt, everyone taking a large sip of wine from a great and ornately carved silver cup with two handles. They hung around, riders and horses together in a group towards the back of the bailey, passing the cup along to each other, making sure no one was left out. Faraz joined them for the send-off, dressed in a splendid and elaborate riding outfit which he had no intention of using for its true purpose, not wishing to join them in the hunt or for a night at the lodge.

As the riders began to mount their horses, mingling into some sort of informal order, Elly dallied at the back of the group, surprising Nell. Wearing her hair loose, Elly carried no weapons but was beautifully dressed in forest green and acted as only focused on socialising. To Nell's further surprise, it seemed that Warwick, also lurking at the back of the party, figured as the centre of her attention.

Nell was more purposefully attired than either Elly or Faraz with her hair tightly plaited, wearing a leather sur-coat and breeches, a bow and a quiver of arrows slung over her shoulder. She was preparing to join the centre of the party, discreetly finding comfort and security amongst the crowd, when she was waylaid by Ed.

"No hiding from you, Nell! I know exactly how good your riding and shooting skills are, so you can join me up front and be my partner. As a pair, we should be able to give my sister and Kaspar a run for their money this year. It's about time I had a companion I can win our private competition with."

Nell looked at him confused as he continued to smile.

"We've always had a private competition at the late summer hunt, scoring points according to the accuracy of the hits on prearranged targets, the speed at reaching particular places and so on, but usually, even Al beats me because I get stuck with some rotten namby-pamby princess who doesn't know one end of an arrow from the other. I figured I'd nab you before Al gets the chance."

He waved cheerily across at both Kaspar and Al as they milled about nearby.

"Kaspar and Allys have won the last four competitions straight. Are you up for the challenge?"

Nell laughed, "Well, with such confidence in me, we can't lose. Of course I'll ride with you. Let's see if we can change your run of luck."

She urged her horse alongside Ed, following him to the front with Marshall in attendance to calculate their score, and paused for the Master-at-Arms' signal to start. Burgess blew on an elegant silver-mounted hunting horn, and the royal party set off at speed, thundering across the small drawbridge tucked at the back of the castle and out into the fields and meadows beyond. It was not long before they entered the forest that led up into the hills and could commence their hunt in earnest.

Nell thoroughly enjoyed her day chasing amongst the fields and trees, sometimes with others of the hunt, sometimes almost alone. It was exhilarating weaving in and out of the undergrowth at full tilt, and the competition added an extra challenge, with some marks harder than others. The third of their targets proved to be a gnarled knot high up on a huge ancient oak tree deep in the forest. Surrounded by a shady glade and standing all on its own, the tree reached out and up to the sky, with a large hollow split in the wood creating a small living cave stretched through its trunk. Finding herself alone, Nell raised her arrow, squinted and aimed through the dappled light.

Suddenly, out of the dark hollow, Warwick emerged, a shadowy silhouette, and flicked a whip. The sharp crack startled both her and the horse. She flinched as it jumped back agitatedly. Caught off guard, Nell lost her grip and fell to the floor. Unhurt but shocked, she gasped when Warwick deliberately strode towards her. In the half light and blocking out what shafts had made it through the forest canopy, he was menacing as he loomed over her, sprawled on the ground, the whip still raised in his hand as if to strike. Then, for one instant, she assumed Warwick would help her up after all; he leant down, dropping the whip hand and slowly lowering his other towards her. But then he snatched it back, shrugging his shoulders.

"I guess you can manage," he sneered and left without any explanation or any apology for causing the accident.

As he exited the glade, Marshall entered. Surprised, he hurried over to help Nell up.

"Are you hurt?" he asked.

"No, thanks, I'm unharmed… just a little shaken," she replied, brushing down her clothes.

"Was that Prince Warwick I saw leaving? Didn't he help you?" Then understanding dawned. "Did he have something to do with your fall?"

"Ugh… yes… but please don't mention anything to Ed yet… I don't want to spoil his day."

"Very well," Marshall agreed doubtfully.

They both paused for a minute, staring in the direction Warwick had just gone, sharing the same questions in their minds although neither spoke. Why had Warwick acted in that way: to course hurt or confusion? And who had he been loitering for: Nell or someone else? Almost in unison, they shook their heads and Marshall helped Nell back onto her horse.

Just then, Ed and Kaspar arrived in the glade together, Allys a few strides behind.

"I reckon we're currently even," Kaspar was saying.

Marshall nodded his head in agreement, "But you all have to have a go at this one now. Nell first."

Smiling as brightly as she could, Nell raised her arrow.

"Good shot, Nell!" admired Kaspar when the arrow hit the centre of the target, and the competition continued.

At about noon, the hunting party stopped to eat: a picnic luncheon by the pool where Nell and Ed had previously swum, but a very different occasion from last time. All around her sat or lay her companions, chatting and eating. Today, nobody indulged themselves with a dip, but some of the more youthful members of the gathering paddled their feet in the cool water as they nibbled on the game pie and fruit cake. Very wary after their earlier encounter, Nell made sure she sat at a good distance from Warwick, but Elly's clear laughter in response to a comment from the Prince told Nell her cousin had no such qualms.

While the afternoon wore on, the hunters resumed the chase, but Nell now made sure she stayed close to Ed, not knowing the directions to the royal hunting lodge and also wishing to avoid a further isolated meeting with Warwick. Ed, meanwhile, was taking a tutorial stance with her.

"Careful with your grip, Nell – steady but light."

"You're making me nervous with such close scrutiny," Nell grumbled, and swivelling in the saddle, she caught him surveying her, justifying her complaint.

"I'm just examining your aim and… balance," grinned Ed.

"That's what I was worrying about!" she rejoined through gritted teeth.

Nell smiled with delight when they finally reached the cabin, and she got her first glimpse of the backdrop to their special evening. It was an elongated building on two levels made from great oak timbers. Inside and out, the beams and columns were carved, painted and gilded with hunting scenes. The ground floor was mainly one enormous room, a hall mostly raised to the roof but with a minstrels' gallery at one end and a huge inglenook fireplace at the other. Other smaller rooms led off along the back wall of the hall, including the game preparation room, a small kitchen and communal servants' quarters. Above these were a series of rooms linked by an arched corridor that overlooked the hall. A few rooms were only big enough for one bed, while the rest housed a collection of wooden bunks. Outside, a beautifully carved wide porch encircled three sides of the building, while a yard and stables were built behind the fourth, back wall. Gabled windows rose into the rafters. With the large number of people it was to hold tonight, the lodge would be a much cosier and more intimate venue than the castle.

When they arrived, trotting along a short, stony path edged with neatly clipped box hedges, Ed gallantly came to help Nell down while a couple of young stable lads stepped forward discreetly from the shadows to lead away their horses.

"I gather that we're ahead of everyone else – I'd estimated that we'd made good time. First to the cabin and with a great score already… thanks to you, Nell," laughed the King, his hands firmly around her waist as he lifted her from the horse, exuberantly swinging her around and down to the ground.

Nell also laughed joyously and instantaneously in reaction. She was not sure but she felt his hands had lingered on her momentarily longer than strictly necessary. She reddened at the sensation that reflection gave her. Ed grinned at her and, flustered with the idea that he had read her mind, Nell blushed even further.

"We usually have a drink while we wait for everyone else to arrive, enabling us to compare scores, falls, disasters, that sort of thing, and then we can go off to our rooms to freshen up ready for supper," explained Ed, as he guided her towards the lodge with one hand resting on her shoulder. "If the weather's fair and warm, like tonight is set to be, we usually have tables put up under the porch and eat outside on the small lawn. We often have a campfire, too, in case the evening gets a little chilly."

Entering the building, Nell wavered in the doorway, letting her eyes adjust to the change in the light. She revolved about, taking in the whole setting.

"It's lovely – a hidden oasis of tranquillity and warmth!" she exclaimed.

Ed beamed back at her, pleased with her approval. He went to an enormous rectangular table in the centre of the hall and pulled a large earthenware pitcher of wine towards him, pouring it into two goblets. Continuing to smile, Ed passed one goblet to Nell. She smiled in response as their fingers casually touched and their eyes met. Gazing at him, she mused on how soft and velvety his brown eyes were. Ed stepped forward, closing the short distance between them, raised a thumb to wipe a smudge of dirt from her cheek and was about to speak when Kaspar bounced into the room with a great clamour.

"Hello!" he hollered.

Instantly, the hall was filled with people and noise as more of the hunting party arrived; the peace Nell had admired was broken. Almost guiltily, Nell and Ed moved apart, taking separate paths around the room amongst their friends, but not before Allys laid speculative eyes on them.

Nell had a wonderful evening. The atmosphere was very relaxed and casual, with no formal seating arrangement or expectations of courtly behaviour. The King seemed to spend the entire evening changing places in order to socialise with all the nobles and courtiers present. A large joint of venison had been spit-roasted outside, and everyone sat around the roaring fire eating pieces of meat, cheese and bread from wooden platters. Nell perched next to Allys on a wooden bench while she surveyed the young men drinking big frothy jugs of ale and chatting laughingly with their friends, usually about their hunting exploits: real or imagined, details carefully recounted or massively embroidered, from today or on former occasions.

The sun gradually sank until the group were illuminated only by the orange glow of the fire and a few strategically placed torches. She was sure that a few couples took advantage of the dark and secretive shadows at the edges of the dining area to kiss and cuddle. Even Warwick was enjoying himself, slouching on the outskirts of the group but, nevertheless, involved with others, and again, intriguingly, often sitting in close conversation with Elly. Once or twice, Nell caught Ed throwing apprehensive glances in their direction, his anxious stare dallying on her cousin's face, and she felt a pang of jealousy at his concern for Elly, realising she wanted him to think that way about her. Nobody ever regarded her with such care and consideration. All she got was a few cool smirks from Warwick which only made her shiver in fear, amazed how he could make her experience that feeling even in a crowded place.

Shifting her contemplation, Nell witnessed Marshall quietly moving away to the shadows of the lodge, approaching Hope where she had been hovering near one end of the porch, ready to assist her mistress if she was needed.

Hope rapidly scanned about her, whipping her head from side-to-side, desperately wishing to find an escape route as the squire came towards her. She had talked to Marshall a few times following their dance at the

Midsummer banquet but only in passing or in relation to her work. She had enjoyed that dance, the warm caress of his hands on her waist as she gazed back into his intelligent, kind eyes. The memory of it pervaded her dreams. Yet, despite the interest Marshall had shown in her, Hope still felt intensely shy, terrified of making a mistake, a fool of herself. She liked him a lot and did not want him to deem her as idiotic. So she had rarely met his eyes since.

"I suspect you might be free to go off duty now, Hope," commented Marshall, having reached her quickly, not giving her a chance to slip away. "Why don't you come with me because this is an evening for socialising and making friends?"

Marshall spoke very gently, respectful of the girl's shyness. He understood her reluctance to talk to him was based in fear rather than dislike because he had a sister equally as timid, and he was determined to bring Hope out of her shell.

Staring warily at Marshall yet unable to conjure up a polite reason not to go with him, Hope panicked about where he wished to lead her in the gloom. Marshall grasped her hand firmly, pulling her after him, knowing she could not resist his strong hold. Hope also realised she would need to be brave, try to conquer some fears, at least enough to talk to him.

Soon, she realised her fears were unfounded because Marshall simply guided her backstage to the stables behind the lodge. She could hear lots of voices as they approached the building which was separated from the servant's quarters by a wide walkway and a small courtyard. It was lit by torchlight, smelt of freshly spread hay, and was filled with squires, stable hands and servants, all chatting, drinking and playing at dice. Hope hung back bashfully but thought it was magical. Marshall, however, strode confidently towards several stalls at one end of the stables, dragging Hope firmly behind him, swapping comments with the others as he did so. One or two grinned cheekily at the sight of his companion.

"Not joining us for a game then?" asked one while he shook his dice noisily in a wooden beaker.

"Nah, he's got other fish to fry," was a reply.

"Well, he's likely to have more fun than us then!" chuckled another.

Hope blushed furiously at the insinuations as she followed closely in Marshall's footsteps.

"Never mind them – they're harmless really," whispered Marshall.

When he reached the last stall but one, he approached one of the horses, a huge jet-black stallion, and gently patting his nose, removed an apple from the pocket bag at his waist.

"He's mine. He's called Shadow," stated Marshall proudly, feeding the apple to the horse. "My father bought him for me when I became squire to the King. It was a great honour – father felt I should have the best steed possible. He serves me really well, so I always try to say goodnight. Here, you can stroke him," and, putting his hand under her elbow, he drew her into the stall closer to Shadow, closer to himself.

Then, holding her trembling hand in his own, he placed it on the horse's flank. The animal felt muscular, silky and warm. She could feel his heart beating calmly and hear his steady breathing. All Hope's fears temporarily melted away in the presence of the horse, a gentle giant like his master. Another horse whinnied close by, making Marshall's stallion bray in response, stamping his hoof.

Marshall laughed, "That's your mistress's grey mare, Star. I suspect Apollo fancies her. I figure she's a little jealous and wants some attention too."

"Have you any more apples?" asked Hope.

Together, they strolled through the stalls visiting a few of the horses before turning in for the night themselves, ready for their early departure. By which time, Hope felt safe and totally at ease in Marshall's company.

Meanwhile, as the fire finally began to die down, the embers smouldering a deep, dark red, people started to drift off to bed, tired from the day's exertions, seeking rest and to prepare for tomorrow's hunt. Nell dawdled by the fire despite the creeping chill, clasping a goblet of red wine, not wishing for the pleasant evening to end. At last, draining the last dregs, she yawned and stretched.

"Time for bed, Nell," said Ed softly.

She almost jumped. Peering around, Nell suddenly realised that they were the last people left. Relaxed and leaning back, hands behind his head as he contemplated the stars, Ed lolled against a log near her, his long legs extended out in front of him.

Spontaneously, Nell went over to sit by his side, a hand resting on his arm with a feather-light touch, and whispered quietly, "I'm sorry about Elly… Warwick and Elly… and how it affects you."

Ed gaped at Nell, surprised.

He sat up and turned towards her, murmuring, "I'm only troubled about his intentions towards her, Nell. I'm afraid I just don't trust Warwick anymore, and I don't want to see her hurt."

Then, for a minute, he stared at her piercingly, as if delving into her mind, before he spoke again, "I'm not sorry for myself. She's pleasant enough company – and obviously rather nice to look at – but I don't have any special feelings for her. Can you guess why, Nell?"

Her heart twisted under his continuing intense gaze and his question. Snaking an arm out, he placed his hand on the back of her head. Leisurely caressing her hair, Ed gradually edged closer to her, his hand moving down to stroke her cheek and the length of her neck. Nell gasped as his fingers swept lightly across her breast and involuntarily her body arched towards his, betraying her. Deliberately, he sought her lips, his kisses demanding and she found herself responding to them hungrily. An instant later, he drew back slightly; she could still detect his heart beating as fast as her own.

Nell felt his warm breath caress her cheek as he murmured in her ear, "I've wanted to do that since I saw you in the pool months ago."

Then he jumped up rapidly and strode lightly into the lodge leaving Nell, stunned and dizzy at all the emotions coursing through her, suddenly feeling the chill that his absence left behind him.

Chapter 9

"Wake up, Nell!" laughed Allys early the next morning, drawing back the curtains and letting in what bright morning light could reach them through the tall forest trees.

Nell blinked and groaned. It was still too bright for her.

The three women had shared a room, but Elly appeared to have gone already. Nell wanted to stay snuggled under the cosy eiderdown, feeling tardy after yesterday's full activity and late night, enveloped in its warmth and soft security. Instead, she stretched reluctantly and yawned, trying to rouse herself.

"I'd love to leave you to sleep in, but my brother would never forgive me – he'd presume it was sabotage – and I wouldn't want you to have the shock of him coming to wake you. Ed's in a jolly good mood this morning but very excitable – he's pacing around downstairs ready for action like a caged cat. He's definitely planning on winning this competition.

"There's a jug of warm water to wash with by the window, and we've been left a platter of fruit and a beaker of lemonade for refreshment when you're ready. Hope has already gone on beforehand with most of the other servants."

Nell watched Allys putting on her gown then struggling to tie it tightly before brushing through her tumbled hair. Sitting up, Nell swung her feet out of the bunk and onto the hard wooden floor, flinching slightly at the cold touch.

"Here, let me help," suggested Nell, and the young women alternated brushing and plaiting each other's hair hurriedly in preparation for another day of riding.

Then it was Nell's turn to wash and dress as speedily as she could. She was still finishing a mouthful of grapes as she left the lodge. Even so, Ed was waiting eagerly for her outside with Marshall, holding her horse, Star, steady. Despite her pleasant dreams, Nell was unsure of how she would be able to face the King after the previous night, the memory of her response alone enough to make her blush, and what she could say to cover any embarrassment. However, she did not have to worry because Ed immediately assumed the lead, apparently only concerned with continuing the hunt as rapidly as possible. Perhaps last night had been, for him, the result of too much ale, something to try and forget or ignore.

"Come on, sleepyhead, most of the party left ages ago, and we need to catch up," Ed complained but smiled broadly at her as he said it. "Al's long gone," and he shook his head ruefully. "Kaspar and I tried to sabotage both his clothes and his partner, but neither appears to have worked."

"A good thing too!" exclaimed Nell. "That wouldn't be fair!"

As Ed assisted her in mounting Star, he added, "The rest of the party are proceeding further down the

89

valley for their picnic luncheon today, but a few of us are intending to go back to the pool for a quieter break. Are you satisfied with that plan, Nell?"

Nell nodded her agreement.

"But no swimming today," she added a little regretfully while adjusting her reigns, and then paused for Ed to mount too.

Nell perused the lodge fleetingly, storing a picture of it in her brain along with the wonderful memories of her brief stay, before they left it behind them.

Today, she stayed close to the King, speculating if they would continue their conversation from last night but noting that, currently, he was intent only on the hunt.

She was aware, too, of several other riders from the party nearby, mostly those who would join them for their more intimate picnic later. Occasionally, she glimpsed Kaspar or Al through the undergrowth who would often share joking comments with Ed. They were all in very good humour.

"You didn't get so far ahead then?" asked Ed when they first ran into Al.

"For some reason, my clothes had vanished," grumbled Al. "I had to persuade my squire to track down – beg, steal or borrow, I'm not sure which – some more for me."

"Aah…" grinned Ed, fingering his tunic, "that would explain my missing sur-coat."

Nell peered sidelong at him, noting how the sheer material of his shirt and tunic clung to the muscles of his arms and chest, especially when the horse moved at speed.

"And my lost boots!" chipped in Kaspar, having to shout between the trees.

"Nope, I only swiped the boots," countered Al in dribs and drabs as he swerved around trunks. "Someone else must be in need of royal garments this morning too.

"After sorting my clothing, I discovered my partner deemed I had other designs on her than the hunt. Fortunately, that didn't put her off from our sport entirely. Unfortunately, it seemed to make her rather amorous, and once we found a quiet spot, it took another half an hour to suggest we should continue with the competition. And allowing you time to catch me up. All I have to say is – thanks!"

"Our pleasure! I know you'll do the same for us sometime," laughed Ed.

Several times during her ride, Nell also spotted the familiar black garb of Warwick amongst the trees. After their encounter yesterday, she found that much more unnerving. She still had not told Ed, and the thought of her fall and the Prince's actions made her mouth run dry.

It was nearing luncheon when they finally approached the clearing around the pool. Nell could hear the hurrying babble of the waterfall. She smiled, envisioning her last more private visit here, and glanced shyly across at Ed. He was busy shouting something to Kaspar who, with Allys, Al, and the young lady Al had brought as his partner, still making sheep's eyes at him, had already arrived in advance of them and dismounted.

Then Ed twisted towards her, "I calculate that we're still doing well enough in our competition and can afford to relax a little, have a leisurely luncheon, maybe even manage another swim after all."

Nell laughed, "You can but I'll stick to the meadow in the present company."

She then tutted as she noticed his clothing, "I'm sure we haven't had that rough a ride this morning, but you look like you've been pushing through hedges rather than jumping over them or going around them."

Holding Star motionless, Nell leant forward to gently sweep away a cluster of small twigs, leaves and dirt that had accumulated on Ed's shoulder, pondering on how he could have done with that missing sur-coat to protect him from the undergrowth. As she did so, Nell heard the unmistakeable sound of an arrow loosed… then in flight.

Everything happened instantly: a sudden searing stab ripped through her shoulder, a force that knocked her forwards and off her horse, while shouting exploded all around her. She hit the ground forcefully. Continuing pain brought bile to her mouth as her face lay in the dirt, stones pressing hard against her cheek. Nell tried to move but lifting her arms, her shoulder, caused another surge of agony.

Somewhere, as if from a great distance, she heard Ed's voice calling 'Don't move!' to her, but there was a soothing blackness that was overwhelming, easy to embrace, and for a short while, she succumbed.

When she came to, the pain still throbbed in her shoulder, and only minutes had passed. Nell found herself sitting up and leaning forwards against Ed's chest, her blood seeping into his tunic; he was holding her steady whilst issuing brisk, firm orders to those standing around them, his voice full of controlled anger.

Nell heard a quiet muttering.

"Don't try to talk," advised Ed gently, but his voice was shot through with anxiety, an instant change from his previous authoritative tone.

Confused, Nell had not realised that the mumbled words she had heard were her own. She did not understand what was happening to her, or around her, and tried to hold back tears of pain and frustration at her own helplessness. She felt a hand grip hers, heard Allys's voice somewhere beside her.

"Don't fret, Nell! We're here… We'll help you!" Allys said, her tears unseen but heard in her voice.

Nell opened her mouth to speak, thought better, and closed it again. She felt another wave of dizziness and nausea. She did not want to be sick over the King, so she shut her eyes to concentrate on what she could hear while trying to breathe deeply, taking comfort from the contact with friends, the closeness to Ed. He was yelling directives to Kaspar and Al, something about Warwick.

Gradually, she became aware that Ed was talking to her again, "I need to get the arrow out, but I can't lie to you, Nell – it will hurt. Once it's out, we can get you cleaned up and bound… and back to the castle as soon as possible."

Nell nodded her head, or imagined she had, and anticipated the agony.

"I'll hold her tight, Allys, while you pull the arrow out – try to make it one swift, smooth movement."

Ed's voice faded and resurfaced in waves.

Almost immediately, Nell felt herself being squeezed in a bear hug. She silently sighed at the comforting warmth and softness, the security. But then an excruciating pain followed, as bad as the original thrust, and for a moment, she let the blackness engulf her again in its sweet relief.

She roused to Ed's voice calling her.

"Nell… Nell… I'm going to cut your shirt – just at the shoulder – to get closer to the wound so that I can wash it… clean it. There seems to be something on the arrow which has got into the wound. Then we'll bind it."

Nell felt a slight tugging while he cut the fabric loose with his hunting knife, followed by more soreness when he tried to wash her wound, then agony once more as Ed had to dig deeper to clean and rinse the gash. Some relief came as cold, clear water from the pool ran over her skin and counteracted a growing stinging heat emanating from her shoulder.

"Hot!" she tried to mutter deep into Ed's chest.

Ed spoke, apprehension in his voice, "There was something in the cut – I don't know if I've got it all out."

Next, there was a firmness when they wrapped fabric around her shoulder, binding her injury tightly. Ed lifted Nell as if she weighed no more than a feather onto his horse, mounted immediately behind her, then held her immobile in front of him while the stallion jolted forward to carry them back to the castle.

"Help me!" murmured Nell, not really expecting to be heard as the words were instantly snatched into the air around her, wondering if she had really managed to say anything at all and, if she had, did it come out as 'Hold me'?

She felt a reassuring squeeze in reply and, once more, let nothingness overwhelm her.

The journey back to Erlwick was mostly a blur of pain, noise and shooting light. For a while, Nell remembered little else until she vaguely woke in darkness, unsure of her surroundings but feeling hot, sweaty and very thirsty. She tried to talk, to ask for water, and to shake off the sheets around her, wanting nothing but coolness, yet no voice sounded out of her mouth.

A firm hand held hers. Someone leant forward and she smelt sandalwood, then cool water splashed her brow. She heard familiar voices all about her, muffled so she could not really make out any words. Tired, she closed her eyes again.

When Nell did eventually wake fully, she heard a strange gentle rumbling noise nearby. Warm golden light streamed through partially opened curtains across what she now recognised as her own bedroom. Still exhausted, muscles sore as if awaking after a fierce fight, Nell rolled her head carefully on the pillow to seek out the source of the noise. As she did so, a sharp stab pulsed across her shoulder, making her wince and bringing her memory rushing back into focus. For a few seconds, Nell closed her eyes and waited for the pain to recede before continuing to locate the source of the noise; when she did, she smiled. Ed lay asleep in a chair pulled close to her bed, his shoeless feet resting on a low table and his head thrown back, snoring. His clothes were dishevelled and stubble grew across his chin. Automatically, Nell reached out a hand towards him, wishing to touch his tousled hair, but the discomfort and a desire not to disturb him made her withdraw again. Instead, Nell watched him, pleased at his presence and liking his unkempt guise.

Allys entered the room and, seeing Nell awake, darted towards her in delight. About to say something, Nell swiftly motioned her silent, pointing at the King.

Beckoning to the other woman, Nell whispered croakily a quick request, "I'm hot, dirty and sticky. Please can you help me wash and change, preferably without rousing your brother?"

Allys smiled, "We'll try our best. I'll just go and get some help from your maid."

With Allys and Hope's assistance, Nell managed to bathe hurriedly, washing away the remnants of blood from her wound and the sweat from her fever. They redressed her shoulder before helping her into a clean chemise. Then Allys plaited Nell's hair while Hope speedily changed the bedclothes. Ed continued to sleep. And, exhausted by the activity but feeling refreshed, Nell herself fell back into a restful, healing sleep amidst the cool, crisp sheets.

Chapter 10

When Nell woke once more, she felt invigorated. This time, the chair beside her bed was empty. Ed had gone. A twinge of disappointment coursed through her. However, it was not long before she was joined again by Allys.

"Ed's been here almost all the time, waiting for you to get better, even nursing you himself to begin with," Allys confessed, catching Nell's glance towards the chair.

Nell flushed pink; that explained the scent of sandalwood she remembered from her vague, fevered dreams.

"But he had some important and pressing matters of state to attend to this morning," Allys said.

She faltered briefly, gazing into space as she remembered.

"You know, I've never seen him so angry – and frightened – as when you were shot. He's usually so calm, unflappable."

"Warwick!" said Nell simply.

"Yes! I expect Ed will want to explain what happened himself. He told me to let him know as soon as you woke up," added Allys.

"Well, let's give him a little longer with whatever he's got to do," suggested Nell. "As you have just said, he's wasted a lot of time on me recently rather than tending to his country, so let's give some of it back to him. I'm feeling a lot better and would like to sit on the balcony, get some fresh air. Although, I will probably be a bit wobbly… Perhaps you could help me walk there?"

"Fine… We'll get you settled with something to eat before I speak to my brother," Allys agreed.

Nell raised and manoeuvred herself gingerly to the edge of the bed before slowly getting out, moving her injured shoulder as little as possible and using her other arm to bear all the weight. Then Allys helped her carefully into one arm of a dressing gown, leaving the other free, gown resting on her shoulder, not wishing to course more pain to her friend. With Allys's support, Nell hobbled over to sit on one of the low wicker chairs on the balcony and stared out at the beautiful day displayed before her: the sky was a clear forget-me-not blue with just a few wispy, white clouds scudding gently on the horizon. A faint breeze murmured refreshingly across her face. Tracking distinctive sounds below her, she could see men practising their skills in the tiltyard.

Nell sighed. She had not been hit in her sword arm, but her injury was sure to affect her ability with a bow, at least in the short term. Her mind ran over the events of the shooting and its aftermath, arousing a string of conflicting emotions. The pain, fear and frustration loomed large still, yet she was certainly pleased that Ed had spent so much time on her. However, she was also horrified at the intimacies that had probably entailed if his sister was right and he had helped nurse her back to health.

Relieved at her mistress's recovery, Hope had brought her a platter of fruit, including tempting, exotic treats such as melon and pomegranate. Not really hungry but unwilling to disappoint her maid, Nell forced herself to pick at the plate, digging out the tiny ruby seeds or leisurely rolling a juicy cube of melon around her mouth. The cook's famous lemonade was very welcome, though, to her dry throat.

A short time later, she heard footsteps approach and Ed materialised on the balcony beside her, also looking decidedly fresher and clean shaven. He stared at Nell, examining the scene in front of him and assuring himself that she really was feeling better. Heartened by what he saw, he broke into a sad smile.

"At last! It's good to see you awake and up out of bed. I have to admit you scared us all because you were out of things for so long!" he exclaimed.

"I assume we didn't win the competition after all," muttered Nell then frowned, puzzled at his words. "What do you mean… so long?"

The King came and sat in a chair beside her, "You've been asleep and feverish, on and off, for five days now."

Nell gasped.

"That long! But what happened? I only have vague memories of events."

Ed's jaw clenched tight as if the memory still made him very irate. It required a concerted effort for him to relax enough and to be able to speak in a controlled voice.

"That's not surprising. You were shot in the shoulder with an arrow. The gash was deep but avoided major blood vessels. We pretty swiftly realised that it had been poisoned, and that's what caused you the greatest problems. We had trouble cleaning it all out, so some must have got into your system, resulting in the fever and unconsciousness."

Ed glanced away, couldn't meet her eyes for a minute while he gathered his thoughts. Then he held Nell's hand gently in his, unconsciously stroking her fingers, before he continued.

"Nell, that arrow wasn't meant for you – it was supposed to be for me, aimed straight at my heart. You just got in the way. You were in the wrong place at the wrong – or rather for me the right – time when you leant towards me, but – with that one gesture – you caught the blow instead of me. I was the intended victim and – without the defence of my sur-coat – I should be dead! You saved my life, Nell… but nearly at the expense of your own."

Nell was shocked at this news of the assassination attempt, scared at the sudden image of what might have happened to either of them.

"But who would do that?" she whispered.

Yet, as she spoke, she already remembered the black clothing amongst the trees and predicted the dreadful answer, one name.

"Warwick!"

"Marshall told me of your encounter with him… and why you said nothing," said Ed with a shake of his head.

"Maybe, if I had told you sooner, we would all have been more wary of him," suggested Nell miserably.

"Well, that's the benefit of hindsight, Nell. It's not your fault. We all know something like this has been brewing for some time," comforted the King.

He stood up and walked away from her, hiding his thoughts and emotions, taking time to compose himself before he carried on. Even so, the strain began to show in his voice.

"There's more to tell you, Nell. My brother got away that day despite all our best efforts, but he did not leave alone – Elly went with him. I think he surmised that marrying a princess would help him, especially after the failed attempt on my life. Little did he guess the truth there! We speculate that they escaped across the border to the north. Goodness knows what havoc he might wreak with help from those lands!"

"Oh, Elly…"

Then some of his words gave Nell pause for reflection.

"What did you mean by 'little did he guess the truth there'?" she asked quietly.

"I believe you have something to confess to me, Nell."

Ed also spoke in hushed tones as if protecting a secret. He picked something up from a table near the bed and dangled it in the light from the window. Nell gulped as she saw the twinkling gold: her butterfly necklace.

"When I had to cut away your shirt, I spotted your necklace," continued Ed, twirling the chain around his fingers. "I understand the significance of this piece of jewellery, even if no one else does… because I was the one to give it to you!"

Contrite, Nell blushed. Ashamed of herself and her actions, she looked away.

Now it was she who could not meet his eyes while she tried to explain, "I'm sorry! I didn't mean to cause trouble. It was one impulsive decision – selfish really – which was simple to make but not so easy to back track from. I certainly never meant to hurt anyone and didn't deliberate far enough in advance to consider how our rouse might end… or how it would be if I made friends with you all. I only wanted… well, I don't know if you can understand… I conjectured – no, knew – how people would see me, how people always see me."

Suddenly gaining a little courage despite the tears glistening in her eyes, Nell glared at him fiercely, spoke a little more forcefully.

"It's different for you! As a man and a king, you are your own master. I have to please my father and my people. I am obliged to make a good match to someone – maybe a complete stranger – who will one day help me rule and protect my kingdom. Wherever I go, whoever I meet, I am seen as the ultimate prize. It doesn't matter if they genuinely get on with me or whether I like them. And I rarely get to see them as they really are. It would be about bartering me – my kingdom – for its security. For once, I just wanted the chance to be myself, to be free of all those expectations and not judged or liked purely because of my status."

The reasons for her choices had begun to sound feeble even to her. Vexed with herself, the situation and feeling utterly wretched, Nell wiped away a few tears. Had Ed's attitude to her changed? Did she detect a coolness towards her? After all, she had lied to him when he had befriended her, opened his home to her. Had she betrayed his trust? Those reflections caused her more pain than the arrow in her shoulder ever could.

"Believe it or not, I do understand, Nell," said Ed, continuing to speak softly. "I would have understood at any time you decided to tell me. I myself don't have as much freedom as you presume. But perhaps you are still learning that yourself. I surmise that, unlike you, I do have more of an option to say no, even if I live under the constant pressure of heavy obligations too. Sometimes, though, I have very little freedom of choice and even less free time. That is why I am not afraid to wield a bit more power when I can. And why my stolen afternoon with you was so special.

"I am surrounded by ministers who constantly remind me that it is crucial I should marry – not just anyone but a princess from an ally to strengthen Torland's position – and produce an heir. And you should hear them since this incident with Warwick! What would have happened if I had died with no offspring and my brother – my murderer – became heir? Yet that is one area in my life in which I insist on taking my time, I want to choose a partner I can share all aspects of my life with, from ruling my country and running my palace to sharing my leisure time and my bed. Hence the recent disagreement I had with my neighbours.

"And that is why I also totally understand the reasons behind what you did. But… I believed I had become your friend, and still you told me nothing!"

Ed sighed as if sad, disappointed, and that tore at her heart. He turned away briefly, his back to Nell, those few minutes feeling like hours to her, and stared out the window without really seeing the view before him.

Then he came back to sit beside Nell and continued, "Never mind… We now have bigger issues! My brother has betrayed me, tried to kill me. His actions nearly killed you too. Elly has gone with him – been disloyal to both of us. It is important that you tell the truth now to all your friends, but I will leave it to you to decide how and when you do that."

A few minutes passed when nothing was said. Both were busy in their own meditations. Nell covered her face with her hands briefly then smoothed one hand over her hair, sighing deeply as she did it.

"What are you going to do about Warwick?" Nell asked eventually, her quiet voice sounding thin.

"I'm not sure yet," admitted Ed. "I suppose that I should wait and see what his plans are, what his next move is, although I don't like only being so reactive again. I suspect he won't be content only to run away and hide, do nothing… But then… I don't reckon I actually know my brother anymore."

He patted her arm distractedly as he got up, and looking extraordinarily miserable and lonely as he stroked his chin, Ed moved away still deep in thought. Nell could only stare after him, guilty at what she had done, hating herself for enjoying herself so much and letting time, and the opportunity to confess to the King, slide. He stopped momentarily before proceeding back into the building.

"If you feel up to it, we would love to have you join us in the great hall for supper tonight. Your position at table will have changed, of course, especially if you let everyone know who you really are."

Nell did make it down to supper. The poison having left her system, she felt much better physically, only her shoulder needing time to heal, the skin and muscle to mend. She sported a large and ugly red welt which was still quite raw and very sore to the touch. However, she knew her head and heart would need longer to sort themselves out, her despondency and remorse time to lift.

First, she realised she had to seek out her friends in order to tell them the truth: that she was Princess Helen of Guthway. Nell set out gloomily, initially to find Allys and Al, Kaspar already in the know, before moving on to other courtiers, even servants, she had grown fond of. She was astonished to find how understanding and forgiving everyone was, adding to her own shame.

During that first supper she spent in the great hall after the assassination attempt, Nell could sense that the atmosphere at court was different, charged with an anticipation, a tension, which hadn't been there before. Everyone was waiting for something more to happen.

For the next week or so, Nell felt deflated with the shock of her injury and the guilt of discovery following the unbridled joy of the hunt. Ed seemed quiet and removed, understandable with all that had happened, the faith that had been broken. Where once his door was usually open of an evening, welcoming company, now it was always shut. She had dithered by the closed door, hand resting on the frame, speculating if she should try to talk with him, but in the end she lost courage and walked away, afraid of rejection. Nell would not have blamed him. Their paths crossed little during the day. The King was either keeping himself very busy with matters of state or remained closeted in his room. He even practised in the tiltyard at different times to everyone else, either very early or very late, with only Marshall, his sparring partner, to accompany him, his fury evident in the ferocity of his attack. During meals, he was uncommunicative and brooding; her attempts at conversation brought little response, but she did not want to give up trying.

Initially, Nell presumed that maybe it was her and what she had done that had produced his new reserve, that she had lost his trust. Had he been so hurt by her childish subterfuge, more than he had admitted to? She had felt he was colder and more remote towards her in particular but was not totally sure if she had read him correctly. Consequently, she sought out Al to ask his advice, recognising his greater insight into his old friend, the King.

"Al, is Ed really so cross with me for deceiving you all?" asked Nell. "He strikes me as quite distant at the moment, and I'm not certain if he's like that with everyone… or just with me."

"Don't worry, Nell! He understands what life has been like for you as heir to a king and recognises your switch with Elly was only a light-hearted, youthful game. I reckon that it did hurt him a little that you had not yet told him the truth, but he is also very angry with himself – that he did not see all this trouble with Warwick coming and had not been able to protect you from his brother's actions. Ed doesn't mean to be unfriendly – it's because he's been so preoccupied, and he's been the same with all of us. I expect that he also doesn't want to be morose and distant when in our company. He just needs some time to get his head straight. This business with Warwick has really shaken him, much more than he'd like to admit. It's knocked his confidence and dented his pride. He always felt that, whatever else, he could trust and rely on family. And don't forget it was a double betrayal – Elly has been false with you both too. Even if she didn't perceive what Warwick planned to do, she was willing to flee with him once she was aware of his behaviour."

Nell sighed, "I can't imagine what I'm going to tell my father and my aunt. I've been putting it off for these last few days."

"I wouldn't fret about that," explained Al. "One of the first things Ed did was to let your father know what had happened." Then seeing Nell's look of alarm, he quickly spoke to reassure her, "He also let King Robert know as soon as we realised that you would get better, persuaded him it was safe for you to abide here to recover. Your father seemed to trust Ed's judgement."

Al smiled gently at her.

"Nell, I know Ed still sees you as a friend. He cares a lot for you. He might not admit it but he was very scared for you – we all were – and he felt events were massively out of his control. Give him time to sort out in his head what is happening with his brother, and then he'll be back to his old self."

As soon as she was able and Burgess agreed, Nell resumed practising her swordsmanship and archery, even her riding. Although her shoulder was not fully mobile, she did what she could one-handed. Her father had instilled in her the importance of being able to fight her own battles in any way she needed to. Moreover, apprehensive herself at Warwick's attack on Ed, the implications it had for all of them and possibly Guthway, she reverted to her lessons with increased vigour.

"Take it easy!" laughed Kaspar, watching her rain blow after blow on poor Burgess whilst working in the yard himself. "Remember you're still recovering!"

Chapter 11

Tensions began to ease slowly over the next few weeks. Following a couple of trips away from court, including one to visit her father, making preparations and having discussions with his nearest and closest allies and commanders in case of war, the King had started to relax and opened up once more to his friends. Although Nell was well aware that Ed was increasing his troops, gathering an army in case it was needed, he had still said nothing directly to her about his plans and had remained slightly aloof with her.

One evening, and not very sleepy, Nell was wandering back to her room with a jug of sweetened, warm milk lightly flavoured with cinnamon. She planned to settle down with a book until, hopefully, with the effects of the milk and the relaxation of her musings through reading, she would begin to tire. Passing near Ed's room, she saw that he had once again left his door open, inviting company. Nell reflected for a couple of seconds, temporarily fearing rejection, but then with the change of atmosphere at court, her desire to make things right and revert their relationship back to where it had been got the better of her. She took a deep breath and knocked tentatively on the door. The King emerged from somewhere on the other side of his room, opened the door further and leant against the door frame. He smiled gently down at her. Nell noticed how tired and careworn he was looking, his face pale and drawn, forehead wrinkled in an almost constant frown.

"I've got plenty of milk if you would like to share it with me," suggested Nell diffidently, holding up the jug.

"I'd certainly enjoy some friendship tonight," Ed replied. "I know I've been stewing too much in my own thoughts lately."

They went and sat by his large arched windows. Although the beginning of autumn, the good weather had continued from the wonderful summer into autumn and it was still very warm. The slight breeze was refreshing through the open window, the silk curtains billowing into sails. Nell saw that the King was not alone; his squire was seated at a desk, head bowed, poring over papers and letters, quill in hand. He glanced up as Nell entered the room. His brow was furrowed too.

"You can go now, Marshall. We've done enough for this evening – we'll finish that tomorrow. The rest will do us both some good," suggested Ed.

Nodding, Marshall hastily piled up the papers and quickly slipped out of the room, leaving them alone.

Nell chose to plunge in and confront what she worried stood between them straight away, before her courage failed her again.

"I'm ashamed about my foolish deception. And I regret not trusting you – you're the last person I would wish to hurt," said Nell very quietly, staring down at her hands lying in her lap. "I had wanted to tell you… I just hadn't found the right time. Perhaps I prevaricated – I was afraid of what you might think of me, how you might judge me, and I also didn't wish to spoil such an enjoyable summer. I'd got as far as telling Kaspar, but then events ran away from me. Instead, I was lying to you when you needed loyalty the most."

"It doesn't matter now," rejoined Ed. "A lot has happened between us. Don't forget that, by taking that arrow in your shoulder, you probably saved my life. I am just sorry for all the pain it caused you."

Now it was his turn to look a little sheepish.

"I have a small confession of my own – I deduced a little of the truth about your deception, that something was not quite right. I was waiting for you to have the courage to trust me… but fate intervened."

"What aroused your suspicions?" asked Nell.

"Initially, when we met, I was confused – the baby I remembered visiting in Guthway had very dark hair, while Elly's is so golden. Although that could have changed, there were other things which gave me pause for thought, like your confusion at the man who resembled Prince Harold. And your swordplay so closely resembles your father's – which I also know well, having been on the receiving end of it – that you must admire him greatly and have studied his work."

He leant forward and clasped her hand in his.

"Nell…" he began.

"Can anyone join in?" asked Kaspar, grinning from the doorway, Allys and Al close behind him.

"Of course," answered Ed, loosening Nell's hand and sitting back again, "but we might need to send out for more supplies if you're joining us, Kaspar."

He then winked at Nell, as they all settled back into one of their evenings of camaraderie that she had missed so much.

"Have you got an outfit yet for tomorrow night?" asked Allys, coming to sit next to Nell.

Nell gaped blankly at her.

"Oh… With everything else, I'd forgotten about the Harvest Supper!" exclaimed Nell, slapping her hand to her forehead as she suddenly remembered.

"Never mind, I'm sure we'll find something for you to wear," laughed Allys.

The next morning, Allys forced Nell to join her in a fleeting foray into town to find new gowns. Satisfied with her purchases, she returned with an emerald green velvet dress embroidered with a coppery thread in a cascading spray of flowers at the front of the bodice, to be worn with a pale green silk chemise.

"You should wear your butterfly necklace this evening – it would really match the gown well," suggested Allys.

Nell was amused at that idea following everything that had happened.

"Did you know that your brother gave it to me?"

"No! When?" gasped Allys.

"When I was a baby," Nell laughed. "A kind of Welcoming present, I guess. He would have been about four."

Allys stared seriously back at her.

"It sounds like a kind of promise to me."

"No! Don't be daft… Just a token of friendship between our families!" Nell exclaimed.

"Well… Perhaps a serious hope then," her friend grinned.

"Allys!"

So, after a long and luxurious soak in a bath brimming with pungent scents, Nell dressed and went to meet the King. When Ed opened the door, he gazed at her with undisguised approval.

"You're definitely looking better. Come in a minute as I'm almost ready," he said, pulling the brocade tunic in his hand over his head as he spoke.

While Ed fastened his velvet sur-coat over the tunic, Nell said, "Here, let me," and stepped forwards to link a gold chain around his waist and to place a small coronet on his head.

Standing so close to him, she could smell that familiar sandalwood soap on his skin. Then Nell gasped as his arms suddenly slid around her waist, pulling her closer towards him. Ed bent his head and softly kissed her lips.

"I was scared for a while by the pool that we'd lost you, panicked as you drifted in and out of consciousness… I deemed that I'd lost exactly what I wanted before I'd had a chance to admit it."

Ed held her even closer, rested his cheek on the top of her head, experiencing the reassuring warmth of her, and breathed in deeply the scent of her. Standing together, listening to his heartbeat and her own pounding faster, Nell shut her eyes, relishing the intimacy of the unforeseen embrace. His hand was softly stroking her back, slowly and deliberately drawing circles down her spine until his gentle caress skimmed the curve of her buttocks. Enjoying the sensation, she nestled nearer to him, her movement feeding a physical response in him.

"Let us enjoy this evening," murmured Ed into her hair, "but I believe that we need to have a serious talk later. There are matters I've already discussed with your father."

Skin scarlet with surprise, pleasure and anticipation, Nell's heart leapt. She lifted her hand to his face, held it against the arc of his cheek and, on tiptoe, reciprocated his earlier kiss with an increasing urgency.

"We'd better go," he groaned, "before I change my mind about emerging for supper at all!"

Nell walked down to the feast feeling extremely happy, lighter than air, arm-in-arm with Ed. The King commenced the Harvest Supper with a thank you to everyone for their diligent work in helping to create and support a healthy economy with plenty of food for all.

"We have been very fortunate in the weather this year," he then added. "And I would also say we were very fortunate not to lose anyone in our recent trouble with my brother. I would like to thank everyone who aided Nell in her recovery, restoring her safely to us. But I fear there may be more trouble to come and that we may have a more difficult year ahead of us. We will need to prepare for those challenges. In the meantime, may you all enjoy our feast while we still have the peace to appreciate it."

The meal was of solid, simple fair: freshly baked bread, soups and stews made from lots of recently harvested vegetables and fresh meat. They followed the savoury dishes with apple pies and pear flans heaped with whipped cream. The music for the dancing tonight was fast and rustic. Ed led Nell onto the floor, proceeding to whirl her dizzily about the hall in his arms. Relaxed and content, with everything good to anticipate, Nell laughed merrily, her hair swinging loosely around her shoulders.

So Nell was off-guard, chatting happily at the table with several friends, when an urgent messenger interrupted the party. He was admitted into the great hall and, despite his mud-splattered exterior from travelling hard, was obviously a nobleman. He hurried forward and, battered and bruised as if from recent battle, bowed on one knee before the King.

"Your Majesty, I must speak urgently with Princess Helen. I have news of grave importance," he said.

"Of course," agreed Ed, gesturing to Nell near him.

Instantly, she rushed forwards, dropping to the floor to speak with the messenger.

"Redvers! What is it? What's happened?" Nell asked, her voice rising in alarm.

Her heart was thumping fast in expectation; recognising the haste in his bearing, she feared bad news. She was only half aware of Ed and others gathered close behind her, listening, and the murmuring around the room.

"Your father, Your Highness, has been badly injured."

Nell let out a faint moan at his words.

"We fear for his life," continued Redvers. "He has sent for you – you must return to Guthway immediately."

"I'll come straightaway. But… how… how has this happened?"

She spoke with disbelief in her voice. Something must have occurred swiftly and without warning.

"We were attacked at dawn, Ma'am, at the weakest point on our eastern border. We managed to beat them back and we're holding our own, but your father was wounded in the battle."

The Earl's eyes shifted uncomfortably to Ed.

"Your brother was there, Sire, leading the enemy attack and striking the fateful blow. Ma'am, we must travel with all speed."

"I won't be long. I'll just gather a few things and my maid, and I will be ready to leave."

Still on the floor, Nell twisted awkwardly towards Ed, all her hopes crushed, all previous desires forgotten in the new crisis and the descent now of that heavy weight of duty upon her shoulders. There was no more escaping her real role.

"I must go to my father and my country."

"Of course you must, Nell," said Ed. "If you need anything – any help – from us… from me… just ask."

As Nell rushed out of the hall, hurriedly followed by Hope, Ed spoke to Earl Redvers, "Please – my squire will show you to a private room and bring you some refreshment while you wait for the Princess. I'm sure you are in need of it. We'll have a fresh horse ready for your journey home too. In the meantime, I will join you – I must find out all that has happened and exactly what we can do to help."

"Our situation is pressing, Sire. The Princess is strong but whether she is strong enough... And our enemy is so many... and your brother so ruthless..."

Redvers shook his head uncertainly.

"You are part of The Alliance, and you will have our support," asserted Ed after he had heard all Redvers' news of the attack on Guthway by their enemies from the north, led by his brother, Warwick.

He was stunned by the ferocity, size and speed of the attack and alarmed at the implications for the rest of the northern borders.

Then, as his squire led the nobleman away, Ed went in search of Nell. He knocked on the door of her room and entered without pausing for a response. He found her talking to her maid.

"Once you've packed, Hope, have our horses brought around to the keep. I'm sorry to drag you home just as you've made friends."

Hope hurried away, carrying some of their hastily packed luggage with her. She felt tearful, eyes stinging and vision blurry, suddenly aware that she did not want to return home yet. However, she realised she had no choice. Before Redvers had arrived, everyone had begun to relax in the servery and Hope had secretly been wishing for the chance to have another dance with Marshall. Now that would never happen.

As she flew lightly down the spiral back staircase, Hope ran straight into Marshall coming up, exactly the person she knew she would miss most. Stopping abruptly, all Hope could manage to say was 'oh' and would not meet his eyes.

"Hope…" Marshall began, moving forward to grasp her hand, but before he could say anything else, she hurtled away, shaking her head, a few tears now falling freely.

Back in her room, Nell had abandoned what she was doing when the King entered and stared miserably at him where he stood, one of his hands resting on the door. In the months she had spent in Torland, her views had totally changed from that initial conversation on marriage with him. Now she knew exactly who it was that she wanted to spend the rest of her life with, almost had the promise of it, the perfect denouement, it appeared to have become impossible. Ed represented everything she desired, everything she now had to leave behind. Nell also shook her head, unwittingly echoing her maid's gestures, as she veered away from Ed to continue what she had to do, not daring to speak for fear of her reaction.

"Nell, before you go, I want you to know that you can always ask for my help. In fact, I will organise some troops to follow as soon as they can. It is extremely likely that things will get tough for you, and I don't doubt that Warwick will attack again, probably rapidly, especially with your father incapacitated. He will see your country as severely weakened now. It seems my brother is bent on gaining power anyway he can and with whatever allies he can muster. With Elly as an excuse, he is targeting Guthway. Nell… I'm sure your father will pull through – he is a strong commander, a powerful man."

As he spoke, Nell pulled on a pair of leather boots, holding back the tears that were threatening to force their way through her control.

"I… I have had a good time here," she started to explain, "made friends and had that chance to be free which I so desperately wanted. But now it is time for me to shoulder my responsibilities, assume more command and put my desires, my freedom, behind me. I have to face the fact that my father has been badly injured, may be dying. He needs me. And my country is most definitely at war. Guthway needs me too."

She could not look at Ed, struggling with her emotions, knowing that duty came first but positive this time that he understood. Nell grabbed her bag, wrapped a travelling mantle around her shoulders and closed the distance between them. Ed dallied in the doorway and, as Nell passed through, she paused so near to him that she could feel his warm breath on her skin, their bodies almost touching. She yearned for that touch whilst she resisted the tempting, magnetic drag towards him.

"Thank you for everything you have said and done, everything you have offered, and what you are already preparing. However, I only request one thing of you at this stage," asked Nell, licking her lips to moisten her dry mouth.

Still too scared to survey his face, admit her fears and emotions, she gazed instead into his broad chest.

"If… if things start to go really badly for us… I will send my sister here for her safety. Please do what you can for her."

"I will care for her like my own sister. Nell…"

Finally, she yielded to the compulsion and peered blearily into his eyes, wiping a tear from her own. He did not say any more, did not need to, just pulled her into a tight embrace, and for an exquisite moment, they lingered, clasped closely together. He leant down, kissed her firmly, warmly, once more before releasing her. Then he let her go into the night for her long and lonely journey home.

ACT 2

Chapter 1

Guthway 1276, 2 years later

Nell gazed blearily out from the roof of the castle's highest tower. Set on a rock that rose into a high outcrop overshadowing the town, the compact castle was a commanding presence with its many floors and dozens of steep towers. Gateways at the lower reaches led out in winding paths and zigzagging, vertical stairs to the bailey, streets and fields below.

Exhausted, Nell had slept little in the proceeding few weeks. Since the death of her father a year ago, her country had been hit particularly hard by their enemies in the north and east, the worst being a series of strong attacks during the last few months, raiding deeper into Guthway. The troops Ed had supplied had helped so far, but also busy fending off strikes in northern Torland, he had not been able to send as many men as he had originally hoped. It was now only a matter of time before their borders were breached and Guthway was overrun by Warwick and his invading army.

Now she watched as the last few wagons filled with women and children, from both the castle and the town, left for Torland and safety. The people had been given the choice of leaving Guthway, starting again as refugees in neighbouring lands, or to stay and hope for the best, that Warwick and his invaders would look kindly on them, still needing servants to wait on them and workers to till the land. Most of the poor had opted to remain, but many of the nobles had left, suspecting they would be treated less gently, with whatever portable wealth they could carry.

Nell contemplated the past couple of years, that last retreating retinue representing the seeping away of her people, power and authority. She had had little time to deliberate freely before; she knew that, if she did, her thoughts would be filled with missing her friends and family. Thankfully, she was too preoccupied to consider how she missed one person in particular, ached for the chance to be near him, to talk with him or to be held in his arms. However, she also understood that, if she ever did meet Ed again, a lot of time had passed and many events had happened to both of them. Inevitably, they would both have changed. Their positions and priorities undoubtedly had altered dramatically. Nell had even been too busy over the last few months to grieve properly for her father. King Robert had never fully recovered from that initial battle with Warwick. Once such a strong man, his wounds had festered and he had lingered on painfully for a year, his life slowly fading into a wrecked shell of his former self.

Nell had received charge of the country as soon as she had returned to Guthway, a queen in all but name. She had gathered what troops she could from their limited population, supplemented by those from Ed, to protect their borders, but both time and men were running out. The army that assailed them appeared to be made from a never-ending supply of tough, fierce soldiers from the north.

Consequently, when King Robert had finally died, at last finding relief from his incessant pain, Nell had initiated a quiet and organised retreat from the country for those who wished to leave. Almost straight after her father's funeral, she had sent her sister, Rae, to Erlwick with most of their family's personal wealth and possessions. She did not want to leave anything she valued to fall into the hands of Warwick and Elly.

"Your Majesty, it's getting cold – please come back to the hall and the warm fire," coaxed Hope from the ladder beneath her.

"Hope!" Nell exclaimed, surprised. "I meant for you to go today in the last wagon. I wanted you away from danger."

"No, Ma'am, I wish to stay with you, to help you, wherever and however that may be."

"Thank you," said Nell, touched, reaching a hand out to her maid. "Go down to the hall yourself – I won't be far behind you."

Nell spun back to the view below her. Now, with those last few wagons travelling west to the pass into Torland or south to the ports, the castle was being run by a skeleton staff of those willing to remain in Guthway and guarded by a small company of soldiers. Nell realised she would have to leave herself at some point soon but dreaded making that final decision to withdraw, accepting defeat and abandoning her country to others.

Ed, meanwhile, had arrived unannounced and in secret at Shirborne, on the south coast of Guthway, with a small company of men. As their ship sailed into port just after sunrise, he stood on the deck with Kaspar and Al.

"She was right," remarked Al, staring out at the compact but pretty harbour full of small white cottages and narrow cobbled streets twisting up to the bright white palace shining above the town almost like a star as the sun bounced of its walls.

"Who?" asked the King.

"Nell. She said this place was beautiful and it was the truth. How sad that we are coming like this – sneaking in like thieves – instead of being here to enjoy it and have fun," Al replied. "I would love to have spent some time wondering the alleyways and walking the beaches."

"No," grimaced Kaspar, "we have come like cavalry to the rescue but furtively rather than charging in openly and much too late to achieve any good."

"If all we can manage to do is get Nell to safety then that will be a job well done," said Ed decisively. "We can stand firm to fight Warwick and regain Guthway another day. As soon as we dock, we ride north to Roxleburg."

They disembarked, acquired horses and a hard ride followed; it was not until early evening the following day that they arrived at the town. The castle towering high on the rock was dark, the roads and houses surrounding it silent. Few lights shone out from any windows, and all doors were firmly locked shut, making the whole place seem eerie. Ed and Kaspar swapped anxious glances. Had Nell left already? Or had something worse happened here? All the men were now on alert.

As they approached the castle along a wide paved road that led up the hill, they could now see that the drawbridge was up and the portcullis down, ready for a sudden attack. A quick glance showed that the walls were intact; there was no damage, so Ed was relieved that no such attack had already happened. Little movement gave any sign of life behind the walls until a horn suddenly signalled their arrival, and a guard yelled down from the gatehouse above.

"Halt! Who goes there?"

"King Edward of Torland, High King of The Alliance, with a company of soldiers, here to see the Queen and escort her to safety," Ed shouted back confidently.

A couple of helmeted heads peered over the battlements. Then a creaking of chains followed muffled voices up above, and the drawbridge was steadily lowered, the portcullis raised, to let them across. The Captain of the Guard approached them swiftly and fell on one knee.

"Your Majesty, welcome to Roxleburg. You will find few servants around to help you, Sire, but if you can find your own way to the great hall, there should be someone around in there to lead you to the Queen."

"I have been here before... but a few years ago. However, I should still be able to find my way to the hall," and Ed signalled to his men to follow him across the bailey while the drawbridge was raised behind them.

Leaving the soldiers sorting out food and water for the horses, Ed, Kaspar, Al and their squires climbed the steep steps to the great square door of the keep on the first floor. Challenged once more at the door, it was swiftly opened to let them in, and they were directed through the unnaturally deserted castle to the great hall towards the back of the building.

The lofty raftered room had only a few torches lit along its flanks tonight, and a little more light flickered off the walls from the great fireplace on one side of the hall where the few inhabitants of the room were gathered. Tall gaunt shadows stretched and danced weirdly in the strange light. Ed reflected that this setting was very different to that of Nell's Welcoming Ceremony.

The castle's occupants stood and waited to find out who the new arrivals were. Almost immediately, however, Earl Redvers, who was amongst the men, recognised the High King and bowed down on one knee, signalling for the other men to do likewise.

"Welcome to Guthway, Your Majesty," said Redvers.

"Please, don't stand on ceremony," asserted Ed, "I don't deem that these are appropriate times for that. Could you tell me where I'll find the Queen?"

"You will find Her Majesty in the kitchens, Sire," spoke another of the gathered noblemen without apology and with more than a hint of pride.

Ed turned to the lord, who was probably in his forties and one of the eldest present, raising an inquisitive eyebrow at him.

"She's very hands on as leadership goes – always has been, just like her father," added the loyal lord.

"Falkner's right," explained Redvers. "With few staff left, it is the Queen's way of doing what she can to help in the present situation. I'll show you the way."

Having arrived at the kitchen after a short walk down a couple of corridors, Ed was poised in the doorway at the top of a flight of stone steps that led down into the room, gazing at the scene below him and Nell, who he had not seen in two years.

He smiled, amused. Nell was certainly exhibiting practical leadership, as she chatted to the few women who had elected to stay behind while standing amidst a great pile of vegetable peelings. As she talked, she chopped carrots and, balanced on a board, carried them across the room before scraping the chunks into a big pot of stewing meat.

Then his humorous smile disappeared to be replaced with concern. Even in the gloom of the ill-lit room, Ed could see Nell's healthy complexion had gone. She looked pale, thin, drawn and utterly weary.

Nell glanced up. She jumped, startled to see Ed suddenly there before her, leaning nonchalantly in a doorway of her home. He was exactly the person she had wanted to see, had, in fact, just been musing about, but certainly wasn't expecting to appear abruptly in front of her as if from nowhere. She wondered fleetingly if she had conjured up a spectre from her own fevered imagination, brought on through lack of sleep, and she held her breath, anticipating that he might vanish at any second, dissipating in smoky wisps into the air around her. But, when he moved, she knew he was real flesh and blood, not a ghost, and she smiled with obvious delight, wiping her hands on her apron before hurrying forward to greet him.

"What a surprise! It's really good to see you again, Ed," Nell said, taking both his hands in hers. "It's not quite the circumstances in which I would have hoped to entertain the High King, mind you," she grimaced, adding with a sigh, "as I'm afraid you see us in the final stages of retreat," and she gestured towards the vegetable peelings where she had been working. "There are not many people left, so I'm pitching in myself. You're welcome to lodge here as long as you don't mind roughing it a bit or putting up with my inexperienced cooking."

"Nell, we've come to help you – to get you to safety – so I don't reckon it would matter what we put up with in the meantime," Ed explained. "I'm sorry we could not come sooner, perhaps have halted the retreat, but we've had a lot more trouble recently along our own northern border to deal with."

Hearing the sympathy, affection and concern in his voice, Nell sighed again, and turning her back on him for a minute so he could not see her face and, therefore, giving her a chance to compose herself, she went to stir the bubbling stew.

"I know you've done what you could for me. I am also aware of what's been happening to you – I've had letters filled with news from both Rae and Allys. It's just that we are too weak… and they are so strong."

Then she concentrated on other matters to steady her emotions, hoping her voice would not crack under the strain.

"There should be plenty of food for all. We have lots of freshly baked bread, too, to sop up the sauce."

There were times when all Nell had wanted to do during the past two years was find some sort of relief in a stream of tears, but she had needed to show a strong face to her people. She knew that if anyone could understand her emotions it would be Ed, yet even now, she did not want to crumble before him, to maintain what dignity she could for a little bit longer. Nevertheless, she ached to experience his strong arms around her, comforting her. So, instead, Nell swung around to face him again, her features carefully controlled not to show her feelings of frustration, sadness or even desire.

"I have sent orders to what is left of our army on the frontline to withdraw discreetly shortly before dawn, putting whatever feints they can devise into place and giving themselves a chance to escape. Meanwhile, we are planning to leave first thing tomorrow morning under the cover of darkness, silently bringing down the curtain on my very short reign. You have arrived exactly at our – my – point of defeat," she said, smiling forlornly at him.

"Well, we will be here to escort you then," asserted Ed.

He was not fooled by her apparent self-possession but respected her wish to maintain her composure. He also tried to change tack in order to help her.

"And I'm sure we can manage one night on a hard floor and with basic food, or we wouldn't be much good as soldiers. Fortunately, we've had plenty of practise recently, and even Kaspar is growing hardened to rough living. Although I expect your cooking is better than you suggest from what I have already seen."

Nell laughed bleakly as she sized him up, noting his lightweight leather armour chosen for speed rather than protection, his sword hanging openly at his side. He looked fit, well and without a scratch from his recent battles.

"I reckon we can still do better than a hard floor – I'm just not sure about a clean sheet and personal service. Allow your men to use whatever they need, whatever they can find. I think we can leave the cleaning up to Warwick," she added ruefully.

As she spoke, another woman entered the room through a narrow doorway opposite, her arms full of wooden bowls and spoons, scarcely able to glimpse past the cradled tableware. She did not see Ed until she was halfway across the kitchen. Suddenly noticing him, she stumbled in surprise, sending her pile clattering to the floor.

"Hello, Hope," grinned Ed, as the woman hastily dropped to her knees to gather the bowls, mumbling anxiously to herself.

Swiftly, he joined her, helping to stack them on the floor.

"Sorry!" he said. "I didn't mean to alarm you."

"She's as surprised to see you as I was. Honestly, I imagined I was witnessing a ghost for a second. Well, I've finished here for now, so I can walk with you back to the great hall," Nell suggested. "You'll find all who can be spared from guard duty will arrive there shortly to eat.

Not that we have many men left. I sent all those I could spare to escort the last of our families and friends to safety. All your men can join us. You too, Hope," she added, smiling kindly at her flustered maid.

"Thank you, Your Majesty," said Hope, dropping into a smooth curtsy while suddenly feeling breathless.

As Hope left the kitchen and proceeded towards the great hall, her arms filled again with the tableware, her heart was thumping violently in her chest. She guessed that, as his squire, Marshall would have accompanied the King to Guthway and was now close at hand. She had continually thought about him, and when Nell had talked about the battles in Torland, she had agonised for his safety. Still desperately shy, Hope had not considered any other man in the same way that she had begun to regard Marshall. Although he had shown a good deal of interest in her, she assumed a man that attractive and of such a high rank would have had a lot of attention from other girls within the past two years, that he would have easily forgotten her.

Silently, she entered the huge room and placed the bowls on a large wooden table against one wall. Searching through the dark at the group of men arranged around the fire, those from both countries mingling easily, joking and swapping experiences, she instantly spotted Marshall. Contemplating how he looked more kind, strong and handsome than she remembered, her face burned as she caught her own reflections, and Hope, embarrassed at herself, briskly left the room.

When they walked back into the hall, Nell ran across the room, heedless of the smooth stone-flagged floor and watching men, to hug Kaspar and Al who stood chatting with Redvers, Falkner and the other nobles.

"It's lovely to see you all," she said. "We can talk more after…" and her voice trailed off, choked with emotions that once again threatened to spill over. "Redvers, can I leave our guests in your capable hands while I see to some other business?"

"Yes, Your Majesty," he replied with a bow.

Ed frowned as he observed Nell disappear into the castle once more, wondering when she would accept a break. They did not see her again until after they had eaten, when she popped her head around the door to speak to them briefly.

"There is plenty of space in the guards' barracks for your men. Hope and I have set up beds for you three and your squires in a few rooms near my own quarters. Hope can show you the way when you are ready," explained Nell.

Ed eyed her suspiciously because he noticed that she was wrapped in a heavy woollen mantle as if she was about to go out, a bulging leather sack over each of her shoulders.

"And where are you going, Nell? As far as I'm aware, you haven't eaten since we've been here. Our coming wasn't supposed to make your job harder."

"Please tell her, Sire, pull rank," piped in Redvers. "She won't listen to me."

"I will come and eat soon, I promise, but there is something I must do before we leave tomorrow, so I really have to do it tonight. And time is flying by," Nell stressed.

"That's fine, but… if you're leaving the castle would you let me accompany you, let me help you? I would be happier if I knew you were safe, and I can only do that if I come too," Ed insisted, holding out his hand to receive one of the sacks.

"Very well!" agreed Nell reluctantly, handing him the heavier load.

127

Once they had stepped outside the castle and were proceeding along the steep road that wound down the rock to the bulk of the town below, Ed quickly understood what Nell was doing when they stopped, almost straightaway, at an inn on the junction with the main road. She acted as if she knew the family well; going inside to find the innkeeper and his family, Nell gave them all a hug before delving into her sack to find a couple of items she had brought from the castle, including a book of fairy tales for the children. They talked for a few minutes, Nell softly rocking the baby on her shoulder, before she left, wishing them luck during the troublesome times ahead. Nell and Ed then continued their journey, visiting some of the town residents who had opted to remain and offering words of comfort and support, along with money or individually chosen gifts.

It was several emotional hours before Nell was ready for her last visit.

"I've one more person to see, and it's the most important visit of the night for me. I'm dreading this one," she admitted, "as it's my nurse from when I was a child. And she was my father's nurse before that. Nana is old and will not leave her home despite all my pleas. My only consolation is that she was Elly's nurse too – we grew up together – and that she will protect her."

"Remember, I'm here with you," said Ed, taking her hand in support and giving it a comforting squeeze.

"It's this way," and she pointed towards a short row of tiny cottages on the outskirts of town.

"Nana," called Nell, knocking at the door, "it's only me!"

"Come in, Nell dear," said Nana, her old nurse, in a wavering reedy voice.

"I've come to say goodbye – it's time for me to go," whispered Nell. "I know you won't leave, as I couldn't persuade you before, but I hope you will accept these small offerings instead," and she gave the old woman the last things left in the sacks, placing them on the worn table. "I worry about you and the cold so here's a thick woollen mantle in the green that you like. And I've brought some bottles of your favourite wine from the castle cellar too."

"Um… I'll accept them… for medicinal reasons only, of course," Nana grumbled.

"And I want you to accept this money to help you through any difficult times that may come because I won't be around to do so," added Nell, placing a clinking purse into the wrinkled palm.

"Very well… but only to keep you happy," muttered Nana reprovingly.

She was eying Ed suspiciously.

"Who is this strange young man? He's rather tall, isn't he?"

Nell laughed despite her fears.

"Nana, this is Edward, the High King."

The tiny white-haired old lady squinted at the King assessingly through pale milky eyes.

"The last time I saw him was quite a long time ago. He's grown somewhat since then – upwards not outwards. It might even have been at your Welcoming, my lovey," commented Nana, leaning forward and patting the Queen's hand.

Nell and Ed glanced at each other and smiled before the King knelt in front of the elderly woman.

"You take care of yourself," he said. "You're important to Nell therefore you're important to me too. I want you to stay safe for her."

"Never mind about me!" snapped Nana. "I'm old, so no one is going to bother themselves about me. But you two are young with your whole lives ahead of you. I want you," she said while poking a finger in his chest, "to make sure Nell remains out of trouble, young man. Protect her for me."

Ed grinned at the old nurse's 'ticking off' while Nell laughed at the vision of the tall, young king bowing subserviently to the diminutive, ancient woman.

"Of course I shall!" he insisted. "That's why I am here – I will make sure Nell gets to Torland in one piece. After all, she saved my life two years ago. This is my chance to repay the favour."

Ed gazed at Nell. Memories flooded back for both of them, good and bad. Staring at him intently regardless of her poor eyesight, reading something in his face or voice, the elderly lady nodded, satisfied.

"Come closer, Nell," she croaked, her expression sad, and Nell went to her old nurse, bending down herself this time, and hugged her tightly.

As they rocked back and forth, Nell finally allowed herself the release of some of the tears which had built up over the months, like the opening of a dam's sluice gates, as Nana softly stroked her hair.

Standing up and wiping the tears away on her cloak, Nell said, "I'll be back to find you some day."

At the door, Nana suddenly called Ed back and whispered something in his ear. Nell could not hear what was said.

While they slowly wound their way back up to the castle, she could not resist asking, "What did Nana say to you?"

Ed looked at her archly.

"That is for me to know. Maybe I'll tell you when the time is right. Your nurse is a wise old bird."

Before they reached the top of the steep road, Ed once again grasped her arm. He stared hard at her. Nell had altered a lot and not just physically. She had left Erlwick young, fresh, idealistic and little more than a girl. Now she was fully a woman with experiences and responsibilities that weighed deeply on her. But then, he expected that he had changed a lot too.

"You did well tonight, Nell – that was a good job done."

Nell felt a flood of warmth from his approval and a tingling charge through her arm where he touched her but could only smile despondently at him, the emotions of the night heavy on her.

Once back by the fire in the great hall, Nell finally succumbed to demand and sat to eat, Hope timidly coming to join her, while the men around them talked avidly about what they should do next. As the decision to leave had already been agreed, all those left in the castle were keen to get to Torland by the shortest route available, via the pass in the mountains. They were to leave soon after dawn with just a light breakfast; baggage, food and horses for the journey were prepared ready for their early departure before they all retired that night. It was to be a fortuitous decision.

Chapter 2

Someone was urgently shaking Nell's shoulder. Despite her overwhelming tiredness, Nell knew she had to wake up, open her leaden eyelids and face the rough intruder. Groggy, her head felt thick and fuzzy with lack of sleep, as it was only a few hours ago that she had managed to get to bed. Nell stole a few seconds to focus in the dingy light before realising the phantom figure looming in front of her again was Ed.

"Nell, wake up!" he called insistently.

She muttered something rude in reply under her breath but sat up anyway and swung her legs out of bed.

"There's trouble," Ed continued, ignoring her remarks. "We can't tarry until the morning – we have to go now. The enemy have broken through."

Nell was now fully alert and started dressing, pulling on and lacing up her gown hurriedly, throwing her riding cloak around her shoulders.

As she yanked on her riding boots, Nell said, "It's fine… I'm ready to go."

They rushed down to the bailey where the rest of the soldiers, swollen in number by the retreating troops, and Hope were waiting for them. Kaspar hastened forward, alarmed.

"We've had further news… and it's not good," he told them. "Some troops from the enemy army are already working their way across the north of the country and, if we aim for the pass through the mountains, they are bound to get there before us… cut us off."

"Well, it appears as if we'll be better off travelling south now, even though it's going to be a longer journey. We should aim for Shirborne," suggested Redvers.

"Right," agreed Ed, "that's exactly what we shall do. Our ship has orders to remain in harbour until the last possible minute. So, if we can get to the port before Warwick's men, we'll be able to leave the country by sea."

Turning briefly to his squire, Ed gave him extra directions.

"Marshall, I want Hope to travel – share a horse – with you. She's not used to this kind of riding, unlike her mistress."

The latter comment he aimed at Nell with a smile.

Bending over, Marshall put out a hand to help Hope mount up behind him. She clung on tightly, arms locked around his waist, nervous of the fast ride and flight from her country yet also scared of the close but comforting proximity to Marshall.

Setting off at speed gave Nell little time to reflect on leaving her home, and she was glad she had already said her goodbyes. It would need almost two days of hard riding to reach the south coast; she was pleased with all that precious practise she had managed to put in at travelling fast cross-country. No one could be given allowances and there would be few rests on this journey, even if Nell would accept any.

They had left long before dawn while it was still dark and did not cease until midday when they broke their ride for a brief luncheon and to give the horses respite. Everywhere they travelled on their way south, either through towns or countryside, was the same: large estates deserted but most of the poorer inhabitants of villages and towns staying put, hoping for the best.

It was midnight before they halted again to rest, stopping out of sight in a woodland clearing. Lookouts were posted intermittently to encircle the make-shift camp. Yet, strangely, almost nothing stirred that night; all was uncannily quiet excepting the very occasional hoot of an owl, the rustle of a mouse in the undergrowth, or the grunt of a sleeping soldier.

Nell slept fitfully, wrapped in a blanket on the firm yet uneven ground next to Hope and surrounded by her nobles, Kaspar, Al and Ed. She marvelled at how Al was out like a light as soon as he put his head down while Kaspar was snoring loudly whenever she woke frequently during the night. She wondered if sleeping rough was part of their training. Equally, though, if she twisted to ease her discomfort or numbness, she would see that Ed was wide awake. Sometimes, he was sitting up, leaning against a fallen tree trunk, alert and thoughtful as he minded the peaceful camp. At other times, he was having a whispered exchange with one of the guards.

She must have made a barely audible noise when Nell woke once more, restless in the early hours, to find Ed again deep in conversation with a soldier at the edge of the clearing. Glancing up, he saw she was awake and carefully picked a path through the inert bodies strewn across the ground to sit beside her.

"I don't believe you've slept all night!" she exclaimed in hushed tones. "You strike me as having been constantly busy."

"I've catnapped," he insisted, "and you've slept more than you presume. I dispatched scouts to find out what's happening, and the news that's come back is not good… from our point of view anyway," he added drily.

As Ed leant forward, a frown wrinkling his brow, Nell admonished herself.

"I'm so sorry," she apologised gently, "I seem to have allowed you to grab the reins and lead us safely through my country. As a result, you have had all the anxiety and not slept a wink the entire night."

Lightening his frown, Ed laughed quietly, "I told you – I catnapped. Don't fret about me because I'm fit and healthy – I can tolerate that burden at the moment. You, on the other hand, have been leading your country in tough circumstances for some time now, and you have been doing a good job but…" and he sent her a piercing stare before continuing, "but – and don't take this the wrong way – I suspect that you are exhausted. When you are that tired you can't necessarily think clearly or make good decisions quickly. I'm here, fresh and capable – I've had lots of practise lately – so allow me to endure the pressures of command. Just let me have a long and uninterrupted sleep if we get back to Torland in one piece."

Nell sighed, "I admit it's good to feel the burden of responsibility lifted from my shoulders. However, I fear that soon I will have no such vexations at all. That will probably be just as unsettling or worse – ironic, I know, after my previous shenanigans. I will have to find a way to repay all your help. I know you say you are fresh, but I am also well aware of the battles you have fought along your own borders. Both your sister and mine have kept me regularly updated. I heard when Kaspar lost his horse in the middle of a battle and the time you hurt your hand… badly. I have been deeply concerned for you… for all of you."

She blushed, suddenly hearing her own words, and looked away.

For a minute or two longer, they sat in silence, mulling over their own thoughts, remembering events or emotions, as they peered across the quiet camp. Ed flexed his fingers as if at the memory of the incident Nell had mentioned and to prove he had fully healed. He had been lucky; many other men had come home disabled… or not at all. Nell also stared at his hand, his long, elegant fingers, and her throat caught at the horrifying images aroused by the notion of battle. Needing distraction, she continued their conversation.

"You said, 'if we get back in one piece,' and that there's more bad news. So, tell me, what is the problem, the difficulty, you have currently uncovered for us?"

"I don't know how," explained Ed with a slow perturbed shake of the head, "but Warwick's army are catching up with us fast and might overtake us at any moment. If they do – which is almost certain – we will be cut off from the harbour too. The town itself is heavily fortified and should be able to hold out for a good long while, but… how will we get to our ship? That's another matter entirely!"

Nell's mind had started racing as he spoke. She knew there was a way in, a secret path that they could use, as long as they could get there without being spotted or raising suspicion.

"There is a possibility," she said excitedly, trying to keep her voice lowered. "Do you remember me saying that the Palace at Shirborne has its own private bay – where I learnt to swim – with access only from the building? Well, very few people outside the family know that there is also a secret stair via the cliffs. I don't believe Elly knows about it – she was never keen on the beach. It's not easy, being both high and sheer in patches, slippery and dangerous when wet, and it's not obvious from the top of the cliffs. It's even difficult to observe from the sea since the steps are uneven and irregular to disguise them against the rocks… but it most definitely exists."

Ed gaped at her in disbelief and delight, declaring, "That's perfect! As long as we can get everyone there without being seen then we've got a chance. We can't move around wholesale like this with the enemy all around us now. I imagine that it would be better if we break up into smaller groups and meet nearer the harbour and the cliffs we're aiming for."

"There are woods on a hill to the east of the town, and the trees edge fairly close to the cliffs. A little temple sits almost on the headland. May I suggest we regroup there, in the graveyard behind it?" recommended Nell.

"Good idea," agreed Ed. "It will give everyone a distinctive target to aim for whilst still providing cover."

Ed studied her thoughtfully. He admired her strength of character, knew the efforts it would have taken to rule her country at this tumultuous time, but frowned again at her pallid complexion and the grey-blue circles around her eyes, utterly different from the Nell he used to know. She looked so vulnerable that he was overcome with a desire to gather her in his arms and protect her.

"Now, unfortunately, with the enemy close at hand, there's no further time for catnaps, let alone sleep. We need to quietly wake everyone up and gather them together for a briefing," said Ed.

Nell nodded. Her eyes felt heavy with tiredness but she could no longer succumb to sleep. She would, however, listen to sense and let Ed assume control. Therefore, following his lead, she started waking the men, ignoring the good-humoured grumblings from Kaspar.

"Listen," said Ed, Nell at his side, "we're going to break down into smaller groups of between two and four men to make it easier to travel at speed through the countryside without comment and to hide if need be. Conceal your weapons and armour, try to imitate travellers or labourers as much as you can. We're all aiming to meet at nightfall in the woods behind a small temple on the headland outside Shirborne. I want you all to study the map – we only have one – before we leave. It will also help if we travel in groups mixed from both the castle guard of Roxleburg and my army, since those from Guthway may have a better idea of the lay of the land, where we're heading. If you need to… ditch the horses and walk. I have to urge the importance of being prompt so that we are all ready to move together at the other end. Also, I must stress the need for secrecy because our enemies could now be anywhere around us at any time.

"Redvers, can you help me split our men into groups? I'd suggest you travel with Kaspar and Al to keep them in line. Marshall, stay with Hope and join Falkner. I'll have Nell with me… Oh… and one more thing – good luck, everyone!"

So Nell loitered in the wings nervously with Ed while the men hurriedly ate, studied the map and then dispersed in their small groups amongst the trees. She hugged Hope, watched her leave clamped tightly to Marshall, and tried to give Al and Kaspar a cheery wave goodbye. Then, when they were the last two people left, Ed brought their horses round for them to mount.

"Are you ready for this?" asked Ed quietly. "I can't promise we'll all get through safely."

"I'm as ready as I can be," she answered with a touch of irony, "leaving my homeland, possibly forever. I can freely admit to you what I cannot tell anyone else – that, at this exact instant in time, I'd rather dwell here like this, living rough in the woods and on the run, than leave for good. I am scared of what might happen next to Rae and me, my people and Guthway. We will have no proper status and no certainty."

She breathed in deeply before changing tack in her thoughts.

"I've passed details of how to find the secret stair to several other members of the group… in case I… we… don't get there in time."

"Well, don't worry about that! I reckon Marshall and I are going to have the easiest task of getting through by travelling with a woman," Ed pointed out with glee.

Nell instantly laughed, "Only if you're lying flat! Your height makes you quite distinctive, so let's hope they don't know that you're in the country… or recognise me, come to think of it."

Ed grinned back at her, and for the first time in months, Nell felt something other than grief, frustration or fear. Her cheeks flushing, she hastily mounted her horse and paused for him to do likewise.

They set off in a steady but roughly south-easterly direction and, when possible, stuck to the cover of woodland, heathland or meadows. If they had to journey by road and deal with soldiers or fellow travellers, they agreed to pretend to be a married couple searching for work. They made good progress, with no sign of the enemy, until they checked their ride for a swift luncheon.

With no one around, they left their horses hidden and secured in a copse of trees and crept across to a neighbouring field to eat their meagre supplies of bread, cheese and fruit, washed down with a little wine. Hungry, they were grateful for anything.

Ed studied her intently then said, "I'm sorry my brother has brought you to this, Nell, hiding in the undergrowth, skulking through the woods and trying to flee your own country. I can only apologise for what has happened to you because of my family. I will do all I can to help you."

Nell faltered mid-bite, "I expect our enemies were seeking any excuse to attack us but don't ever ask me to forgive Warwick for what he has done. I can never forget how my father suffered – and for such a long time – before the end."

Startled, Ed looked up from his food at the sharp note in her voice, something he had never heard before.

Nell turned away, could not meet his eyes with tears in her own.

"When I got home from Torland after your brother's first attack on Guthway," she said, "I found my father to be very ill, and although he recovered from his initial injuries, he was never quite the same again. It was as if there was an invisible poison in his wounds, too, that seeped through his body, contaminating his mind, and he gradually died, sometimes in bouts of excruciating agony."

She stared miserably at the bread in her hand, suddenly unable to eat, a lump dry in her throat.

Ed reached for her hand, offering comfort, "Nell, we may have been late in coming to your aid, but you are not alone now. I can only repeat what I said before – you have all of our support… my support."

Nell gasped with surprise but not at his touch. Facing the road, she saw what Ed could not.

"There are soldiers on the track – six of them – and they're walking along by the field. We're really close to the track… so they'll discover us for sure. In fact, they've probably already seen us."

"Hmm… right then…" muttered Ed slowly, yet thinking rapidly as he spoke, "if we can make them assume we're no threat, just peasants… Umm… You're just going to have to trust me on this one, Nell…"

Without further explanation, he hastily grabbed her wrist, hauled her up and ran across to a nearby haystack with her. Surprised, Nell then found herself thrust back onto the straw and Ed dropped down beside her.

"Well, you said I needed to lie flat so that I wouldn't be recognised," he chuckled.

His eyes sparkled mischievously, almost as if he was enjoying the challenge despite their present extreme danger. He carefully observed the approaching soldiers as he spoke.

"Now… I'm sorry about the next bit, but it's all a part of the rouse of being a harmless courting couple."

Immediately, Ed rolled over towards her, squashing Nell against the rough, scratchy straw, and kissed her. It was long, leisurely and teasing as he nibbled along her lips, and much more intimate than required for the task. His mouth was warm and soft against hers. Astonished, she gawped back up at him and saw amusement in his eyes.

Briefly, he lifted himself on to one elbow and suggested ironically, "It might help if you act as if you were taking part, enjoying it even."

Straightaway, in reaction to his words, Nell curled her arms around his waist and dragged him back down towards her. They kissed again and, this time, Nell felt herself responding, her body melting into his, as the soldiers drew level with them.

"It's just a rutting couple," they heard one of the men state crudely. "Let's leave them to get on with it. If only we could all have such fun."

As Ed's hand casually caressed her side, Nell forgot all about the soldiers and their peril. Instead, she was only aware of an urgency, a need, within her own body. Hungrily, she answered Ed's kisses with her own. His mouth was demanding, forcing her lips open. She raised her leg, arched her hips, craning eagerly towards him, wishing to get closer, fully aware of the growing response in his body.

Suddenly, Ed pulled away, twisting up into a sitting position, his back to Nell.

"I fancy they've gone now," he said, his voice sounding hoarse. "I'm sorry, Nell, I didn't figure that ploy to go quite so far as it did. It was the only solution I could concoct on the spur of the moment to allay any concerns the soldiers might have had about us. We should delay a few more minutes until they're definitely clear, and then we can get going again."

Nell nodded, speechless; it took her a good few seconds to remember precisely what he was talking about. She had forgotten what they were doing, where they were going, because she was so wrapped up in the kiss and the caress of his body against hers. When he drew away, she felt cold and empty, aching for and craving that closeness, incomplete.

They sat for those few minutes in silence, composing themselves.

Confused, Nell stared at Ed's back, taut and muscular, and wondered what exactly had just happened. Even though she was brought up a princess, she was not ignorant about the facts of life. The King was a powerful man with strong physical needs. She knew there were occasions when he had acquired a particular sort of female company during her time at Erlwick Castle. Of course he would respond to what she had unexpectedly offered, but she could no longer hope for anything more serious, permanent or respectable for herself between them. Clearly, he cared about her still, but it could not be as much as he had once, due to the effects of distance and time. What's more, her circumstances had now totally changed, altering their possible relationships. Yet, however he felt about her, these passed two days and the last few minutes told her that this was still the one man she wanted to be close to, to spend her life with. And that physical ache in her body left her with the sense that what had just transpired was unfinished business.

After a few minutes, Ed stood up and peered cautiously around the haystack before finally pivoting back to face Nell. He coughed to clear his throat.

"Well, the enemy are certainly around, so we'd better be even more vigilant from now on," said Ed, and he smiled softly down at Nell, leaning forward to pick a piece of straw out of her hair, making her stomach flip. "Obviously, it did help me a lot to be travelling along with you. I don't know if I could have managed that trick with Kaspar… or enjoyed it quite so much."

Ed gripped Nell's hand to assist her up.

"We can go now," he added quietly.

Thoroughly disconcerted by the incident and the tumultuous emotions aroused, Nell shook out her gown while she tried to conceal her true feelings, too embarrassed to gaze directly at him.

"We'd better get moving then. We don't want to waste any more time. I imagine we'll be the last to arrive at this rate," muttered Nell.

Ed regarded her with a measured sideways glance, a smile continuing to dance about his lips.

"I don't think I'd call that a waste of time," he said, making Nell blush at his inferences.

Chapter 3

Nell was right. They were, in fact, one of the last to arrive at the graveyard, having ditched their horses surreptitiously in a field near to a small farm. Kaspar greeted them as if he had begun to get anxious for their safety.

"At last!" he said, confirming their suspicions. "We were wondering whether to send out a search party for you. It wouldn't do to abandon the Queen of Guthway and the King of Torland to their own devices and aim for the cliffs. Losing two reigning monarchs seems a little careless, even for me. Everyone else has arrived safely, but we're quite a big band, so I didn't know how much longer we could delay. I'm glad you're here now though."

"So are we!" laughed Ed. "Well, as we are all here, we can proceed to the cliffs straightaway. Lead on, Nell."

"Can you give me five minutes?" she asked and, without pausing for an answer, Nell grabbed Hope's arm and dragged her away, disappearing over the low moss-covered wall in the direction of the stone building.

When they returned, the men were all rather surprised to see that they had changed. No longer wearing a gown, Nell had swapped her skirts for a male shirt, tunic and breeches. She was followed by a very self-conscious Hope who was dressed in a similar fashion but, unused to such attire, hid behind her Queen. The girl moaned a little, blushing profusely, when Marshall, grinning, gave her a sign of approval.

"Well, there's no way I'm climbing down that cliff in a skirt," Nell stated defiantly.

"I don't mind," commented Kaspar. "Somehow it suits you, Nell. Well, we're in your hands now, so… please lead us on to our secret destination."

They crept under cover of the decreasing light of dusk, slinking across the small field between the temple and the cliff top. Instantly exposed and highly visible, a strong wind whipped around them as they reached the cliff edge and began to head purposefully back towards the harbour. Nell constantly studied the cliff top, scanning for something specific, a sign, and beginning to panic that she wouldn't find it. Suddenly, she halted by an old, gnarled tree, stunted by the salt-laden breeze continuously blowing from the sea, which grew against a large pointed rock.

"This is it," she whispered, searching ahead and then all around her, scouting the horizon for trouble. "It may look like I'm going straight over the cliff but there's quite a wide ledge just a short way down – you'd probably reach it without stretching," she said, eyeing Ed archly. "It's just a matter of taking it steadily and gently. Once down, the stairs are to your right as you face the cliff. They're quite random in size and distance apart, and the path they follow down the cliff face winds about rather a lot. Of course, if it's been particularly wet and windy, the steps may also be very slippery. The best thing is for everyone to remain focused on one step at a time. Climb slowly and carefully, assessing with your feet and hands all the way. Stay alert – I'll relay any instructions for particularly tricky spots as I go. At the bottom, we arrive on the rocks around the corner from the bay. Obviously, the route's then easier if the tide is out. I don't know what the situation will be like down there. I'll feed that back too. Right… here goes!"

Nell cautiously approached the outcrop of rock, maintaining half an eye on the path, and sat gently on the brink of the cliff. She could hear the woosh and boom of the crashing waves below her but refused to look down. Taking a large gulp of air, she gradually edged herself around then, testing an overhanging branch of the tree before trusting to it, she held it firmly and gingerly lowered herself, stretching until the tips of her toes touched the stone ledge below. Carefully, she let go of the branch above her and, as she swayed backwards slightly, readjusted her weight and balance to lean towards the cliff. Nell relayed initial instructions back up to the men waiting patiently above. Inhaling deeply again, Nell moved swiftly along the ledge, hugging close to the stone face and still avoiding peering down at the turbulent sea broiling beneath her. When she found the first step of the ragged stairs with her foot and began to test her way down each step, Nell called up her progress and became aware that, to her left, someone else was already descending onto the ledge.

Making headway was slow and painstaking; Nell needed to gage the distance between each step and balance herself accordingly as she travelled down the staircase, while sending directions back up the queue of descending men. Occasionally, she would come across a step that was broken or very wet and slippery, and for one heart-stopping instant, her foot would flail around in thin air. Then she gripped the rocks more firmly and persevered, warily reaching out to find her next safe foothold.

Halfway down, a sudden shower of stones and a loud shrill gasp, told Nell that someone had slipped badly. Everyone stopped, gargoyles clinging tight against the cliff, heads tucked in, pausing for the dense but abrupt hail to finish. Nothing further happened and Nell, reassured, continued on her steady progress to the bottom.

It felt like forever before the sound of waves smashing against the rocks grew closer and she began to sense a fine mist of brackish spray dampening her skin. In reality, it was minutes.

Finally reaching the bottom, Nell delayed for a moment, heavily breathing in the salty spume after the mentally draining descent, until she realised the next person was right above her, and she needed to move hastily out of the way to let him land. Nell gazed around. Seeing with relief that the tide was still fairly low, she clambered across the rocks before jumping into the shallow waters and paddling through the surf towards the sandy beach.

Exhausted, Nell sat on a smooth sand bank and waited for the stream of men to follow her. Watching, she realised that it had been Al immediately shadowing her down the cliff.

"That was quite a bit of exercise you had in store for us," grinned Al, flexing his fingers to alleviate the stiffness after their extra workload. "One or two points were quite taxing – awkward angles or broken steps requiring a good stretch."

Al wavered as he saw how Nell was surveying the men coming ashore with a wrinkled brow and pursed lips. Her frown lightened fleetingly when Hope emerged, struggling through the water at Marshall's side.

"I slipped! I nearly fell but Marshall caught me. He saved me," stuttered Hope, chalk white and continuing to clutch the squire's guiding hand.

"Thank goodness he was there," said Nell, smiling her thanks at Marshall while giving her maid a comforting hug, before her eyes reverted back to searching the sea with redoubled apprehension.

Al, studying her troubled face, guessed her concern was for Ed, so he spoke to allay her fears.

"Ed insisted on being last, wanting to see everyone down safely, and of course, Kaspar remained with him. I shouldn't imagine the King would have much trouble, though, extending his long frame over awkward distances."

Yet now it was his turn to feel uneasy because the row of men had faltered and come to an end, but still there was no sign of Ed or Kaspar. Both Nell and Al approached the last soldier wading ashore.

"I'm sorry, Your Majesty, but we had a little bother as I was about to go over the top of the cliff," explained the man before they even had the chance to question him. "We spotted a couple of soldiers walking the cliff top on a patrol. I had time to duck down on to the ledge, but King Edward and Prince Kaspar had to dive for cover back into the field. They should follow on soon, once the coast is clear."

Nell sat back down and scanned the rocks where the bay curved round the cliffs and out of sight. With a sharp intake of breath, she realised the spray from the thundering waves was reaching further, the water rolling higher across the massive tumbled boulders because the tide was coming in… and coming in fast.

The minutes ticked by and her fear grew.

Meanwhile, at the top of the cliff, Ed and Kaspar were hunkered down in some undergrowth. Trapped, they were trying to stay as quiet and invisible as they could.

Sitting by the path, they had been waiting calmly for their chance to descend. The last of their men had just begun to drop to the ledge and Kaspar had started to rise to his feet when Ed had yanked him hastily back down.

"A patrol advancing our way," hissed Ed. "Take cover!"

Maintaining a low profile, the two men shuffled back awkwardly to the feint protection of some shrubbery at the edge of the path, well aware that it would take only a quick glance from the soldiers, who would soon draw level with them, to be spotted, despite the growing gloom. Ed felt they were sure to hear the pounding of his heart. He groaned inwardly and grimaced at Kaspar when the two soldiers came to a halt exactly parallel to where they were hiding. In response, the Prince raised his eyes to the sky and shook his head when the patrol seemed to be settling into a deep conversation.

"Why did the Captain send us up here?" protested one. "Surely any action will be nearer the harbour, and we'll be well out of it."

"I agree, but it's not wise to complain," said the other. "I'd be surprised if Shirborne didn't surrender soon anyway, and we won't see any fighting at all."

"Maybe… but you never know with this country…"

The two nobles waited in hiding for the conversation to end, without a word but alert and ready to react.

Minutes continued to tick by sluggishly while the soldiers talked.

Suddenly, one of the men shrugged his shoulders and ushered his partner further along the road, away from the harbour. But, just as Ed and Kaspar felt they could relax, that same soldier began to twist his head for one final scan of the land behind him. Sharing the same thought, that they were likely to be caught so it was now or never, they jumped to their feet and charged towards the patrol.

By the time the two soldiers realised what was happening and drew their weapons, it was too late. Employing their body weight, momentum and the shock of surprise, Ed and Kaspar crashed into them, wrestling them to the ground. Kaspar drew his sword and thumped one man with the pommel, knocking him out instantly, while Ed punched the other unconscious with his bare fist. Then he winced ruefully, shaking his previously injured hand, as it smarted once more.

Clambering up, Kaspar gasped, "I really could do without this! I thought they'd never move, grumbling about their patrol shift. I've got stones stuck in my face, and my arm has gone numb."

"Talking about grumbling…" grinned Ed, smacking Kaspar's shoulder. "Cease your griping as we've still got plenty of work to do. We need to secure these men safely to buy ourselves more time before they're missed and found. And we need to get down that cliff!"

Each hauled a soldier, now a dead weight, the short but uneven distance to the temple. Fortunately unlocked, they were able to dispose of their hefty load in the middle of the building. They used some of Nell's abandoned garments as makeshift hand ties. Then they dragged out a solid, heavy pew, upended it and used it to wedge the door firmly shut. Even if the men escaped, the King and the Prince should have disappeared without any indication of where they had gone.

After a short breather, aware of the further hard work yet to come and the dim light, the two friends vanished over the cliff edge without the aid of Nell's guidance.

"Aah…" hissed Al suddenly through his teeth, "that's them now."

He was right, as at last, two figures materialised with some difficulty on what remained of the rocks. The water was now deep at the edge of the bay. After a brief hesitation, they dived quickly into the rough waves and swam the increased distance until the sea became shallow enough for them to wade sluggishly onto the beach. Nell sighed with relief once her two friends stood before her, dripping from head to foot and grinning inanely.

"Catching you up needed a little longer than expected," chuckled Ed, shaking the water off his arms and legs, reminding Nell of a large, shaggy, playful dog. "We had to hide from a couple of Warwick's guards with little cover. And that field was quite uncomfortable."

But he ceased laughing when he saw Nell's ashen face.

"Yes, and I thought the guards would be there forever. They stopped right in front of us and gossiped for ages like a couple of old biddies. I was just waiting for them to glance down and notice us. I don't know how they didn't," chipped in Kaspar as he squeezed a splash of water from his shoulder length hair.

"And then we had to climb done the cliff stairs without any of your support which was quite hairy in parts, but especially when we reached the bottom and realised the tide had come in and almost covered the rocks," added Ed. "Still, the swim was refreshing."

Kaspar strode towards Nell, soggy arms out in front of him as if to embrace her.

"Urgh! Stay away!" shuddered Nell, warding him off. "I'm wet enough. Thank goodness that's done. I really believe that you two are enjoying yourselves. No one would suspect that you've been in danger of capture from Warwick's men. Now, we just need to hope we don't get attacked by the Palace Guard. There's a path from the cove that meanders back up through an informal, layered garden to a terrace behind the building. Halfway up is a high wall and gate. In times of peace, it's unguarded and open, but today, I assume it will be closed. I'd better go on beforehand again to show my face so we'll be recognised as friendly, even if I don't resemble a queen."

With dusk setting in, she walked with Ed beside her along the path which climbed and wound through terraced gardens, followed at a short distance by the rest of their group. Their progress had obviously been detected because a large guard had accumulated on the crenulated wall, weapons drawn ready to repel an enemy, awaiting their approach. However, Nell was recognised almost at once despite her damp masculine clothing, and with a discreet hand signal, the soldiers were dismissed and the gate opened. The Captain of the Guard dropped on one knee in deference to his Queen and spoke apologetically.

"Your Majesty, we weren't expecting you, were apprehensive for you, but are delighted you have managed to reach us safely after all. The town is completely surrounded, and more troops arrive every hour. We thought there was no way in or out, except by sea, and didn't reckon that you could get through to us. We are anticipating the enemy will attack us soon, maybe even barricade the harbour with ships of their own. Therefore, we have been clearing the town of anyone who wishes to leave before the serious trouble commences. Thankfully, that hasn't happened yet, but we're watching as much of the coast as we can in readiness."

He turned to Ed.

"Sire, your ship is still anchored in the harbour awaiting your return, although it is prepared to set sail at any minute."

"Good! That's as I envisaged," answered Ed. "I'll send a message to the Captain shortly, letting him know our plans."

"Thank you for your concern," said Nell before issuing further orders. "Inform whoever's left of the castle staff that we will eat here tonight and, after a few hours' sleep, will leave Shirborne while it's still dark and before our enemy has a chance to acquire ships of their own. Hopefully, they don't even know we're here yet. Make sure there are enough ships ready for all those who wish to leave. I am happy for the guard to retreat with us and abandon the town to the enemy. Shirborne is dear to me, and I would rather this beautiful place was left intact for our possible return someday than have it laid to waste in a protracted battle. Although, I hate the thought of Warwick enjoying these particular spoils."

The large group moved further up and onto the top terrace where they could admire the view behind them. Nell focused on Al beside her who was staring around himself at the Palace that even now gleamed slightly in the growing dark; tiny crystal particles embedded in the wall sparkled when caught in the glow of torchlight. His eyes fell on the terrace patterned with bright mosaics and voluptuous coloured glass beads, softened by flowering creepers and fruiting vines that grew in unruly tentacles along iron-worked trellises and arbours. Rich scents tarried on the night air, mingling with a gentle salty sea breeze. He heard, rather than saw, water bubbling through elegant marble fountains and cascading down the layers of garden. The mellow sound attracted him to look out beyond the high terrace at the view across the town and towards the harbour below them to the west. He could just make out the shapes of several large ships in the harbour, miniscule lights swaying on the decks, including their distinctive Torland carrack.

"I talked to you about the beauty of Shirborne and its Palace in happier times, Al," Nell's voice was muted and mournful as she spoke. "I'm sorry you will only get to see it at night and with few torches to shine on its treasures."

"I can still appreciate the craftsmanship and artistry of the garden and building around me," Al reassured her, "and I am sure I will one day get to see it in all its true glory."

"Then you are more certain than I," she replied.

The Captain of the Guard led them into the building and surrendered them to the care of the Palace Steward in the great hall. The vaulted room opened directly on to the terrace through a series of tall glazed doors with stained glass panels which would dapple the room in colourful light during the day. The group rested there while sleeping quarters were hastily arranged for all the men. Nell guided Ed, Kaspar and Al along to a series of grander, private rooms next to her own.

"Ed, I'm putting you in my father's old room. It's still filled with some of his things, so please feel free to help yourselves to anything you might need. I suspect you could all do with a change of clothing to get comfortable after our rough night and soaking. A maid will soon bring you all some clean, hot water to wash with."

A short while later, there was a knock on Ed's door. He opened it to find Nell standing there, once again in a gown, her hair waving in shining locks down her back.

"Would you mind if I came in and confirmed that all our most precious family things have gone?" she asked. "It's one thing leaving my country to your brother but our personal items are quite another."

Ed perceived that a bitter tone had crept back into Nell's voice and he contemplated her regretfully.

"No, of course I don't mind a little last minute packing. As soon as you are done, get someone to carry it all down to my ship," he suggested.

He had already washed and changed his breeches and was just selecting a clean, dry shirt and tunic. Trying to ignore his rather obvious and magnetic physical presence near her, Nell wondered around the room scrutinising shelves, peering into cupboards and poking through drawers. Seeing these simple items of her father's brought memories rushing back and she almost felt as if his presence was in the room. She was standing at the neatly carved and inlaid dressing table, picking up a couple of pieces of jewellery and a book, then circled about to face Ed. When she did, Nell jolted with shock. Transiently, in the dim light and wearing his clothes, Ed's resemblance to her father, something about his jaw line, was uncanny. But the seconds past and, with longer and closer inspection, she could see the differences: his height and colouring, the shape of his nose and the missing muscular bulk and wrinkles of years.

Gulping back the sudden tears down her dry throat, Nell crossed the room towards Ed. Fumbling, then picking out something from her clutch of rescued items which she spilled onto the bed, Nell seized his hand.

"I don't want to leave this as spoils of war. It was a favourite of my father's, and I reckon he would be keen for you to have this – he liked and respected you a lot," she murmured.

She slipped a gold ring on one of his fingers, and he studied the deep terracotta lozenge of cornelian etched with a lion rampant.

"Thank you, Nell," said Ed, touched by her words and actions.

He held her hands in his for a little longer, tried to catch her lowered gaze.

"Everything really will turn out well in the end," he tried to reassure her.

Avoiding his eyes, Nell continued briskly, "I've found my father's old Sige set too. It's rather beautiful, carved from colourful onyx, agate and marble and stored in an ebony box inlaid with silver. I know Al's been using a tatty and broken one he's had for years, so I'll bring it as a present for him. I'll get all the things I've found packed, and then I'll see you at supper. It'll certainly be good to have something warm to eat tonight."

Picking up her bundle of treasures, Nell left hastily with Ed studying her retreating back thoughtfully.

Consequently, he was concerned an hour later when Nell did not arrive at supper as promised while everyone else was tucking in to plates of food and jugs of beer. He watched as Marshall protectively cared for the timid Hope, surrounded by the more raucous squires and soldiers, but Nell remained absent from the meal. Excusing himself, Ed went to find the Captain of the Guard.

"Have you seen the Queen? She seems to have gone missing on me once more," he enquired.

"Yes, Sire. Her Majesty is on the town's ramparts," came the surprising reply.

Further unnerved at this news, Ed followed the Captain's directions to one of the tall towers that broke up the wall surrounding the town. He could see Nell as he approached, a slim figure huddled in a dark mantle amongst a couple of patrolling guards, thrown into relief against the navy sky by a lit brazier.

"Nell, what are you doing up here?" he admonished gently once he had reached her. "You could be putting yourself in danger from an arrow."

"Again," she stated flatly.

Taking in her words, Ed paused and perused her.

"You need to have a decent, warm meal inside you and a good night's sleep at this physically and emotionally tough time… and, having spoken to your old nurse, promised her, I see it as my duty to take care of you. Come away from here, Nell… There's nothing to see."

He grasped her arm firmly, trying to steer her away.

"Oh… but there is," she said, her voice unusually cold and hard, resisting his pressure to move. "He's been here for ages, pacing the perimeter of the wall, leering up at the Palace… hungry, gloating and prowling like a wolf."

"Who?" asked Ed, but a stab in the pit of his stomach told him he had already guessed.

"Warwick! It's almost as if he knows we're here and is lurking, anticipating his victory to be complete," Nell said miserably.

Ed looked down from the parapet and instantly spotted a black shape standing immobile, armed and staring up at the battlements, searching. As Warwick scanned the wall, he suddenly saw his brother. For a few minutes, their eyes locked in a silent, distant battle. Then Ed pulled Nell back from the crenulations, willing to break the contact and lose this fight.

"Let's leave Warwick, give him the stage – alone – in his triumph. He knows I will not let this rest here. Come, Nell, you really do need something to eat," he insisted, tugging on her arm again.

This time, Nell reluctantly followed.

Their supper in the great hall was good yet the atmosphere was strange. All ranks mixed in together, the men joked and laughed but any lighter moments were broken with sombre thoughtfulness. Nell kept the jugs of beer flowing but they all retired early in readiness for the very early departure the next day.

For a while, Nell sat in front of her mirror, brush in hand, gazing intently at her reflection. She had been deliberating for a long time and had come to a significant decision about her next course of action. She would not sleep in her own bed tonight. She would finish what was initiated earlier. She would go to Ed and, by giving her body to him, bind herself irrevocably to the King, whatever her future might hold. Nell steadied her nerves and gathered her thoughts, rehearsed what she wanted to say. Then emptying a goblet of wine for courage, she quietly slipped out of her own room to stand outside his. Taking a deep breath, she knocked emphatically on the door.

Ed had already gone to bed, still partially dressed as was his habit when in the field. He was surprised at the interruption, even more so when he opened the door to find Nell. She was dressed ready for bed, her feet bare.

"Nell!" he frowned. "Is there a problem?"

She shook her head, her unbraided hair undulating in glossy skeins around her shoulders, as she entered the room. Finding words difficult despite her practise, she spoke hesitantly, trying to get her viewpoint across. While she did so, Nell walked across to the window, untied her dressing gown, slid it off her arms and laid it across a chair beside the balcony.

Ed's frown deepened.

Nell bravely carried on, "I have cared about you deeply for a long time… Once I might even have had hopes… of more… but after today… my life, my situation, my expectations… will be very different…"

Ed took a step forward, began to speak, but Nell raised her hand to silence him. She was determined to carry on, without interruption.

"I wish to give myself entirely to you tonight… as I might once have done as your wife. I want to do this while I am still your equal… and I am free to do so… to choose."

As her words slowly trickled out, Nell loosened her chemise and the supple fabric slipped easily over her soft, smooth skin to the ground, pooling around her feet in a swirling eddy.

"Nell…" Ed groaned, sensing an instant physical response to the vision of her silhouetted naked in the window against the night sky, her hair ruffled and nipples hardened by the draught, while wondering quite how to react to this situation and save her from both herself… and him.

His first instinct was to rush forward, envelope her protectively in his arms, giving her rapidly cooling body warmth from his own. However, he quickly realised his mistake: the touch of her silky skin, her gentle curves against his muscles and the sweet smell of a floral perfume inevitably aroused him further.

"This is a massive decision… and one that can't be reversed," he murmured into her hair, closing his eyes and breathing in deeply the scent of her.

"I know… but it is my choice. It is what I want," asserted Nell, deliberately nuzzling her body closer against his.

"Oh, Nell…"

Ed embraced her tightly, fitting her body against his, lifted her chin and kissed her tenderly on the lips. He picked her up easily in his arms and carried her to the bed.

Three hours later and Ed was already dressing, without any sleep and ready to withdraw from Guthway. Nell had left the room an hour ago. He stared down at the rumpled bed, reflecting on what had happened there, his eyes lingering on the small smudges of blood, evidence of her maidenhood, something she could never get back. He sighed, making a mental note to himself that he would, somehow, make everything right for the pleasure he had enjoyed this night.

Only a few minutes ago, Kaspar had popped by. Working out what had happened, Kaspar had been angry with him, furious at the King's weakness and its result for Nell. After a few choice, terse words, he had quit his friend in disgust.

Ed rubbed his brow as if his head ached. Another bridge to mend.

Once again, they were leaving before dawn. A plate of uneaten pastries lay discarded on the dressing table. Having packed and sent everything they needed to the waiting ships, Hope bustled around the room doing nothing in particular and avoiding Nell's eyes. However innocent she may be, she knew something of her Queen's emotions and had figured out where Nell had been, what might have happened. Deciding to withdraw discreetly for a few minutes and go in search of Marshall, Hope left her mistress some hot water to wash with.

Nell dressed very carefully in one of the best gowns she could find of deep blue velvet, trimmed with lace and embroidered with pearls. She had found a small white-gold coronet to wear and wrapped a fur-lined black velvet cloak around her shoulders. She was determined to enter Ed's country resembling every bit a queen, even if she did not feel it, would no longer be one. The costume would also help her to keep calm, since she was nervous of meeting Ed again after last night whilst also terrified at the prospect of departing her country, possibly forever. She had to ignore her fluttering stomach in order to leave Guthway with as much dignity as she could muster.

Once dressed, and on her maid's return, Nell called Hope over to the almost empty desk. Only a long piece of parchment, curled at the ends and filled with several different styles of elaborate handwriting, lay on the polished surface. Hope recognised Nell's signature and seal stamped at the bottom of the page.

"Hope, I have a special document for you," said Nell softly. "There is a copy now locked in the Palace vaults. You have been more than a hardworking and loyal servant – you have been my friend. This document shows that I have reinstated your family with a peerage, something I believe is well overdue and have made sure has happened while I still have the power to do so. For the next hour, at least, you are Lady Shirborne and this region of Guthway is yours. You are no longer my servant, but while I am Queen, you are my lady-in-waiting. When we reach Torland, you will be my companion and my ward – I will make sure all your needs are met and will hold a considerable dowry for you."

Hope gawped at Nell in astonishment, her mouth open, having difficulty taking in exactly what she was saying. Nell clasped her hand and placed in it a heavy white-gold necklace with a thick chain and a pendant designed as a cross in a circle, studded with diamonds and pearls. Then she pushed a matching ring onto Hope's index finger.

"These are the symbols of your office. Wear them with pride, Hope, because you deserve them."

"Thank you… Thank you, Your Majesty!" exclaimed Hope breathlessly, holding the jewellery to her chest, tears sparkling in her eyes.

"Make sure you are ready to leave – sort yourself some clothing and accessories from those I, my sister and Elly have left behind that will work better with your new status – then enjoy the short time you have as Lady Shirborne," smiled Nell.

Having already sent on her last few possessions herself, Nell made her own final visit around the Palace and the town. She walked around the terraces and gardens, down to the cove and back, eventually meandering through the cobbled streets of the town down to the harbour. Then, having spoken to the dignitaries of the port, wishing them well, Nell dallied at the side of Ed's ship where it was moored in the harbour. She stood still until all the men who had travelled to Guthway from Torland, all the soldiers and nobles from Roxleburg and all the guards from Shirborne had boarded the carrack and other waiting ships. Only when the Captain of the Guard had retreated up the gangplank did Nell finally, regretfully, leave the solid land beneath her feet, the country of her birth, behind.

Ed waited for her at the top of the ramp to receive her symbolically onto his ship. He grasped her hand steadily; their eyes met and she managed to hold his gaze without wavering, although the pink of her cheeks deepened with thoughts of last night flooding back. When Nell was safely onboard, they pulled away from shore, sailing for the harbour exit. Once clear, they knew the remaining townsfolk would be free to surrender the port to Warwick, preserving its beauty from attack.

As soon as they left the sheltering walls of the harbour, the waves grew larger, pitching the ship from left to right. Most people proceeded down into the bows of the ship for security but Nell stayed put, watching as Guthway gradually, almost imperceptibly, grew smaller and more distant on the horizon, signifying her retreat from the main stage.

Having issued whatever orders he needed to, Ed came and settled himself noiselessly next to her, his left hand wearing her father's ring rested gently on her right where it lay on the rail of the ship, and he gave it a compassionate, reassuring squeeze.

They continued to stand there together, Nell gripping the rail, until Shirborne had completely faded away into the horizon. Ed explained that the ship would sail in a large arch around the bottom of the mountain range that divided their countries. Where the foothills of the mountains fell into cliffs, massive jagged rocks created dangers for unwary travellers who sailed too close to their treacherous teeth.

As they ultimately swept passed the mountains and away from Guthway, Nell felt overwhelmed by sadness, anger and a sense of personal failure. She had wanted to be strong, independent and to lead her country, but she had had to retreat, leaving her country to Warwick. She could no longer avoid some tears escaping and rolling down her cheeks. Then, as a wave jolted the stern, her shoulders heaved in unison and sobs crashed through her resolve.

Ed was regarding her with immense pity, a gaze that caused her a strange mixture of emotions: embarrassment and shame but also a small twinge of gratification. Her pride made her wipe away the tears and straighten her back. Nell could sense his eyes still on her even without glancing in his direction. He knew life was going to be tough for her; she had left Guthway a queen but was entering his country a wealthy yet landless noblewoman. He passed her a piece of cloth for her tears, placed an arm compassionately around her shoulders and led her down to the cabin below deck.

ACT 3

Chapter 1

From the moment they landed in Torland, Nell was continued to be accorded the utmost respect, but she felt the difference within herself. Everyone would know who she was and what she was doing here. A queen without a country to rule meant she was effectively no longer a queen; a great irony when it had been the role she had been so quick to divest herself of when entering Torland two and a half years ago.

"Well, we don't have to rush so much now," commented Al, "so we can stop off at my place overnight on the way up to Erlwick. I can introduce you to my family and repay your hospitality, Nell," he grinned, "but I can't promise to make you such a good stew myself."

"Thank goodness! Al doesn't need to because he has a great cook," laughed Kaspar. "He loves reading but just can't follow a recipe – I know from bitter experience. But you'll certainly like his library because he has books from floor to ceiling and plenty of comfy seating."

Nell smiled back, heartened by their genuine friendship.

They journeyed throughout the day and by late afternoon they arrived at the outskirts of a busy market town overlooked by a huge circular stone castle on a hill top.

"Here we are… my home," said Al with more than a hint of pride. "We can finally all have a long and peaceful night's sleep."

As they wondered into the town and up to the fortress, many people abandoned what they were doing to view the procession of nobles and soldiers, gawping at first then bowing when they realised that not only was their lord home but their king too. Some peered with open curiosity at Nell and the foreign soldiers.

"We have more time tonight – I'll arrange a bath for you, Nell," said Al. "I'm sure you'll welcome the chance to freshen up properly."

"Have one yourself, Al," remarked Kaspar, grinning at his friend. "You didn't get a chance for a proper soaking in the sea yesterday unlike Ed and I – you could definitely do with a clean up after all your exertions."

"And I'm sure I can find space for you to sleep in a pig sty or dung heap somewhere," replied Al, acidly.

Nell loved the look of this neat, round castle with its series of smooth, regular, circular towers. Everywhere seemed trim and tidy. Al showed her up to a room almost at the top of one of the towers, an exhausted Hope trailing behind them, her eyes enormous with surprise at everything new she was seeing. He stopped at a room on the way to Nell's and knocked on the door. An older woman with long blonde hair, streaked with white and pulled back into a loose plait, opened the door.

"Albert!" cried the lady, hugging him to her in delight. "We weren't expecting to see you so soon."

"I know, mother, but we've had an unforeseen detour."

His mother's eyes slid passed his shoulder towards Nell, intrigued.

"This is Nell, Queen of Guthway and Rae's sister. I've told you all about her already," and Al winked at Nell as he spoke.

"Oh, Your Majesty!" said his mother, curtsying to Nell. "You are welcome to our home. I met your lovely sister when she visited us last harvest time."

"Oh no, I'm not a queen anymore! My position has changed somewhat. I gather we decided on Lady Guthway for now, so please, consider us equals," insisted Nell, taking the other woman's hands in her own. "I've also heard about you. It's a delight to finally meet you, Lady Linnet."

"I've put Nell in the room above yours for the night. Ed and Kaspar will be in the east tower with me," mentioned Al.

"The King… the King's here?" Linnet squealed, instantly flustered at the mention of Ed. "Oh, my! I'd better make sure everything's properly prepared for his room and the meal this evening. I'm sure you'll like your room, dear," she added to Nell, patting her hand. "It's one of the best. I'll meet with you again later at supper, and we can talk further then. Al, dear, if you see your sister or brother, please send them to me as I'm going to need their help with all these extra guests," and she scurried away in the opposite direction, suddenly urgently busy, all other concerns forgotten.

"Perhaps I shouldn't have mentioned Ed's name since its thrown mother into a huge panic," said Al reflectively. "At least I didn't mention exactly how many guests we have – that really would have sent her reeling. Still, she's right – your room is a nice one. High up and on the south side, it has a good view across the town and countryside. Oh… and if you come across a young blonde minx hiding somewhere in your room, or anywhere else for that matter, that's bound to be my sister Pippa. Here we are…"

Al showed her the room. It was light and airy with gold damask curtains, matching bedcover and a detailed tapestry depicting a unicorn in a forest glade sewn in yellows, blues and greens. She grimaced at the irony: she was no maiden now to attract such a creature. Nevertheless, Nell felt the room was imbued with a restful atmosphere that echoed the woodland clearing.

"It's lovely, Al, really peaceful. Listen, I took my father's Sige set from the Palace at Shirborne – I wasn't going to leave it to Warwick – and I want you to have it. I know how much you enjoy a game and how you are in need of a new set. Here…" and she handed him the boxed carved stone set from her canvas travelling bag.

"Thank you, Nell, that's really thoughtful of you," replied Al, touched. "I'll treasure it and put it in the library where I often potter about when I'm home. I'll leave you now and give you a chance to freshen up."

Shortly after Al had gone, a maid arrived and started to fill a wooden tub with buckets of hot water. Hope immediately went to help.

"No, Hope," insisted Nell firmly, "I want you to go to your room – you'll have a nice one of your own now – and rest. You're exhausted too! I'm sure the maid will show you the way. I'll ask someone to send you some suitable clothes, and you can get ready for supper too."

She smiled at the girl's startled face.

"Now you are a lady, you must eat with us."

Hope hesitated but Nell continued to insist so finally, curtsying, she left.

"A little lavender essence, my lady," explained the maid on her return as she tipped a small amount of liquid from a green glass bottle.

167

The pungent scent filled the room as it hit the water, and Nell came to swirl the essence around the tub with her finger tips. Appreciating the peace and time alone, she could not wait to get in, wash away all the dirt, sweat, frustration and sorrow of the last few days. She also washed away the remnants of the intimacy she had shared with Ed but the memory of his tenderness and affection last night would persist with her for a long time. Tired, Nell almost wanted to cry again. She submerged her head under the water, enjoying the heat as it stung her scalp. Raising her head up, water running off her hair and down her back, Nell gasped a welcome breath of air. As her ears cleared, she heard a muffled noise. Alert, she stared around the room. One curtain ruffled as if with a slight breeze, but the other stayed motionless. Nell could see two small leather shoes peeping out from beneath the curtain fringe and guessed they belonged to Al's elusive sister.

"Hello," said Nell. "Now I suspect that you are Pippa. My name's Nell, and I could do with some help. I won't let on that you're here, but my maid has gone, and I need someone to help me – pass my towel, help me dress and sort my hair. Please could you do that?"

A pale elfin face peered out from behind the curtain, with a smattering of freckles covering her pert, upturned nose.

"Oh, thanks… My towel is over there on the bed," and Nell pointed at it without making a fuss or requiring any chatter in response.

Pippa had been watching when the company arrived. Part of her wanted to rush down, jumping three steps at a time to greet her brother and his friends, hear all their news of any exciting action as she would normally have done. She knew Al and Kaspar would have been fearless in facing the enemy but felt sure the King would have been braver.

These men had always been her heroes. Pippa studied them practising their sword skills whenever she had an opportunity, tried to copy what they did, but particularly sat in wide-eyed admiration and youthful hero worship of Ed's skills. She loved it when he commented on her own abilities or offered a helping hand to show her what to do.

Out on the battlements, Pippa had been pretending to fight when the group's approach had been trumpeted. Discovering that there was a queen in attendance today, she had looked down at her homemade armour and sighed miserably. While her mother despaired and said her brother indulged her too much, any noble women she ever met, excepting Princess Allys, always regarded her with scorn, dismissing Pippa as a childish tomboy. Her only option to avoid more glances of disdain or disappointment had been to run and hide. Yet now she was trapped in the same room as this queen, and once discovered, she had no choice but to come forward and show herself.

The girl, looking young for thirteen, slunk forwards. She went to pick up the towel and brought it over to Nell, peering out from beneath her unruly, fair hair. She loitered at a distance, out of reach, as if expecting to be grabbed and held prisoner.

"Thank you, Pippa," chatted Nell easily to the girl, completely ignoring her armour. "I came here with your brother, Al, today… Did you hear him earlier? He's a good friend of mine. Once I've towel dried my hair, can you help me brush it through and plait it? It's got so long it's difficult to do myself, and it does have a tendency to get tangled. I fancy it's probably about time I trimmed it."

Pippa nodded and, reluctant to speak and unable to escape but not wishing to act rudely, went to find a brush.

"Which gown shall I wear?" asked Nell, continuing to engage the girl. "I wore the blue velvet here. It's fairly clean, so I could wear it again. Or I could choose the dark red brocade which is a personal favourite of mine – it might give me the bit of colour in my cheeks that I need. What do you think?"

"The red one," whispered Pippa, shuffling her feet nervously on the floor, surprised at Nell's obvious friendliness and respect for her views.

Nell grinned at having garnered a response from the reticent girl. She was making some headway with her.

"I love your armour by the way – it's a little similar to something I had once in leather that my father had made for me," she continued, smiling at Pippa's sudden amazement. "I'll have to show you what I wear in the tiltyard when you next come to Erlwick. But I wonder if you ought to remove it before you go down to supper – even when we are at war, it's not quite the done thing to wear armour in the hall."

"You really practise in the tiltyard?" asked Pippa, moving closer.

"Of course! I didn't ever want to just stand by and observe battles but fight for my country myself, alongside my people, and my father understood that. In fact, he respected and encouraged it."

By the time Nell was dressed and ready for supper, Al's sister was merrily chatting with her. Both of them jumped slightly when there was a knock at the door, and Pippa fell silent again.

"Can I have a brief word, Nell? Hello, Pippa," said Ed entering the room and spotting the girl.

Pippa gaped at him, awestruck at his sudden close presence.

170

"It's safe, sweetheart, neither of us will tell on you," Nell reassured the girl. "Thank you for all your help. You can escape now and hide somewhere else. Though, I do hope to see you again at supper, and we can discuss our training further."

She continued to smile while Pippa scuttled rapidly from the room. Yet, as soon as she was gone, Nell felt tense at the impending conversation, alone, with Ed.

"Nell, I wanted to have a quick word with you, as soon as possible, about how we're going to deal with your people while they're in Torland… and, of course, your status."

Ed sauntered over to the window as he spoke, and Nell automatically followed him. She wondered how much of her status he was planning to refer to.

"I was going to suggest asking your nobles, such as Earl Redvers and Lord Falkner, to hold some of my forts at various places along my northern and eastern borders. They could gather what men are available from your dispersed peoples to help swell the garrisons and patrol the area. They would be able to run the castles and the surrounding lands as temporary homes of their own while securing the borders for me against our joint enemy. It will give them a surety, a status, right from the start yet will also help us. But I wanted to run this idea past you before I offer it to your men. Do you agree?"

Nell thought for a few minutes then nodded slowly, "Yes, I can see that would work. It would give them a solid purpose while we wait for our chance to return to Guthway, keep them armed and ready yet offering you extra men exactly where you currently need them most. They are all good, loyal commanders, Ed, and will support you to the hilt."

Nell paused briefly, stepping out onto the balcony and gazing over the town below, before spinning back towards him and continuing with a question, "But what about me?"

"As I have stated previously, Nell, you and your sister will always have a place of safety – no, a home – with us. And it is my brother who is responsible for your current situation. Moreover, you are our friends and are always welcome in my castle."

Ed stared at her, knowing the next bit would be hard to say, harder to hear.

"But, as you have already gathered, your status has changed… in some eyes at least. My ministers get annoyingly technical about these things, and as you are no longer the incumbent monarch on the throne of Guthway, they say that we should – temporarily, at least – refer to you as Lady Guthway instead. It will never change how we regard you as a person… a friend."

He swallowed hard, and she knew his next comment would refer more directly to them.

"Everything else… we'll take a day at a time."

So that was it, no promises of anything more, just friendship: all that could be offered to a mere landless lady. Nell's heart sank and tears threatened to spill over, stinging her eyes.

"Nell…" Ed's voice was concerned.

He wanted to find a way to reassure her while being wary of giving her close physical support after last night, further endangering their friendship and Nell's position.

She swung away from him, gripping the balcony tightly as if to steady herself, "It's fine, Ed… It really is! I'm sure I'll get through this. Worse things have happened to many other people, and as you have pointed out, I have both family and friends here. And I'm not poor."

Nell let out a long sigh.

"I was just contemplating the incongruity of my situation. Last time I came to Torland, I wanted to hide my status because I was anxious about all the attention my rank would afford me. This time around, I come to your country and all that rank has been… stolen from me… And now I know I will miss it – would want all the responsibility and heartache it entails back – not for the position itself but because of how I could use its power to protect the people and places I love."

"And it was my brother who snatched it from you. We owe you so much. And who knows what Warwick will do with all that power," spoke Ed quietly, shuddering at the notion.

"I won't get any of those offers of marriage I so abhorred now. I'm protected from that at least," she added, suddenly laughing at the irony, but aching at the limitations she speculated it now put on her relationship with him.

"Nell!" exclaimed Ed, slightly bewildered at her jumbled reactions and shaking his head. "Yesterday…"

"Right, let's go down to supper."

Nell leapt back inside hastily, not wanting to hear anything else.

"What's more, I do still have the hospitality of friends to enjoy," and Nell smiled at him, acting as happily as she could while linking her arm through his.

Chapter 2

Travelling at a more leisurely pace, it took another three and a half days before the group finally arrived at Erlwick and the city could welcome its king home.

When they reached the castle, Nell was delighted to see her sister fit and well, standing next to Allys, waiting for her on the familiar terrace at the front of the keep. Dismounting, Nell ran up the steps to greet Rae, the sisters hugging amidst the tears of their bitter-sweet reunion.

"I'll accompany you back up to your old room, Nell, and you can tell me what's been happening," said Rae.

"Oh, I'm coming too," added Allys. "I've been starved of decent gossip since you've been gone."

"I don't believe that!" laughed Nell.

The three young women proceeded into the castle, arms linked, with Hope close behind.

"I hope you know what you've done," laughed Kaspar, "because that looks like trouble to me."

"It's good that Allys gets on well with them both," said Ed, "since she hasn't always seen eye-to-eye with visiting ladies at court."

Kaspar snorted with laughter, "That's because they're not your usual pampered princesses thanks to their father and the precarious nature of their country. They have to be tough. That appeals to Allys… and, let's face it, to all of us."

As the women headed back to Nell's room, passed at least one minister muttering ominously in the shadows, Allys explained that they were to have a feast tonight.

"I know things have gone badly for you in Guthway, and I know it's all the fault of my dreadful brother, but we wanted to celebrate your safe return. We had a message to say you were all unscathed and on your way, so the cook has been very busy in the kitchen. I thought it would be fun if we could all get ready together."

Allys contemplated Nell thoughtfully for a short time.

"I expect it's been quite a while now since you've had much female company other than Hope."

"Yes, you're right. Excepting Elly's mother – who just seemed to mope around until she retreated to her country estate – most other ladies of the court left soon after Rae." Nell sighed, "I could do with some more light-hearted chat. It makes a change from agonising about the lives of the soldiers guarding the border."

Then she added in surprise as they reached the doorway, "My room… it's exactly the same!"

"Yes," explained Allys, "my brother gave orders to leave it untouched – except for a dust and brush up, of course – in case you returned. I'm afraid he felt it very likely, especially once you sent Rae here. He wanted to give you something familiar – homely – to come back to.

But, for my part, I'm very pleased to see you, whatever the circumstances. Rae and I have already become good friends."

Focusing on Hope, Allys reached out her hands to grasp those of the former maid, "And, now you are a lady, Hope – congratulations, by the way – we've sorted out a lovely room for you further along this corridor – much bigger than the cupboard you had before – so that you are still close to Nell. I will show it to you in a minute."

"Then let's gather together what we need – gowns, perfume, jewellery, some light refreshment – and meet back here again in an hour's time. That'll be long enough for me to have a bath after my journey," suggested Nell. Then she added with a wicked grin, "And long enough for us to prepare Hope for her first formal banquet."

As the other women left, temporarily leaving Nell to the ministrations of her new maid, she shut the door, and leaning back against the solid surface and exhaling in a whistling breath through her teeth, she surveyed the shrunken nature of her kingdom. She was pleased to see the familiar furniture again, many personal items such as books, clothes and knick-knacks that she had left behind in her need to travel lightly and swiftly before, all now giving her the sensation of warmth and security that Ed gauged they would. She knew, however, that it also represented the change in her life. Nell understood she would be considered with less significance than she used to be here. Those turbid glances from the ministers were a forewarning. She thought she could bare it, find a way to make a new life for herself while she was amongst such good friends.

Pulling herself together, she smiled at her new maid, Blythe, and started asking her questions about her family, discovering Allys had considerately chosen a girl from Guthway, one of the many refugees needing help to resettle.

While Nell once again washed the trials of her journey away, she finally felt that she could relax, let all her grief, tiredness and stress swirl free into the warm water around her, and she allowed some tears to flow for one last time. Now she could leave all her responsibilities behind her, let someone else endure that pressure. Then she sat up suddenly, guiltily, in the bath, slopping water over the sides, realising that she was lumbering Ed with greater burdens. She knew she must continue to help in any way that she could or that he would allow.

When Allys, Rae and Hope arrived giggling at her door in their dressing gowns, Nell, now composed, was already swathed in perfume to compliment the essences of her bath and wore a cream silk chemise.

"Blythe is settling in well. She managed a good rummage in the kitchen – she's made friends there already – and has brought up some fresh lemonade and sweet treats – nougat and honeycomb – so please help yourselves," invited Nell. "I've found some fine ribbon I'd like to try braiding into your hair, Rae."

"Oh, do me too, if you've got enough!" pleaded Allys.

"Only if you tell me all that's been going on between you and Kaspar, Allys," laughed Nell.

Then, sighing ruefully, she peered down at the gown she had chosen which was hanging loosely on her diminished frame, however tightly she laced the seams.

"It's not Kaspar and I providing all the recent gossip," giggled Allys in reply, enveloping a bemused Hope in a cloud of fragrance.

"What do you mean?" asked Nell and then gasped as she discerned her sister's pink cheeks. "Rae, what's been happening? Should I have let you come here on your own?"

"N… nothing," she stuttered in reply, "it's only… there's someone… someone I rather like… He's someone you like too," she added imploringly before hanging her head, pink cheeks now burning scarlet, fretting about her older sister's reaction because she wanted her approval.

"Well, Allys, I deduce that I will need your help on this one – I think you had better tell me what's been going on," Nell laughed again.

"As your sister is as interested in books as you are," Allys grinned, "Rae has been spending a lot of time in the library and, therefore, a lot of time in the company of one Albert, Earl of Langford. And now they appear to be seeking each other's company outside the library too."

Nell grabbed her sister's hands, delighted, wanting to encourage her.

"Rae, I couldn't be happier… especially if the feeling is mutual. We'll have to keep an eye out for any signs of that later. Al is a good man and, now I've met them, I know his family are lovely too."

While the women continued to get ready, helping each other with their hair, selecting jewellery and other accessories, cajoling Hope into a more expensive outfit, Allys decided to probe Nell.

"And what about you?" she twinkled mischievously. "You've spent almost a whole week in my brother's company. I'm pretty certain you two were growing fond of each other before you left for Guthway. Has anything of that old spark been revived?"

Nell let out a long breath as she twined the last ribbon through the small plaits hanging loose in Allys's hair, a slight resignation creeping into her voice. She certainly could not admit what had happened between them in Guthway or the sickening sensation that had grown since. However kind Ed's words and attitude towards her, she noticed he avoided meeting her eyes earlier. She was not sure if he was ashamed of what had happened, ashamed of her.

"It doesn't matter how I feel or what I might wish for, I'm no longer in a position to choose. Neither is Ed. He is the High King, remember, and his ministers hold a lot of sway concerning matters of state. His relationships are a matter of state. I have wealth but I no longer have any land and, therefore, little real rank or power at court… or at least that's how it'll be seen by many."

"Oh, Nell, Ed doesn't think like that!" exclaimed Allys.

"The King might not but others do and he always has them, his position and his country to consider," asserted Nell. "Ed has always put the priorities of Erlwick and his people first – you know that. And so he should. I am more aware and understanding of that now than I ever was before. And don't forget that a lot has happened to both of us since I was last in Erlwick… Things – emotions – will have changed."

"Well, we'll see," said Allys more optimistically. "At least you're still friends."

The women commenced down to supper together, but as they reached the bottom of the stairs before the great hall, Al almost bounced over towards them, grinning more than Nell had ever seen him do before.

"My lady," he addressed Nell, "would you mind if I had the pleasure of escorting your sister, Rae, into supper?"

"I'd be delighted," smiled Nell back at him.

She glanced at Allys, and they giggled together while Al walked towards the hall with a beaming Rae on his arm.

"What's so funny?" asked Kaspar when he and Ed approached them.

"Nothing that concerns you men," said Allys tartly, "I believe that it's time for you to escort me into the hall, Kaspar, as you have badly neglected me for a fortnight or so now."

Ed studied his friend and his sister while they also moved away, arm in arm.

"I'm surprised Kaspar still wants to honour the agreement our parents made and marry Allys. She gets cheekier every year. I have actually said I am content for them to opt out if they wish but both strike me as happy enough with the arrangement."

"Maybe Kaspar likes someone with a bit of spirit," suggested Nell.

"You're right, of course. I don't reckon a mouse would suit him... or her either come to that. Hope, I have arranged a suitable companion for you to go into supper with, Sir Ralph," Ed told the girl, a further adjustment to her new life which made her moan a little and her shoulders sag.

He then glanced across at Nell.

"You're looking lovely tonight, Nell – I am honoured to be escorting you into our little feast."

Blushing, Nell accepted his complement, while not totally believing its accuracy, and his arm then walked with him into the great hall, past the overtly disapproving glare of Caldwell.

Chapter 3

Nell had a glorious evening talking and dancing with her friends. The following days continued in a similar vein as she settled back into the routines of life at a busy court with many young nobles currently in attendance. She especially enjoyed the resumption of the late evenings spent in the company of Ed and her friends, now joined by her sister, Rae. She began to recover from the exhaustion and grief of the past two years.

While Nell appreciated her increased leisure, she also worked harder than ever with Burgess, the Master-at-Arms, improving her prowess with both sword and bow. Whatever else might happen, she had no intention of accepting events in her life so passively again and fully intended to be involved in any battles to come, whether in Torland or Guthway, and however she could.

Ed was aware of the large amount of her mornings she spent in the tiltyard. If he had any concerns, he said nothing, guessing where this new passion and hard edge came from. He too filled many hours there sparring with Marshall; he was also devoting more time to his commanders and his army. It was becoming increasingly obvious that the King was preparing for war. As more of his time was consumed with military matters, the day-to-day running of the castle fell to Nell who was keen to shoulder this duty for Ed.

A couple of months into their new regime, Ed found Nell and Hope in the stables and pulled her aside. Gazing at her sideways, he acted a little apprehensive about what he had to say.

"Thanks for all the hard work you've put in so far since your return to Guthway, Nell, which has helped me concentrate my efforts elsewhere, but I'm sorry to be causing you more work shortly," and he coughed slightly as if clearing his throat. "We are expecting guests next week. We need to make sure they have suitable rooms befitting their status and that their retinues are also housed appropriately. We will also be planning to amuse them properly with a series of feasts and entertainments. Could I leave the bulk of the household arrangements to you?"

"Of course you can, Ed. Now my responsibilities have eased, I'm happy to do anything to help yours which have increased greatly. Who are our visitors?" asked Nell and she observed with wry amusement the King shifting nervously.

"My ministers wished to invite several of our allies and their families – especially their daughters, apparently – to bolster support against our enemies."

She heard him gulp as if embarrassed.

"With all that has happened, they are pressing for me to marry and produce an heir. I presume that this is their idea of a way to hurry me into finding a suitable match. Still, on the bright side, Al's family will also be joining us at court for the duration."

Ed stared passed Nell's shoulder and would not meet her eyes. He was painfully aware of the hurt he might be causing by this revelation. He cared about her too much and wanted to shield her from any repeat performance of the intimacies they had shared; that's not how he wanted their relationship to develop. He certainly did not wish to gradually transform Nell into the role of his mistress; he had already destroyed a passion and lost a child in that way, causing both immense grief and heartache.

Yet, he wasn't quite sure how it could develop further, especially now his ministers were badgering him to unite through marriage with a strong ally. Caldwell had made it perfectly clear they were pleased there had been no official, public commitment between Ed and Nell two years ago, leaving options open for what he perceived would be a better alliance.

Meanwhile, Ed felt he needed to distance himself from Nell in order to protect her from what had happened between them, ensure it didn't happen again. He had agreed to his ministers' shenanigans as he conjectured a harmless dalliance, or two, with other women, distracting him and avoiding being alone with Nell, would be a good way of achieving this. He still had no intention of being bamboozled into an alliance he did not want.

If the thought of entertaining foreign royalty bothered Nell at all and the knowledge that Ed was supposed to find a bride elsewhere pained her, the news that Al's family were coming delighted her. It was his family who arrived early and were with them on the terrace for the influx of the first royal visitors from neighbouring lands. When the grand carriages which bore King Regan, Princess Moira and their retinue ceased at the bottom of the steps, Nell mulled over the rumours she had heard that the Princess was a great beauty like Elly. Even so, she was surprised at the audible intake of breath from the waiting men when Moira emerged from the carriage wrapped in a fur-lined mantle.

'Here we go again,' thought Nell wryly.

The same age as Nell, Princess Moira carried herself with a poise and elegant grace that none of the women on the terrace felt they could hope to achieve. Her lustrous black hair was wound in one long, thick plait twined with silver thread and glittering beads that contrasted sharply with her blossom-pink and white skin. Her lips were full and rose coloured while her curling black lashes framed her bright emerald-green eyes. Everything about her was perfect in size and shape, completely flawless. When she spoke in response to Ed's words of welcome, her voice was entrancingly melodic. The other women instantly felt insipid and insignificant in contrast. Beautiful like Elly but otherwise much worldlier, Moira had every intention of acquiring the most powerful man in The Alliance for herself and, understanding her allure to men, knew exactly how to attract him. She dipped in an elegant and carefully calculated curtsy; Moira leant forward to reveal a low cut, exquisite satin gown that barely concealed her voluptuous breasts, a smile sensually curving her lips.

All the men's eyes, all their attention, were magnetically drawn to this beautiful woman. Nell was sure she could feel the glee radiating from Caldwell at his already assumed success in allying this princess with the King.

"Well, we might as well vanish," remarked Allys acidly when Kaspar strode forward to welcome Moira while Ed greeted her father.

"I think she's horrible," stated Pippa, taking an instant dislike to her and pinching her brother Godwyn who stood gawping, mouth wide open. "Quit drooling, Wyn!"

"Hush," said Nell, her hands resting on the younger girl's shoulders, because she saw Ed bringing the guests towards them for introductions. "Let's give her a chance – she might be really friendly."

However, she spoke without conviction, perceiving the look of disdain that flitted over the Princess's face when she was presented to the women of the court.

"Nell, I have described to my good friend, King Regan, how you've helped with preparations for their visit. I've also explained that they are to have a rest from their long journey tonight and that we will be holding a banquet in their honour tomorrow. Would you walk with Regan and show him to his quarters?" asked Ed.

"Yes, Sire. Your Majesty," and she curtsied to Regan before continuing, "I hope His Majesty, King Edward, also informed you that we are holding a tournament next week. Would you be willing to participate?"

"Maybe, my dear, if my back holds out. I'm afraid I have not kept my physical strength like your father did, but I still have some ability with a sword," smiled King Regan.

"There is a magnificent tiltyard here at Erlwick and an excellent Master-at-Arms who would give you any help you need. You might bump into me there – I'm giving the Earl of Langford's sister, Pippa, swordsmanship lessons."

Regan raised his eyebrows in surprise as they turned to enter the keep, but before he could say anything further, a rider suddenly clattered urgently across the bailey.

"Your Majesty!" called Redvers in automatic address to Nell while he dismounted swiftly.

"Excuse me a minute, Sire," Nell said to Regan and went to talk to her nobleman who had dropped on one knee before her.

"Why is he showing such deference to her, speaking to her above you and the High King?" asked Moira, perplexed, and loud enough for Nell to hear even though she was walking away. "She no longer holds such rank."

Ed gaped at Moira, momentarily perturbed at her attitude, while Rae glared icily at the Princess, hurt for her sister's sake.

"Now, my dear," spoke Regan indulgently, "she is still of royal blood and that nobleman, I deem, is one of her own. Presumably, he has news of some importance?"

"Yes, that is right," confirmed Ed, "he holds one of my major forts on the border with Guthway. I must speak with him too. Please excuse me. Kaspar, will you see to our guests?"

With a quick nod, he joined Nell to hear the news of Warwick's massing troops and experimental skirmishes along the border.

Chapter 4

By supper of that evening, all their royal guests had arrived, were welcomed and settled into their rooms. The banquet on the following night, in celebration of such a large gathering, went without a hitch. Nell organised for lanterns and torches to be set on the terrace in front of the fortress, the layered gardens along the side of the building and the courtyard behind the great hall, once again allowing greater space for everyone to spread into, making the most of the glorious summer weather.

She had arranged with the cook to provide a feast of many courses fit for the visiting royalty, music during the meal and dancing after. At five in the afternoon, Nell went to check on proceedings in the kitchens before getting ready for the evening. Half an hour later, Kaspar was passing through to sneak a little light snack when he found Nell helping model some marzipan sweetmeats.

"Nell! Shouldn't you be getting ready for this evening by now?" he exclaimed.

Nell laughed drily.

"I find it relaxing to be involved in a practical activity. If I'm focusing on these roses, I'm not reflecting on – or stewing over – anything else. Besides, it wouldn't really matter how long I take, or how carefully I prepare tonight, nobody is going to heed me next to Princess Moira. Isn't that right, Pippa?" and she passed a piece of almond paste to the girl hiding out of the way of the kitchen staff under the table.

"Well, I'll promise to notice and dance with you, Nell… and you," he added to Pippa, crouching down to talk to her.

Kaspar was as good as his word, and having danced with Allys, he came to collect Nell from where she sat next to another visiting monarch, the elderly King Storr, and was working hard to prise some conversation from his plain and timid granddaughter, Princess Ingrid.

"You do look beautiful tonight, Nell," remarked Kaspar, "you have a grace and dignity that was missing from the young woman in disguise who dwelt with us two years ago."

Then he frowned a little.

"Unfortunately, there is a greater sadness in your eyes too."

Nell laughed, despite the earnestness in his voice, "I've never been described as beautiful before… That was always reserved for Elly."

"That is because her beauty is bright and obvious from the start. Yours is quieter and more unassuming, the kind that gradually grows on you until you wonder how you never perceived it before," commented Kaspar. "Your face matches your personality and they are altogether more restful. I reckon that every woman has some beauty in them. Consider Princess Ingrid – some would say her countenance was plain, but her hands and feet are small but exquisitely elegant and maintaining beautiful time tapping out the music. I've always believed that it's who you are and what you do that makes people special and attractive – internal beauty. Yes, Moira is stunning to look at, but you wouldn't find her chatting to a child like Pippa in the kitchen, and I know which I judge is better."

"Thank you," said Nell, so genuinely pleased and respectful of what he had said that she did not argue with the compliment given as she normally would have done. She thought how lucky Allys was in her betrothed. Instead, she just laughed and added, "Don't call Pippa a child or she'll go for you!"

Then her eyes drifted over to where Ed was once again dancing with Moira. He had monopolised her all evening and had barely talked to any of the other female guests yet. Nell frowned. She accepted that he wouldn't be dancing with her, but this discourtesy towards the other royals and nobles present was highly unusual in the King. His manners were normally so impeccable. For someone so reticent in his regard for princesses, tonight he was undoubtedly as captivated as, almost, every other man in the room by just one woman.

While Kaspar danced next with Pippa as promised, Nell walked around the room, ensuring everyone was happy like a model hostess, pausing to talk to King Storr again for a few minutes and persuading Princess Ingrid to take a turn about the floor with Al. As Kaspar predicted, she moved beautifully to the music. Ed was still dancing with the Princess, so Nell, her head throbbing slightly, decided to get some fresh air and wandered out to the courtyard. She nodded at a few people but did not stop to talk anymore, wishing for some time to herself.

Sitting by the raised marble pool, she watched the silvery fish dart in and out amongst the weeds. She inhaled slowly and deeply. The cool breeze that whispered around the cobbled yard cleared her head. She was there a little while before someone came and sat beside her. She did not need to glimpse across to recognise the long lean legs and she caught her breath, suddenly dizzy again.

"I missed you in the hall, but I can understand your disappearance – it is rather warm in there," said Ed. "I wanted to thank you again for all the hard work you've put in for tonight because it's been such a magnificent evening. In fact, I wanted you to know how much I appreciate all you have done around the castle during the past few weeks – you have really helped me out." Then he grinned at her, "Thanks especially for the marzipan. The roses are particularly beautiful."

"Ugh!" she winced, "Kaspar told on me."

"I would like you to come back inside and dance with me."

Pleased, Nell smiled at him.

But then, laughing, he added, "I think Pippa might lynch me if I don't!"

Her stomach dropped like a stone, dismayed that he had not asked her from his own desire. Still, Nell enjoyed the touch of Ed's arm, strong and warm around her waist, as he guided her back to the hall. But, once they were whirling about the floor, she could not help noticing that Ed's eyes kept drifting across to Moira, dancing elegantly with Al, and this time, her disappointment was so intense it was as if her breath had ceased, lungs squeezed tight, empty of air.

Ed, meanwhile, stared mesmerised at the Princess, reflecting on how she was the most beautiful woman he had ever seen and, despite everything, including his better judgement, considered how a marital alliance with Frisged would certainly strengthen his country in these troubled times. He sighed silently. In normal circumstances, he would not have even remotely contemplated marriage yet. He still felt so young and that he had so much more to learn about kingship. He would like to mature into his role first and have time to choose the right woman for the position of his queen, someone more companionable than Princess Moira appeared to be. However, these were not normal times. His thoughts focused back on Warwick. Unconsciously, Ed's arm tightened protectively around Nell's waist.

As the dance finished, Moira suddenly surfaced at their side.

"Ed, dear," she said serenely, placing a hand proprietorially on his arm and peering earnestly into his eyes, but without even a glance at Nell, "I'm so hot. Can you show me somewhere cool to sit for a while?"

"The courtyard is looking very pretty tonight, or you can go out on the terrace. There's a fantastic view across the city from there," suggested Nell.

"Please show me somewhere quiet," continued the Princess significantly, completely ignoring Nell and moving her body between her and Ed, blocking her out of the conversation.

Moira's hand darted forward to stroke his and then twined her fingers through his. With a small shrug of his shoulders and a whimsical smile at Nell, Ed walked away with Moira and hardly a backwards glance. Nell breathed in some deep lungfuls of air, trying to keep calm and hinder the strange queasy, dizzy feeling assailing her again. She spun around to find Pippa staring at her.

"Right," said Nell decidedly, "you are going to dance with me," and she scooped her up and off around the edge of the great hall.

Chapter 5

Nell saw little of Ed over the next week. He was spending a lot of time with Moira, virtually ignoring the other visiting princesses, while Nell was busy with her own plans. In the evenings, when there was not a banquet or ball, she still met with her other friends, often in the library or one of their rooms, but no longer with the King.

So Nell found herself constantly drawn to the tiltyard. In her mind, she said it was her own desire to practise but, in her heart, knew it was the one place she might see Ed without Moira present. Yet that advantage was bitter-sweet: her almost physical need to see the King was tempered by the fact that Nell could only see him amongst others, as he joked and laughed beside the knights and squires he sparred with.

With the tournament fast approaching, everyone had much to do in preparation and the tiltyard was continuously busy. Many of the young men at court were eager to show off their prowess and were constantly practising, aware also of the possibility of impending battle. The tournament was to be staged over three days.

A temporary arena for the jousting was built in one of the fields near the castle and surrounded by a fair, with a couple of other smaller arenas marked out for events such as archery and wrestling, many of which were open to all comers. Competitions were to be conducted throughout the day and into early evening with a small marquee set aside for luncheon. However, they would all return to the castle for supper.

On the first day, Ed, as High King, opened proceedings with a short joust then retired to the royal box to watch the other nobles take their turn. Allys, Rae and the visiting princesses all got to hand out favours to the young squires performing bouts that morning, but there was no sign of Nell.

"No Nell? That's very remiss of her. Even her mousey companion is here… although I don't know why Albert lets his sister mingle with the servants like that," uttered Moira in disgust.

"Hope is no longer Nell's servant and is, nevertheless, from a noble family," explained Allys, but Moira coughed deep within her throat to voice her disagreement, as if Hope's recent history was enough to make her a social outcast for ever.

Pippa was indeed standing with Hope beneath the royal box, hanging over the guard rails, eagerly analysing the activities of the squires.

"There's Marshall, Hope," chatted Pippa excitedly, pointing at one of the armoured men who had ridden out tall and proud into the arena. "He's really good, isn't he? No wonder Ed chose him for his squire. Oh, and that horse of his is a beauty!" She whistled to show her approval.

Hope whispered a 'yes' in response to Pippa's comments but her eyes were shining, willing Marshall to perform well, her heart in her mouth every time he jousted or fought with a sword. Yet she need not have fretted as Pippa was right: the King's squire was one of the most able fighters there. At the end of one run, he swivelled around and for a second he was staring straight towards her, his eyes locked with hers. His eyes twinkled, suggesting a smile beneath the helm, and she blushed, her stomach churning in response.

Although her status had changed since her return to Erlwick, she continued to meet Marshall when their master and mistress were in company together or bustling about their errands in the anti-chambers and corridors. Yet, scared again after the period of distance between them, she rarely spoke to him. If she knew his eyes were on her, she fumbled clumsily like a toddler and blushed in embarrassment at her own ineptitude. Hope still wanted him to like her but was scared to show her own emotions, worried about rejection.

Just as they all sat down to luncheon in the colourful marquee draped in royal standards and coats-of-arms, Nell suddenly materialised looking slightly rumpled and flustered.

"We missed you this morning, Nell," said Ed. "Where were you?"

"Oh, wandering around the fair… I lost track of the time," but Nell would not meet his piercing gaze, afraid of what he might read there, so busied herself with reaching for a bread roll and some thick cut slices of ham instead. "Still, I'll come back with you all after luncheon because I can't wait to see Kaspar knock you off your horse. And, of course, I'm expecting Al to give you a run for your money too," she teased, quickly changing the subject.

"I wouldn't be so sure of that!" laughed Ed.

He was not completely happy with Nell's reply, especially when he spotted Burgess whispering something to her, passing a note during the meal, but she would say no more.

Nell kept her word and returned with the others to the royal box, enjoying the afternoon's entertainment when the knights and lords were to take to the field. She bet scits with Allys, Rae, Pippa and Wyn on who would win each bout, continuing to disagree about who would prevail between Kaspar and Ed. Nell insisted loudly that it would be Kaspar, citing his greater upper body strength and dexterity, but in her heart she hoped it would be Ed.

"No, my brother is generally stronger, more determined, over all. He will win," Allys insisted firmly.

The two men galloped at full tilt towards each other, lances held out straight, and for once, with both her friends in danger, Nell had to close her eyes. Nothing happened: they had missed each other and had to wheel around and ride again. For a second time, they thundered towards each other. With a massive crash, they made contact this time. Both wobbled in their saddle but maintained their balance during this evenly matched contest. On the third run, Nell's eyes tight shut once more, there was a tremendous reverberating crack and both men fell to the ground. The cheering crowds were instantly silenced, and Nell glanced up anxiously, peering between her fingers. As Kaspar hobbled to his feet, Ed remained lying motionless in the dirt. Nell gasped, her hands clenched into fists as a picture of what might happen to her friends, to Ed, flashed into her mind. Within seconds, the King had risen to a roar of approval from the stands. The moment had passed, but for Nell, the image and fear lingered.

For a while, the two friends battled on with swords: temporarily, Kaspar impressed as having the upper hand but then Ed would revolve it around, neither giving the other advantage. Finally, with a fast, clever and dramatic twist of his wrist which Nell could not quite catch, Ed knocked his opponent's sword from his hand, and now weaponless, Kaspar had to admit defeat and surrender. A second great wave of cheering went up around the entire stadium. Out of breath, the King shook hands with his friend, and then they proceeded back together towards the preparation tents, passing swords and helmets to their squires on the way.

As he entered the royal box half an hour later, Ed was greeted with applause and cheerful, complimentary comments. Moira squealed with delight and rushed towards him, enthusiastically exclaiming about his clever swordplay. Over her shoulder, his eyes locked with Nell's. The only person not cheering, Ed was startled to see the fear and strain on her pale face, realised to what level she had been afraid for him. He wanted to reach out to her, reassure her, but surrounded by others, he could not contact her.

He only caught up with Nell later, at the end of the day. After a delayed supper, Ed had retired to bed wishing to get an early night ready for the tournament tomorrow, but he found that, with adrenaline still pumping, he could not sleep. Finally, with midnight passing and neither Marshall nor a servant around, he decided to get himself a drink from the kitchens. Even at that hour, there were many people working in the kitchens, preparing more food for all the visitors, so he was not surprised to see a figure hunched over a large mound of bread dough, pummelling and twisting it on the dusty table. Only as he drew nearer was he amazed to find out that it was Nell.

"What are you doing, Nell?" Ed asked, incredulous.

"Kneading dough," she answered shortly.

Then, groaning, knowing that would not be enough to satisfy him, she stopped and wiped her hands on the linen apron she was wearing.

"I couldn't sleep and coming here, into the kitchen, keeping busy, always relaxes me… as I explained to Kaspar a few days ago."

"Nell… today… the fighting… it meant nothing," he muttered, guessing at her fears.

"Yes it does because it's all play and practise for war… and that's what is coming soon. When I saw you lying there, I felt cold, frozen, as if it was real. I have lost my father and my country – I don't want to lose any of you now, my friends, but… especially…"

Nell stuttered to a halt, could speak no longer. Instead, she stared down miserably at the dough, poking it with one finger.

Ed crossed the rest of the floor that lay between them and gathered her to him in a warm, reassuring and compassionate hug.

"That is not going to happen," he asserted firmly.

Too late, he remembered his self-imposed ban on close contact with Nell, except in public. The feel of her body in his arms, her warmth, the smell of her freshly washed hair, even the dough, attracted him and he felt his own body stirring in response. He breathed in deeply her glorious scent, evoking memories of their night together, and his arms instinctively tightened about her.

Behind them, footsteps fell softly on the kitchen steps, pots and pans began clattering, as servants re-entered the room. The pair broke apart abruptly, almost sheepishly, regaining their composure in front of others.

"Saved…" muttered Ed huskily, continuing to stare deeply into her eyes and not explaining who.

Ed coughed to clear his throat.

"Nell, leave the bread. You need to sleep or all these fears will be compounded and get the better of you," he stated.

Nell's heart raced within her chest. She could still feel his body even though he had moved away. Reluctantly, Nell agreed to his suggestion and followed him out of the kitchen and back to her room. Once there, she lay on her bed and stared blankly at the ceiling. With fresh desires pumping through her body along with her heart, she definitely had little chance of sleeping now.

The following morning, Nell was once again missing for the first few hours. After their talk the previous night, Ed was intrigued about where she had gone, but with Moira hanging adoringly on his arm, his attention was kept busy, and admittedly, he was enjoying the Princess's flattering conversation. After watching another joust, though, Ed managed to speak with Burgess, and the information the Master-at-Arms gave him led the King out to the archery arena, Marshall at his side. When they arrived, he realised the second round of the open archery competition was underway. Although a dozen or so men were lined up shooting, his scrutiny was absorbed by one slight hooded figure performing well in the middle of the row. He smiled to himself, pleased with his secret knowledge. Then he felt a tug on his sleeve. Pivoting, he saw Moira gazing up at him admiringly with wide emerald eyes, a couple of ladies-in-waiting in toe.

"I missed you," Moira murmured earnestly, her words lilting musically. "I wondered where you had disappeared to. What are you doing out here?"

"Oh, it's always good for me to see and be seen," he replied evasively. "I also had something to investigate."

"Well, while we're here, perhaps you could walk me around the fair. You're not jousting this morning, and we have an hour before luncheon. I love shopping, and as you said, it's good for you to be spotted around and about."

As she talked her voice became breathier, she leant revealingly further towards him, her eyes larger and rounder as she leered up at his face.

"My pleasure," said Ed, succumbing to her flirtation. "Marshall, stay and let me know how things pan out here. Keep a special eye on the little one in the middle."

Then, placing his hand over Moira's where it rested on his arm, he ushered her back out amongst the market stalls. Some sold food or household goods, but many traded accessories like leather belts and bags, scarves and jewellery. As they passed one such stall, Moira squeaked with delight.

"Ooh, look at these pretty, dinky trinkets… They're simply perfect for wearing during the day. I'd love to have one to go with this dress."

"Well, then," Ed laughed, acting on the spur of the moment, "as you put it like that, we shall have to get you one."

He picked up a particularly pretty bracelet of three woven ribbons of silver studded with fat, round amethysts. Gallantly, he slid the bangle over her wrist. Suddenly spotting a matching ring, Ed impulsively picked up the second piece of jewellery too, paying the stall holder handsomely for the pair. As they headed back to the royal box, Moira kept pausing to admire her new jewellery, her eyes glinting brightly at the sight of the ring. Pippa, sitting nearby, glowered at Moira sullenly while the Princess showed everyone her gifts.

"Oh, please come and look at my gorgeous ring, Caldwell," called Moira to the minister when he entered their box and waving her hand eagerly in front of him to admire it. "Dear Ed bought it for me – I think it shows something special between us," she hinted suggestively. "I just know everyone's spotted it, senses it too."

"I've got a bracelet similar to your one from the same stall," declared Pippa, and she could not resist speaking loudly enough for everyone to hear. "Nell bought it for me to wear at the end of tournament feast. I expect lots of ladies have got them today."

Pippa smiled a little smugly, knowing she had hit her mark, as Moira threw her a dark glance.

For the afternoon, the main stadium was to be transformed into an archery arena with the final of the open archery competition preceding a similar contest for the nobles.

"It's a shame we have to sit through the commoners' rounds first – I'm excited to see how you fare with a bow, Ed. After observing your superb swordsmanship, I deduce that your archery will be brilliant too," flattered Moira.

The other women groaned at her blatant fawning, but Ed smiled at her indulgently.

"It's good to encourage new talent, and of course, anyone with real promise can be hired by my Master-at-Arms. Shortly, we will need all the skill we can muster. Which reminds me, Kaspar, pay close attention to the youngster in the green hood. I observed him earlier. He has a sure aim – he's a possibility for the top prize."

"Who? The green hood and brown breeches? Have we come across him before? His stance looks somewhat familiar," commented Kaspar, staring closer and more intently at the archer. "Hm… I gauge that that broader lad next to him will be stronger, control his aim better."

"Willing to bet a munc on it?" asked Ed.

"If you're happy to lose it!" rejoined Kaspar.

Several others joined in with the banter and betting which ensured they all viewed in growing fascination as the competition played out in front of them. Once again, there were twelve bowmen to begin with, but some fell rapidly by the wayside, leaving a smaller number of more serious contenders to fight it out over increasing distances. Finally, it came down to a straight shootout between the young lad the King had highlighted to Kaspar and another, who appeared to be just a few years older.

Both shot well, easily matching point for point until the youngster made an error, perhaps through tiredness at the end of a long and challenging day, and plucked the string to send the arrow awry. Applause rang out around the ground for an entertaining match and a worthy winner as Ed beckoned the two young men towards him.

"To the well-deserved winner of this year's competition which is open to all, I give a hefty bag of silver thrums and a place in my guard if he wishes it," proclaimed Ed, and the watching crowd cheered again. "And now, for the excellent runner-up… perhaps he – or rather she – could reveal her true identity?"

The hooded figure dropped her cap to display a coiled up plait of long brown hair, and Nell grinned at the gasps and murmurs of surprise and amusement throughout the stadium.

"I thought I recognised your handling of the bow. Oh, well done, Nell!" exclaimed Al.

"Good shooting, Nell!" laughed Kaspar, clapping with delight, "I probably couldn't do so well myself, as you will no doubt shortly see. And I now owe Ed a munc," he added ruefully.

Nell laughed.

Moira stared at Nell with a mixture of disgust and disbelief, but Nell happily ignored her while she shared stories and experiences with her friends before it was their chance to shoot. When the squires finished their competition, Ed spoke to her as he prepared to compete with Kaspar, Al and others.

"That was good work, Nell, but I am rather concerned about where you might be going with this."

His brow was wrinkled in deep furrows.

"Oh, nowhere… It's just something my father would have liked," Nell answered, but he noticed that, once again, she could not quite meet his eyes.

Chapter 6

The rest of the tournament continued to go well with the King and his nobles displaying their prowess on horse and foot with a variety of weapons, interspersed with the competitions which were open to all. It all ended in a grand feast at which King Regan and the other royal guests were to bid farewell. Only Princess Moira was to stay on enjoying life at the High Court, much to the satisfied presumptions of Ed's ministers who saw it as a very promising sign, along with the ring.

Moira did her utmost to monopolise Ed's time and attention. Sometimes she requested he escort her out around Erlwick and the surrounding countryside, but often she just demanded his company at the castle, alone. She would frequently refer to the jewellery he bought her as if it was part of some unspoken agreement rather than a purchase made spontaneously.

"Isn't it a beautiful, little thing," she oozed animatedly, twisting and admiring the ring on her finger. "I don't mind telling you, Nell," Moira whispered confidentially, "as a woman who can have few such prestigious hopes herself now, that this is more than just a gift. Dear Ed is such a wonderful man and so sweet to me."

Even as she blinked at Moira's dismissal of her relationship prospects, Nell's stomach felt as if it was clenched in a cold, hard grip. What hurt more than Moira's words, however true, was the fact that Ed cared less about her, had never given her such a symbol of affection from his own choice, not even her butterfly necklace. Stunned, clutching that pendent, she had to shake her head and reconfigure her thoughts. Not only was she still a wealthy noble in her own right, which gave her plenty of marriage options if she wanted them, but who knows what her future might hold, possibly even a return to Guthway. A lot of her future was now in her own hands.

The King did not seem to mind all the attention; in fact, he acted as if he enjoyed the compliments Moira lavished on him. Busy with either the Princess or affairs of state, Nell saw hardly anything of Ed and thought it was just her who was missing his friendship, until she confessed to Al one day whilst playing a game of Sige.

"I miss the times when we used to meet and chat in Ed's room," Nell murmured quietly.

"So do I," agreed Al. "We embarked on a game a week ago which became quite involved, complicated, but haven't had time to finish it."

"I thought that you and Kaspar were continuing to meet with Ed even if I wasn't!" exclaimed Nell, now more alarmed and distracted from the game.

"I wish!" muttered Al, frowning, sharing his own anxieties about their friend with her. "We hardly see Ed either. When he's not busy running the country, he's holed up with Princess Moira, squirreled away from the rest of the court. This is just not like Ed. Kaspar's convinced Moira's bewitched him – it's all I can do to prevent him searching her room for evidence of charms, potions and broomsticks. The only time we get together with him is in the tiltyard, and then, as you well know, he trains hard, as if the devil was behind him – and maybe he is – so even then we don't talk much."

"Ed looks so tired and serious!" Nell cried. "I had hoped he at least got a chance to unwind with you and Kaspar, voice and, therefore, unburden his concerns to you. I know how draining it is being too absorbed in – driven by – one thing. He could do with some time away from his total obsession with Warwick. I'd rather he didn't attempt to regain my country if it makes him ill."

"Don't think like that, Nell. He knows Warwick is not going to cease until they face each other now, and that his brother also has Torland in his sights. Therefore, Ed has no choice but to continue. Unfortunately, I reckon he still believes there may be some truth in the things Warwick said to him – that he is a weak leader. It's not correct, of course, but those words stung deep – and he feels all these troubles are largely his own fault. It's certainly not yours – his choice, remember!" asserted Al.

"I understand that sense of personal failure all too well – I feel it myself! I suppose Moira offers him some diversion," murmured Nell without any humour. "Although, she's not the female companion I would choose for Ed. She doesn't enjoy a lot of the activities he does, doesn't strike me as very practical or very mindful of affairs of state."

Al delayed a little, mulling over his next comment but also considering how much he should admit to Nell.

"The King hasn't seen so much of Kaspar because they had a… slight falling out… a difference in point of view."

"About Moira," speculated Nell, knowing how Kaspar felt about the Princess.

"Yes… Ed acts as if he's rather fixated with her just now, possibly to the detriment of other things."

But she surmised there was more that Al was not telling her.

Al knew Kaspar felt the King had treated Nell badly in Shirborne, and that he was continuing to do so with his attention to the Princess. Furthermore, the talk in the council meeting he had attended the other day all centred on the ring Ed had given Moira and the promise Caldwell was sure it indicated. Caldwell had even begun to suggest that anything less than a confirmed betrothal could be considered an affront by Frisged. Flummoxed, Ed had not denied that these were his intentions and, presumably with his thoughts elsewhere, for once was not assertive of his own views or position on a possible marriage; he seemed to have lost some of his self-belief.

Then, after a month when they saw virtually nothing of the King, Moira fell ill and, too feeble to be seen, retired to her room with her small entourage. For a week, with Moira incapacitated, Ed reverted to his former self and invited company. On the second night, with his door left open, Nell grabbed the opportunity to visit.

"May I come in?" she enquired, knocking lightly on the door.

"Yes… yes please! I could do with some straightforward, light-hearted companionship. I've had a heavy meeting with my ministers this afternoon – my thoughts are thick and muddied," he answered, frowning at the memory.

Nell slipped in silently and sat opposite Ed, nervously perched on the edge of a seat. Official papers were scattered all over the table and even across some of the chairs.

"You look exhausted," she said, studying his face. "May I…?" she then asked hesitantly, gesturing towards the notes. "You can't relax properly surrounded by work."

He nodded and Nell gathered up the paperwork into one tidy pile, which she stashed away on a side desk out of sight, before pouring Ed a drink from a large silver jug.

"You're working too hard," she stated simply. "I know you have a lot on your plate right now, but the occasional night off wouldn't go a miss."

"You can talk!" Ed spluttered through a mouthful of wine. "This from the girl who was half dead on her feet when we arrived at Roxleburg."

Ed grinned, despite the apparent criticism, and Nell could not help smiling in reaction.

"And look what good a rest has done for me – I'm double the size I was on arrival here," laughed Nell, gesturing to herself. "Seriously, though, I had no choice… but you still do."

While she poured herself a drink, he asked what she had been busy doing this week and, within minutes, they had relaxed back into a friendly conversation. Soon they were joined by the rest of their friends, all seeking an opportunity to renew their friendship with Ed, and by the end of the evening, the King was laughing again, his face suddenly lightened and younger.

"Thank the heavens for Moira's fever!" muttered Al under his breath to Nell.

As the week drew to a close, Ed was sitting with Nell on one of the side terraces overlooking the city, basking in the warmth of the sun's rays on his face.

"I'd almost forgotten how to have fun and relax," he said softly. "I've been so bound up with other things – other people – I'd almost lost how to have a decent conversation. I've missed our chats, Nell – I've always found you really easy to talk to."

"But you've had Moira to keep you company!" she said surprised.

"Yes… She's lovely to look at and has such an entrancing voice to listen to, but… well… we don't especially have a lot in common and don't particularly share the same interests. And she's quite demanding, insisting on one-to-one attention all the time."

His words gave Nell a secret pleasure and, fleetingly, sitting close beside him in the warm evening, her heart sang. She had to drag her emotions back to earth, reminding herself about the ring he had given Moira and the promise it now symbolised, especially to his ministers and, maybe, even to him and his people.

The following day, having all met up in Ed's room after supper, Pippa persuaded them all that it would be fun to play a game of hide-and-seek in the castle.

"I suggest sticking to the keep or we'll never find anyone. That's going to be hard enough as it is!" laughed Kaspar.

"Let's put a time limit on it then – if you're still hiding after a couple of hours, you definitely win, Pippa," added Ed.

"I bet I can guess exactly where she'll be," asserted Wyn scornfully from his position sitting cross-legged on the floor.

"Now then, little sister," said Al, "off you go. You'll get a slow count to fifty, and then we're coming for you."

"Hide well – we'll be searching every nook and cranny," Kaspar called after her as she scuttled out the door.

"That'll last forever!" groaned Wyn.

"I thought you said you knew where she would be," laughed Al.

"You're playing too, Hope… you and Marshall," insisted Ed, making the girl jump at the sudden mention of her name.

Hope blushed profusely, guiltily, as Nell's speculative gaze fell on her where she sat quietly sewing, aware her own eyes were more on Marshall, sitting just feet away from her and working on some papers, than on the garment in her lap.

"Come on, Hope, we're under orders," grinned Marshall, putting his work aside.

Hope sighed heavily, tucking her sewing into a bag, while Kaspar commenced the count. Everyone immediately dispersed in different directions at fifty, trying to work out where a thirteen year old might hide. Hope started out towards the great hall and the main state rooms of the castle. Hastily, aware of the deep, dark shadows in the vast chamber, she checked under tables and peered around pillars. Then, standing in the middle of the cold, empty room with its myriad of black recesses, Hope trembled. There was no sign of Pippa, so she hurriedly retreated and headed across to the library opposite, relieved to be in a smaller, brighter space. A fire crackled in the grate, ready to welcome passers-by. Everywhere was silent except for her own gentle breathing, not even the sounds of the other seekers reached her here.

Slowly walking around the tables and chairs, her fingers ran along the top of a bookcase until they met a small, gold embossed, leather-bound book. She picked it up, opened the pages to the middle and started reading a familiar love poem.

"One of my favourites," said Marshall over her shoulder in a hushed voice.

Hope leapt in shock, nearly dropping the book and knocking his chin at the same time. She had not heard him enter the room, yet he stood so near to her that she could feel his breath against the skin at the back of her neck. She did not dare to spin around because he was so close they would be practically in an embrace.

"So… Nell makes sure that all her maids – or ladies rather – can read?" he asked curiously.

"She approves that I can, but I come from a good family, and it was my father who insisted I learnt to read."

"You haven't told me about your family yet," remarked Marshall.

"My father owned land in the moors on the eastern edge of Guthway, some of the first lands to be captured by our enemies. I was born and grew up in Roxleburg, but my father always talked about how beautiful his homeland was. He always seemed so sorrowful, was desperate to return, but died fighting alongside King Robert protecting our borders."

Hope's voice grew quieter and quieter until Marshall could barely hear her. A silent stream of tears began to trickle down her cheeks. Wishing to distract her, he leant forward, reaching his arm around her to take the book, and commenced reading the poem out loud.

"Her tresses flowed in shining golden waves, Swirling in silken rivulets about her pearl-white neck…"

Hope shivered, unsure if it was the words that gave her goosebumps, the timbre of his low voice as he spoke them, or the cool of the night.

"There's still a bit of warmth in the fireplace," said Marshall quickly, spotting her shudder. "Let's sit next to it, and we can continue reading. I expect the others can persist in their search without us. They probably won't even notice we're missing."

This time, he laid his hand gently around her waist, guided her towards the secluded corner by the fire without pausing for her response, then tugged her onto his lap as he sat down. He proceeded to keep his arm around her, clasping her close, while he read the rest of the poem.

Nell, meanwhile, was climbing the winding flight of steps to the next floor where her room was. She walked along the corridor, moving away from her own room towards another series of turrets and towers, inspecting behind doors and curtains as she went.

A flicker of colour and movement out of the corner of her eye made Nell suspect that Pippa was disappearing down another staircase. But the treads only lead down a few steps before twisting onto a long balcony that ran precariously across from one tower to the next, then curled down to the lower floor.

Slightly disorientated, Nell scanned around only to realise she was on a small colonnaded landing a stone's throw from Moira's room. As it happened, the Princess was sitting, wrapped securely in a large woollen blanket, on her own balcony and chatting loudly to her lady-in-waiting, as was her habit. With her back towards Nell, Moira did not see her, but her voice carried clearly through the tranquil night air.

Nell withdrew gradually so as not to attract any attention, hoping to retrace her steps, but then, recognising her own name, she stopped as motionless as one of the columns she lurked beside, except for the sudden thumping of her heart.

"And can you believe what Nell was wearing that day? What was she playing at dressed as a boy like that? You'd never guess she is royalty by the way she looks," sneered Moira. "Her skin is so brown – she must spend most of her time outside like a peasant. And fancy learning to shoot in the first place. It's so unnecessary for a woman in her position. I hear she can use a sword too. What's more, she's being a terrible influence on that little Pippa who needs all the help she can get to become a proper lady, poor dear. That child needs a firm restraining hand – not encouragement to perform like a monkey in all those masculine activities.

"What dear Ed – or even that gorgeous Kaspar – sees in Nell to be friends with, I don't know! She does herself no favours with those simple gowns and the modest jewellery she wears, yet she's wealthy enough to have the latest, dazzling fashions and stunning stones. Have you seen that quaint butterfly pendant of hers? Honestly, I don't know why Ed feels so sorry for her and obliged to house her when she does neither us nor herself any credit.

"Umm… Maybe she uses something else to entice him," Moira suggested viciously, and Nell gasped sharply. "Well, presently, I'm happy for Ed to… play with her as much as he likes. After all, once he marries me, Nell will be totally forgotten. I assure you that lots of things will change once I assume control in this castle… and perhaps I can persuade her to leave, find a backwater where she'll be satisfied with her lot."

Horrified at what she was overhearing, Nell tried not to make a sound as tears began to slip slowly down her cheeks, echoing Hope's. Is that what everyone thought of her: a ridiculous tomboy who had no place at court? Engrossed with her own misery, Nell did not realise she was not the only person to overhear the conversation.

Ed had been searching the darkened, empty rooms above the Princess's. Noiselessly, he had come out onto the balcony and could hear every word that was said but remained hidden in the dark shadows. Glancing about, he could see Nell even though she did not discern him. Hearing Moira's unkind thoughts, his heart went out to Nell, wishing he could tell her it was not true. He felt an overwhelming anger at the cruel and unnecessarily malicious things Moira had said.

Then the Princess focused her contemplation on him.

"Of course, that jewellery the King gave me is as good as a promising ring… or, at least, it is with the way I've talked about it to everyone. Caldwell is four-square behind me."

As she listened, Nell's hand unconsciously crept to the butterfly necklace hanging at her own throat, as much a promise made by their parents.

"Dear Ed is already so attached to me, spends all his free time with me, that I'm sure I can persuade him to send Nell away to another castle somewhere. Regardless of how she looks, I don't trust his friendship with her one bit. I think it would be better to remove her to a safe distance, further away from Erlwick, the court and the King.

"I would never lose my head in such a way as Ed has done with me. He's quite enchanted with me, but I don't want to love anyone. That makes life so complicated, and you lose all your control. The King is handsome enough, thank goodness, or I probably wouldn't bother at all. It's his position – the authority and wealth it brings – that interests me. If he loves me and presumes I love him then all the greater power belongs to me."

"It's getting cold, my lady, we really should be going back into the warmth," suggested her lady.

"Fine… but I'm fed up with being cooped up in this hole of a room. That's another reason to move Nell – her chamber is so much better than mine and right above the King's."

The voices tailed off as the figures retreated into their room. Wiping her eyes, Nell was shocked at all she had heard but was unable to work out what to do for the best. Confused, hurt, shoulders slumped, she slowly and dejectedly headed back over the bridge into the main castle.

Ed continued to stand motionless on the balcony, dallying and deliberating. He was not as attached to the Princess as she assumed he was, but he was equally as concerned with the impression his gift of jewellery had created. He knew from the comments his ministers made that it was being considered seriously, but up to now, he had not commented, seeking an easier path. He was cross with himself. Small trinkets, they now posed a big problem yet had only been a sudden pleasantry to a beautiful girl… and one that he now deeply regretted. He had let Moira's beauty distract him from the anger and guilt he felt about his situation with both Warwick and Nell.

He sighed heavily. He recognised one more thing from his anger at the way Moira spoke about Nell: his desire to comfort his friend. Ed finally understood and acknowledged to himself where his true emotions lay.

Hurrying back to his room, the game completely forgotten, Ed reached the junction of a corridor and the main passageway when Nell rushed passed, clearly distressed. Abruptly, he grabbed her arm and jerked her towards him in the shadows. Losing her footing, she squealed slightly as she steadied herself against her unforeseen captor. Flummoxed, she gaped back at Ed, surprised at his sudden appearance and acutely conscious of how she must look. Eyes red, her tears were obvious as she glared defiantly up at him, glistening streaks dripping down her cheeks and sliding off her chin to dampen her gown. He cupped his hands around her face and gently rubbed the tears away with his thumbs.

"Don't cry, Nell! You have nothing to be ashamed of… nothing to feel sorry for," Ed murmured softly.

"You… you heard her?" whispered Nell.

Ed nodded. With Nell before him, all he wanted to do was comfort her, but as he gathered her in his arms, a stronger physical craving engulfed him. He bent to kiss her brow, then her cheek, mouth and chin, following the trail of tears. Leisurely and tenderly, one finger echoed the line of his kisses before continuing down the contour of her neck, across the gentle slope of her shoulder blade and around the outer curve of her breast.

She gasped in surprise at Ed's change of tack from comfort to desire, but she followed it with a moan of pleasure, and he took full advantage, transforming his anger at Moira into passion for Nell. As he kissed her forcefully, Ed slipped his hand inside her chemise to stroke her hardening nipple, making Nell groan into his neck and nestle against his body. Deftly, he opened the door of an unoccupied guest room behind them with his other hand, nudging her inside before shutting and locking it firmly to avoid interruption.

Chapter 7

The following few days after the game of hide-and-seek passed in a hazy dream for both Nell and Hope but for slightly different reasons. Neither knew how the game had finished or whether anyone had found Pippa.

Hope mulled over the pleasant few hours she had spent leaning against Marshall's firm, broad chest and reading poetry, appreciating his distraction from grief, finishing with the caress of a gentle kiss planted on her head and the trace of one scarcely skimming the nape of her neck. She had hardly seen him since, but whenever she did, Hope could not resist granting Marshall a shy smile.

Nell had also spoken little to Ed, with more pressing issues of state looming, but she walked as if on air, hugging the memory of those hours spent alone with him, entwined intimately on a narrow bed.

"Nell!" exclaimed Allys in exasperation. "You really aren't with us today – head in the clouds," she said as Nell continued to float down the High Street, while she and Rae had halted outside a draper's shop.

"Oh," was all Nell could manage, blushing.

Rae stared at her sister curiously. She had never been a daydreamer before. Always interested in the present, the real world, and always level headed, Nell was her sensible older sister. What had changed? She had a few suspicions.

Nell bit her lip guiltily. She had never previously kept secrets from Rae but felt this was not a story she wished to share. Part of her wanted to keep the memory of those intimate moments with Ed completely private, something special for herself. Part of her was only too aware of Moira's innuendo that had hit so close to the mark. Perhaps she was little more than a plaything for Ed. However, maybe she was content, currently, to snatch whatever closeness he offered. It was certainly not a debate she wanted to get into with anyone since battle was imminent.

During the time following Nell's return to Torland, more and more reports were sent from the border detailing skirmishes until, finally, the news they had all been dreading, but anticipating, came. A messenger arrived one morning from Redvers who held the fort at the end of the valley through the mountains to Guthway; Warwick had a small army on the march, and he was poised to cross the border at the other end within two days.

Straightaway, Ed mobilised his troops, sending some cavalry, foot soldiers and archers on in advance to support Redvers' own men. From the start, it became obvious that he fully intended going himself, leading his army front and centre, and furthermore, that Kaspar and Al would accompany him.

Deeply concerned for her friends, Nell paced the library, too beside herself to read or pay any attention to the books she adored. The image of Ed immobile on the ground during the joust returned to haunt her.

"Stop, Nell, you're wearing a path in the rug! Don't panic – nothing is going to happen to us. We have all practised for this and have been here before," asserted Al who sat in a chair, a book balanced open on his knee, tracking her relentless stride back and forth across the room.

"But if only I had something useful to do… to help!" Nell cried.

"Knowing you are all safe back home is enough for us," said Al.

Nell bit her lip and said no more. She did not admit to Al that she already had plans of her own in hand. There was no way she was going to reside at a distance from the action, not knowing what's happening, when it was a battle involving her country, her people and her friends.

"Don't be so dramatic," admonished Moira to Nell as the afternoon progressed, and it was time for the nobles to leave with the rest of the troops, travelling through the night in order to reach the valley before Warwick. "Come down and say goodbye at the gate. This is what men do – go to war."

Nell glared at her, no longer willing to mask her dislike for the Princess following the overheard conversation. She felt Moira sounded very cool, flippant, as if this was no more than another joust or hunt rather than a battle putting their friends in danger.

"No! You do things your way and I'll do them mine. I'll say my goodbyes separately, when and how I wish," Nell insisted.

So, after an early supper, Ed and his friends were at their last preparations and nearly ready to go when Nell came to say goodbye.

In turn, she held their hands as she kissed them, wishing them, "Godspeed."

There was little else she could say, little else they needed to hear.

Then, as they assumed their positions to lead the troops, Nell put her alternative plan into action. The second group of archers were placed at the back of the army, giving Nell a chance for a brisk change in time to join that band of men before they marched out of the castle. Several of the men around her, including Burgess, knew what she was doing, but Nell, already packed, once again disguised herself as a young man. Away from her friends and towards the back of the army, nobody seemed to notice in the dark except for Pippa who, having wondered where Nell had gone at this critical time and burst in on her friend when she was changing, now stood by silently, observing her leave with tears in her eyes. All the other women were busy watching the nobles and their men march out of the gatehouse. They didn't notice that one of their own number was missing.

Hope had wished to speak to Marshall, say something, before he departed but had not been brave enough. Since their escape from Guthway and the night when they read poetry together, she had begun to care deeply for him and blushed for other reasons than fear whenever she saw him. However, she was well aware that he was a handsome, spirited and well respected nobleman, while she was a shy mouse who, until recently, had been just a servant.

Catching up with Marshall as he left the King's room, readying himself for the journey, Hope could do no more than run up to him and clasp his hands.

"Stay safe," she muttered without even meeting his gaze, before running off, choking back a tear.

Bemused, Marshall gaped after her as she fled.

The army had to move speedily in order to reach the border before Warwick's men. As the two countries had always previously been friendly allies, there was no formal barrier across the wide valley. Even travelling at top speed, it would take over a day and a half to reach the border; as soon as they arrived, they had to rapidly get into position because the enemy was already advancing into the end of the valley.

Some of the archers were sent to the hills on the right where Nell found she had a perfect view of events on the battlefield below. Almost immediately, they were forced into action when Warwick sent his cavalry charging into one side of Ed's men, hoping to unsettle them before they had a chance to prepare for the onslaught or rest from their journey.

Nell's heart was thumping and she choked back a gasp, momentarily wondering what on earth she was doing here before responding promptly to shouted orders. Letting loose an arrow into the attacking enemy, Nell had no more time to consider her position. Now she only had time to think about the next arrow, and then the next.

While Ed sent his own cavalry to chase down Warwick's, regrouping the scattered infantry under a hail of supportive arrows from the archers, Kaspar held firm on the left.

Al immediately put a plan they had already devised into action. While Kaspar kept his men together, Al, in the centre, was to pull back, making it seem like they had to withdraw after the initial onslaught. As Ed regrouped, it would resemble the beginnings of a chaotic rout. With glee, a portion of Warwick's army charged forward, overexcited, presuming they had easy prey. But, as soon as they moved, they found themselves enclosed by Al, the back of Kaspar's troops and the reserves under Redvers, who had come in from behind to support Ed on the right. Clearing the central troops, Kaspar and Al moved forward. Half the archers supported them, while the rest, like Nell, covered the men directly below them.

She was watching the scene unfolding in horror.

Ed and a few of his men were surrounded following the early attack, the reserves still battling to get through to them, while Warwick was baring down on him with malicious intent. Warwick's face was darkened with hatred to match his black armour, a sharp contrast to the Torland army's shining plate mail and arched helms, as he forced his way ferociously through to reach his brother. Both men were tall enough to stand out in the seething mass of soldiers, but Ed, busy fighting for his life, had not seen Warwick break through behind him. Then, just as the reserves reached them, Ed, already battling three men and holding them at bay with only Marshall at his side, was hit by Warwick.

Snaking up to his brother, Warwick quickly stabbed him in the side with one hand, thrusting a thin, sharp blade between the metal plates.

Close enough to be heard, even in battle, Warwick sneered, "Who's the king now?"

Then, using the same knife, he expertly cut and flipped off Ed's helmet, almost in one movement. Seizing the opportunity he'd created, Warwick raised his arm, bringing his sword down brutally onto the King's naked and vulnerable head, aiming for the kill. Simultaneously, and fortunately, Ed fell away, reeling from the initial injury, only catching a cut to his face and a glancing blow to his shoulder from his brother's weapon as he lurched towards the ground.

Warwick chanced a rapid perusal of the battle progressing about him. With the Guthwayan reserves now in support and on the attack, he promptly retreated from the increasing danger, happily leaving his brother for dead.

Spotting Marshall standing protectively over Ed's prone body, Redvers and his soldiers hastily rallied around the fallen King, and Al broke off with a small band of men to strengthen them.

"Burgess," called Nell, still shooting and anxiously watching events from above, "I could do it."

"Do what?" asked the Master.

"I could get to the King on a horse and get him out of there... Help him to safety. You know what my riding's like," she pleaded.

"Fine... but you really have to be quick. We'll give you cover," said Burgess.

Slinging her bow over her shoulder, Nell ran hell-for-leather down the hill to a place where she knew some horses were tied up ready for messengers. Grabbing one and mounting it, she used all her skill and rode into the action, weaving amongst the soldiers to where she knew Ed lay bleeding. She mumbled a prayer, amongst a few expletives, as arrows fell harmlessly all around her. When she reached the King, Nell yelled for help. Without blinking at her sudden entrance in the middle of the battlefield, both Al and Marshall heaved Ed's limp body onto the front of the horse while Redvers held back their attackers.

"Looks like you're in charge, Al!" Nell shouted as she wheeled about to leave, ducking as one arrow bounced lightly and harmlessly off her gambeson.

Once again, Nell darted through the soldiers, not ceasing until she had passed the battlefield. Briefly she paused, fumbling with the straps as she hastened to take off her gambeson, hauberk and tunic. She replaced the gambeson but dropped the hauberk to the ground, lightening her load. Then she cut and ripped the tunic as best she could. Removing some of Ed's armour, Nell rolled a large portion of tunic into a bundle, pressing it against Ed's side, tying it tight in an attempt to stem the blood. She held another piece to his face, suppressing the rising bile and trying not to glimpse the gaping wound that ran down his cheek. Not wishing to waste any more time, Nell rode rapidly on to where she knew a field hospital had been set up temporarily at a safe distance from the conflict.

Chapter 8

On arrival, several people rushed over to help her. They carried Ed into a tent to be seen by the surgeon who instantly came to tend him. Nell stayed at his side to help. Taking a dagger to Ed's shirt, she tore a ragged cut to rip it off his body and then found some hot water to wash the wounds, allowing the surgeon to treat him more thoroughly.

"The King's lost a lot of blood but they're both clean cuts. He's very lucky! Someone up above must have been watching out for him – the blade didn't damage any organs or major vessels in his side. His ribs and shoulder blade are going to be bruised on that side, too, but he should be safe once I've treated the wound, sewn him up and he's had plenty of rest. The wound on his face is a bit trickier. It's not too deep but I can't sear it to halt the bleeding. I'll also need to use more stitches in the hope of lessening the scaring and some ointment to help with the healing." He shook his head a little. "If he wakes up he'll be dizzy… As I said, he's lost a lot of blood. He'll also be very sore and probably in a fair amount of pain.

See if you can get some fluids into him, my lady, when he wakes up… and keep him warm."

The surgeon worked swiftly in concentrated silence, knowing he would soon be needed elsewhere, while Nell, afraid, tried to calm her shaking limbs as she mopped blood and changed scraps of linen.

"All done," said the surgeon, relieved to have completed his most important task with reasonable success.

Walking away to his next patient, already waiting and requiring urgent treatment, he veered back briefly, "When the King's settled, we would be pleased to have your help. There are plenty of others who need their wounds cleaned and patched, ointment smeared on, dressings changed or even just some help having something to eat or drink. We're very short-handed here."

She nodded affirmation in response.

Nell gently rubbed some cream into Ed's wounds, the slightly sweet smell of yarrow reaching her nostrils. Although unconscious, his eyes flickered when her hand lightly fluttered across his face and he twisted his head away, muttering. Nell bit her lip, blinking back a tear, not wanting to course him further pain. She then dressed the injuries with clean linen, binding them tightly. Several young lads responded to her call, helping her carry the King's long frame into the next tent and placing him on one of the improvised beds. Covering him with a large woollen blanket, Nell smoothed a lock of hair from his pale forehead and choked to see him look so forlorn and vulnerable.

Nell sat for a few minutes, staring at him miserably in his restless, pain-filled sleep, unable to wish away his injuries, but then a cough reminded her of the other casualties, and realising there was little more she could currently do for Ed, she decided to follow the doctor's orders. Nell worked her way around the tent seeing if she could help anyone in anyway. Some soldiers she left to sleep, others she made comfortable by fetching blankets, washing wounds or changing dressings. One or two were beginning to get feverish and Nell had to find cold water to mop their brows and cool them down. So it was timely when a woman appeared carrying a black iron pot.

"This is a special infusion, my lady, containing willow bark and ginger, amongst other things. If you could get a dose of this down as many of the patients as you can, it'll prevent them getting over heated or feverish and may ease their pain. Thank you for all your help, my lady, as we're rushed off our feet," she added with the best curtsy she could whilst still carrying the large and heavy cauldron. "I'll be back soon with some soup and bread for those who can manage it."

With that she passed the pot and several small cups to Nell and was gone. Straightaway, Nell set about her new task of aiding or cajoling as many men as she could to drink the special infusion.

By the time Nell had returned to Ed on his makeshift bed of straw bales at one end of the tent, his eyes were open, but he was gazing about the place perplexed at where he was. His face, what could be seen beneath the bindings, was drawn and white with the pain. He was even more bewildered when he saw her.

"Nell?" he queried huskily, puzzled at her sudden presence beside him.

Ed tried to sit himself up but only winced in agony, falling swiftly back down again because of the throbbing wounds, bulky bandaging and light-headedness rapidly taking effect.

"No," Nell spoke firmly, one hand temporarily placed symbolically, but not heavily, on his chest, "lie still!

I'm under orders to give you some of this medicine – it'll help ease the pain."

She moved her hand to gently raise his head slightly, and with the other, she lifted a cup of the infusion to his lips. He drank deeply, greedily, his mouth parched. Seeing this, Nell went to get him a beaker of water.

"Here you go," she said and Ed swallowed gratefully.

He continued to frown, confused to see her there.

"What…?" he began to ask her, but while she hushed him, the surgeon reappeared.

"Ah, Your Majesty's awake, good… good." He came close to inspect the King's wounds and feel his pulse. "I bring great news – that young whippersnapper, your brother, has been sent packing for the time being. The rest of your army should arrive shortly to be patched up as necessary before returning to Erlwick. By the look of you, Sire – much, much better than I had hoped you would be earlier – you could perhaps return with them, just not under your own steam, I'm afraid. Still, I'm sure this admirable young lady will take excellent care of you. She's done an outstanding job so far. I'll be back to check on you before everyone leaves."

As he walked away, he spoke briefly to Nell.

"I'll make sure you have plenty of clean dressings, ointment and some of my infusion to take home with you. Keep the wounds clean to let them heal properly… Oh, and make sure the King rests otherwise he could reopen his wounds."

"Easier said than done!" laughed Nell.

Having settled Ed once more, Nell continued to travel around the tent for the next few hours helping the wounded men. At one point, as she passed near the

King's bed, she realised that he was examining her every move and smiling despite his pain.

"The best thing you can do, Your Majesty, is to try and sleep a little before everyone else arrives making lots of noise to disrupt you," she declared primly. "You know what Kaspar and Al will be like."

"As you wish, nurse," said Ed and, still smiling, shut his eyes.

When Kaspar and Al eventually walked in, almost straight from the battlefield a few hours later, Ed had managed a further sleep and something to eat. He was intensely sore but eager to move and assume control once more. He persuaded his two friends to assist him in sitting up. Then he pressed them to tell him everything that had happened during the battle once he had been hit. Afterwards, Ed had to ask the one question that still baffled him.

"Why is Nell here?"

"Well, we're not entirely sure ourselves. We conjecture that she disguised herself and snuck in with the archers," explained Al. "But you should be grateful she did – it was Nell who came to your rescue with some nifty riding, grabbed you and carried you here."

"Ha!" he laughed. "So it was her chance to save my life. I presume that makes us even again. We seem to keep helping each other out." The laugh hurt and he ruefully touched his fingers lightly to his face. "That's the end of my good looks, I guess."

It was Kaspar's turn to chuckle.

"What good looks? If anything, a scar should be an improvement, add interest to your face. I'll send Marshall in to help you get ready. He's been dithering around like an old maid outside, keen to see how you are."

A couple of hours more, when everyone who needed it was patched up and fed, the army was ready to

228

leave, returning to Erlwick. A large section of men had been left at the border to bury the dead and support Redvers in case Warwick tried to invade through the mountain pass again, to build new battlements if needed. The walking wounded were to travel in wagons with the rest of the army, and Ed was planning to join them. The remainder of the injured were to lodge overnight until they could be moved more safely and comfortably the next day.

"You need to be up front and lead this cavalcade," asserted Kaspar. "Let your people see you and know that their King is alive and well – sort of – after the battle. I think I might be able to rustle up a trap if Nell can drive you."

So Ed, still tired, snoozed in the back of a cart during the longer, slower return journey. Then, as they approached Erlwick early evening three days later, he swapped places to sit next to Nell in the trap, in advance of Kaspar and Al, the rest of the cavalry, infantry and archers. More wagons of wounded followed behind them.

"I'm surprised I managed to sleep in the slightest with all those bumps you found in the road," teased Ed. "You might be a good horsewoman but you're a lousy carter."

Nell pulled up sharply, bringing their wagon and the whole procession behind them to a sudden halt.

"Well, if you're not happy, you can always get out now and walk," she suggested with a nod of the head and a raise of her eyebrows.

Ed just laughed, then scowled from the pain that caused.

"You deserved that," Nell stated, yet she was delighted he was obviously well enough to joke around, so much better than those first frightening moments after the attack when he had lain inert on the horse next to her.

She smiled with pleasure.

It was only when they reached the city and found the streets filled with cheering crowds that Nell suddenly felt self-conscious. Although she was the only woman in the whole train, she did not feel very feminine and knew she looked a mess. Having been so busy, she had not had the opportunity to change. She was still wearing the clothes from her masquerade as an archer but without the tunic and hauberk, the rest covered in dirt, sweat or blood. Her hair had been braided to help tuck it out of the way but now it hung down with loose, straggly tendrils.

Ed, too, was suddenly very aware of how he might appear with a large thick dressing bound around his head. He tried to sit further upright, acting more alert and commanding, with one hand touching his bandage and the other gripping tightly to the backrest.

As if she had fathomed his thoughts, Nell said, "It doesn't present as too bad. And we tried to keep the dressings to the minimum. It shows that you have been through a fight and that you meant business."

"But I failed to see the battle through," he grimaced from unjustifiable shame.

"Not because of any fault on your part – I saw everything, remember. You were deliberately targeted by Warwick and his troops. You were outnumbered."

"It'll be different next time we meet," said Ed with an icy edge to his voice.

Nell shivered at the thought that there might be, probably would be, another fight to come.

When they rode into the castle, Nell stopped the trap in front of the busy castle steps where ministers, noblewomen and servants alike anticipated their arrival. Hope blanched white as, surveying the troops, she spotted the injured King and feared for his squire. Beside her, Pippa nudged her side and pointed at Marshall where he rode behind the knights. Relieved, Hope could see he was unscathed.

"Marshall," Nell called, also twisting back to find the squire, "please help the King to his room. Whatever he might say, he needs to rest and it's already late. He has been through the millstone over the last few days and has lost a lot of blood. And I certainly don't want him doing anything that might cause his wounds to reopen."

Ed began to protest, but Nell was very firm, "Hush! If you don't behave, I'll circle this trap around and transport you straight back to a hospital. Everyone needs to rest but especially you. The victory feast can wait until tomorrow." The King looked mollified while Nell focused her attention on the other knights, "And that's my orders for everyone. After a good night's sleep, we'll all be in a better state to enjoy it."

Kaspar and Al grinned back at her and they nodded in agreement, but Nell had detected a surreptitious glance pass between them, arousing an inkling of suspicion that they might be up to something. She shrugged her shoulders dismissively.

The second Ed was helped down from the trap, Allys hared down the steps of the keep and hurtled towards him. Nearly bowling him over, his sister just stalled herself in time, spotting the bandages and examining him with alarm.

"It's good, I won't break, just be careful where you hug me… and don't squeeze too tight!" he laughed.

Allys gingerly put her arms around his neck and momentarily laid her head against his shoulder. Ed affectionately ruffled her hair.

While Marshall assisted Ed to his room, a very thankful Hope offering help in toe, Nell stayed back to talk to the castle steward about the wounded men, discussing how they were to be cared for, and the victory feast for tomorrow. She asserted that, despite what she had said, plenty of meat, bread and beer should be laid on for the soldiers tonight too. By the time she climbed the steps, her feet leaden and her back aching a little, most people had gone back into the castle but Princess Moira still loitered. Having welcomed her brother, Al, Pippa also then lingered to greet Nell. As they walked passed Moira, they could not help noticing the glance of contempt she threw in Nell's direction.

"Oh, good grief! Do you see the state she's in?" gasped Moira to her lady-in-waiting, her voice barely lowered, so Nell could not avoid hearing what was said. "What an absolute disgrace to be seen like that."

For once, Nell could hold her tongue no longer. Pivoting sharply, she strode back to Moira and pointed at the stains on her clothing.

"See this… and this… and this… That is the blood of dead and dying men. Their blood is not a disgrace. No, I don't mind being seen like this because every one of them, whether the King or a lowly foot soldier, is worth ten of you!"

Nell marched into the keep, not looking back at the gawping Princess. Once inside the building, she leant against the wall and caught her breath as her usual reserve was restored; she flushed as she remembered her words.

"I shouldn't have said that," she moaned out loud but to herself.

"Why not? Maybe it needed to be said. Good on you, Nell, for having the guts to say what you believe," declared Al from where he had watched everything in the shadow of the doorway, now stepping forward to join her and Pippa.

Nell felt she couldn't keep her eyes open. She was exhausted and all she really wanted to do was sleep, but while she bathed and changed, washing away all the dirt and trauma of the last few days, she had to relive those events again and again for Allys and Rae. They kept pestering her until she had told them everything she could remember several times over. Jealous, she gazed blearily at Pippa who had curled up on her bed and was already fast asleep.

Eventually, she got them all to leave, but she did not go straight to bed. Instead, she tightened her dressing gown around her, collected the various ointments and other items she needed that were piled together in a basket, asked Hope to bring her a pitcher of fresh water, then went upstairs to Ed's room. Knocking on the door and entering the room on the King's answer, Nell discovered that Ed was alone too, except for his squire. Marshall had helped him to bath and change but had left redressing his wounds to Nell.

"I have been abandoned," explained Ed. "I imagine Kaspar and Al had other plans for this evening." He then smiled at her guiltily, whether because of their actions or for revealing their secret she did not know. "Both seemed very hale and hearty, and I have a suspicion that neither planned to follow your orders of resting tonight – sorry, Nell. In fact, I believe they mentioned meeting some of the other commanders down at the Cobweb Inn for an 'all-nighter'."

Nell groaned heavily in exasperation at his words but was not surprised at their need for exuberant celebration with adrenalin from the battle still running high.

"They'll be shattered tomorrow – I won't expect to see them before luncheon. Now… I'll be as gentle as I can with you," promised Nell while he patiently waited for her ministrations.

"I'm all yours, Nell," he said in a whisper that she could barely hear but with an insinuation that made her blush.

Once more, she rubbed the soothing, healing cream into his wounds. Although she tried to be careful, he was still very sore and could not help wincing in pain occasionally, teeth clenched tight to avoid a hiss escaping. Hope brought in the pitcher of water before retiring to a discreet distance in case she was needed again.

"You must try to drink plenty of water if you wake up during the night, Ed," she explained, "because it'll help with the dizziness. And have some more of this infusion straightaway. I imagine you're feeling sore after the ride – which was so rough according to you – the bath and my manhandling of your injuries. I'll leave you a beaker of it, so you can have some more early in the morning. I've left orders with Marshall to come and fetch me if you have any problems during the night."

Ed smiled indulgently while she issued her orders, but then he grimaced at the slight stab of pain it caused.

She raised her eyebrows, "As I thought… I'll cover and bind all your wounds again for tonight, to protect them while you sleep."

Nell searched across the room to check that Marshall was listening but tutted when she saw he was otherwise engaged, absorbed in a hushed conversation with Hope. She continued her instructions.

"But the doctor suggested that you can have a lighter dressing tomorrow on your face which will be a lot more convenient and comfortable, as long as the wound's kept clean. I would suggest binding it heavily again if you are at risk of getting it dirty or you are wearing anything tight or hard which might chafe. I expect you'll be back riding or training in the tiltyard sooner than you should, but please delay it as long as you can bear."

She studied him up and down squarely.

"Don't bother wearing a belt or sur-coat for tomorrow's feast – just a silk shirt will be adequate as it's warm enough." It was finally her turn to grin before carrying on. "It might suit you – especially with the scar as well – and give you a certain wicked quality."

Ed grumbled a little, "There's no point anyone marrying me for my handsome face any more. It'll have to be for my charming personality instead."

Nell gaped at him, surprised, and asked seriously, "What other reason is there?"

He grabbed her hand and, softly kissing the back of it, exclaimed "Thanks for that, Nell! And I suppose there's always my throne to lure the hordes. Remember what you told me about its power to attract? I will rely on that.

"Please stay with me for a few minutes at least and eat something. I know you want me to rest, but the kitchen has sent up a great bowl of steaming broth which I can't manage on my own and everyone else has left me alone for the night."

"Very well," agreed Nell, "just for a little. I am rather tired but I must admit I'm also very hungry too."

Sending both Marshall and Hope away, they sat companionably eating the soup and soft stewed apple, sweetened and flavoured with nutmeg, until their tiredness intensified, overwhelming them.

Swaying slightly herself, she assisted Ed back to his bed, lying him on his good side under the silk sheets, and he was almost asleep as soon as his head hit the pillow. Inspecting his slow, rhythmic breathing, Nell decided to tarry a while, to check he was really settled for the night. She could not resist the temptation to lie on the sheets beside him, feet curled under her, feeling his warm breath on her cheek. A mistake, she fell asleep quickly too.

She awoke feeling chilly and aware of a leaden weight across her chest. Blinking in the dingy light of early dawn, she peered bewildered around the room until she realised where she was and that the heavy pressure was Ed's arm slung casually across her body. Nell lay motionless for a minute to enjoy the sensation of security that weight gave her, the warmth from his body and the gentle sound of his breathing. Finally, as gently as she could, Nell lifted away the errant limb and slipped unheeded from the room.

Chapter 9

When Nell awoke a second time, she quickly realised by the bright sun glowing through her window that it was already mid-morning and much later than she had planned to get up. She began to get dressed hurriedly when Allys emerged with a bowl of steaming porridge.

"Don't rush, Nell. I've already seen to Ed with his ointments and bindings, so take your time… you've earnt it. I've also been into the kitchens to oversee the feast – you don't need to concern yourself about that either. Everything is in hand – I don't want to see you anywhere near the kitchens. I'm under direction from Kaspar to make sure you also get a chance to relax too."

"And you always do what you're told!" laughed Nell.

"Maybe not, but you are going to do so today," emphasised Allys, firmly.

Allys came over with a brush and, while Nell ate her porridge, she brushed out then plaited her hair.

"Thank you, Nell," said Allys quietly, "for bringing my brother home."

Nell grasped Allys's hand in understanding and harmony.

Off duty for the day, and certainly not intending to go to the tiltyard herself, Nell decided to have a walk through the gardens on the south side of the fortress. It was a maze of paved walkways among dry-stone walls, trim towering hedges, trellised flower beds and canopied paths full of flowering climbers, scented roses and fragrant herbs. With shadowy corners, sunny seats and the occasional fountain or statue, it was the perfect place to find a quiet spot to sit, read and meditate without interruption.

She found a small bench tucked into an alcove and surrounded with blousy white roses wantonly spilling their perfume into the still air. The sun reached inside to warm the secluded corner and a few fat bumblebees buzzed lethargically around the flowers. Nell sat and opened her book, appreciating the peace and quiet of this compact but secluded space in a busy castle. Hunched against the back wall of the alcove, engrossed in her book, Nell did not sense the sun gradually creeping away from her corner, the shadows extending and her nook cooling and darkening.

Suddenly, she lifted her head. Someone was walking through the square of garden nearest to her. Not wanting to be seen, Nell withdrew, hiding further from view, but could not resist peeking out to see who was passing. It was Princess Moira, her voice once more carrying so clearly through the still air. Nell barely breathed as she listened to Moira's words, wondering what poison she would spew.

"Even if he is the High King, I don't think I could bear to marry him now with that great, ugly scar he'll have on his face. How could I look at it every day? It would make me nauseous! I certainly wouldn't want to share a bed with him. Mind you, his wealth and position would sweeten that problem if I kept him to his promise.

"Now Kaspar, on the other hand… he's very handsome and an heir to a great kingdom. It's a pity he's already betrothed. But then… things can change… Maybe I can work my magic and focus my considerable charm on him."

Nell was shocked at the callous way Moira spoke about her friends, reducing them to non-sentient beings with no free will of their own. She was determined to fight Allys's corner, but was pretty sure Kaspar knew of, and could withstand, Moira's cold-hearted, calculated scheming. He was also too fond of Allys to pay attention to her flattery. Wasn't he?

Within minutes, the malicious pair had gone. Now suddenly feeling the cold of the shadows, Nell shivered and got up, deciding to move to a warmer, more cheerful place. Leaving the alcove, she spun sharply to walk through a small gateway only to bump slap into Ed. Both were slightly startled at the other's presence. Ed, preoccupied, had been looking rather gloomy. Nell wondered if he had overheard the Princess's words and whether, with the emotions he must have for Moira, it had hurt him.

However, he just smiled as he gazed down at her and grabbed her empty hand.

"Come with me, Nell," he said, "as it seems we're both at a loose end today. You can see that I'm following your orders," and he indicated to his shirt dangling free. "I'm also trying to relax a bit, although that isn't currently very easy for me. I've found the perfect sunny spot though – there's a small patch of grass we can sit on and it stays in the sun most of the day but, because it's tucked away in a corner with only one entrance, few people pass through it. Come and talk to me."

She let Ed guide her to the hidden lawn. He was right; it was filled with sunshine, and the surrounding walls kept off any breeze. Nell wondered how she had not found this peaceful place before. Sitting on the grass did not strike as quite enough, so she could not resist stretching out, arms behind her head, to soak up the warmth all over her body. She noticed Ed also chose to lie down, if a little more gingerly. Nell perused him as he carefully sat down then positioned himself on his good side. Her eyes fell on his concealed muscles, hinted at by the gentle folds of his shirt, and his chest where the silk draped open. Instantly, her mind was flooded with the memories of all the times they had shared intimately together: by the waterfall, in the haystack, at the palace in Shirborne and here during the game of hide-and-seek. Observing that Ed was eying her thoughtfully, Nell looked away, flushing, wondering if he had read her thoughts.

"Do you miss your home… the castle and the country?" he asked unexpectedly.

"Of course I do! Don't forget, I hadn't been to another country before I came here to Torland. But the castle is really only bricks and mortar. Most of what is important to me – what's left of my family and friends – are here." Sighing, Nell surveyed him, met his deep brown eyes. "I sometimes worry about Elly. She isn't really bad, just easily swayed. And she's somewhat delicate, wouldn't fare too well under hardship or cruelty. She's not as tough as me," and Nell smiled an almost bitter smile.

"Nell, that's not true," said Ed, extending his hand out to hers. "You may be tough and assertive when you need to be but that doesn't mean you don't care or feel intensely. By your own admission you are concerned for Elly. Many others would just say – tough luck to her!" At Nell's horrified face, he immediately added, "But you needn't fret, I have had word that Warwick married her and treats her very much as his Queen. Don't forget that she is your uncle's daughter – he also sees her as legitimising his position in Guthway."

He stared passed her for a short time, as if contemplating the need to prune a shrub, before adding, "And I believe they now have a child on the way."

Nell was initially alarmed by this news, anxiety for her cousin growing, but she also acknowledged the truth in what he was saying and that Warwick would be proud to have an heir. She sneaked a sideways peek at Ed; was that a note of yearning she had detected in his voice?

While they lay and talked a little longer about the latest developments, they heard footsteps entering at the one gate into their hideaway. Looking up they saw an astonished Kaspar and Allys. Kaspar was carrying a jug of wine and two beakers. Nell guessed they had planned to find a private place for themselves.

"Rumbled," laughed Kaspar, deliberately not making it clear which couple he meant.

"Join us and we can share," suggested Ed, warily raising himself back up to a sitting position.

So the four friends sat chatting well into the afternoon until Allys suddenly gasped.

"Oh, heavens! We've got the feast tonight and we need to get ready!"

Ed laughed, "I don't reckon I need to bother too much. I can't charm anyone with a face like this at the moment. I might as well go as I am."

Nell studied him, concluding that he definitely must have overheard Moira's words.

"Even if you're not bothering, brother, we are," asserted Allys, "so Nell and I will leave you to it."

With that she grabbed Nell, laughing, and tugged her back towards the castle.

Chapter 10

Whatever Ed might have said, he did present as having made an effort after all. Nell thought he looked handsome despite the still swollen, ugly red welt on his face. He wore a cream silk shirt under a lightweight, baggy dark blue tunic which hung loose and was embroidered around the hem. He wore fine, matching blue hose and the whole outfit gave him a roguish air.

Before they sat to eat, Ed spoke a few words, reminding them of why they were celebrating but also what might still be to come.

"We have had a turbulent week, but we have made it through, mostly in one piece." Ed gingerly touched the wound in his face as he spoke. "I would like to thank all who supported us and were involved in the battle at the Guthway Pass, defeating my brother and pushing him back across the border. I would also like to thank those who nursed the injured, including those who unexpectedly turned up to do so!" and with that he looked directly at Nell where she sat beside him, placing a hand gently on her shoulder. "Most importantly, I would like to raise a glass in remembrance of those who have not returned home, who gave their lives for Torland."

Everyone raised their own glasses, and for a moment, all were quiet in their own thoughts and memories.

Therefore, not many people were surprised when, following the meal, Ed turned and asked Nell to lead the dancing with him. Moira did not seem in the least perturbed by the King's choice since she made her own beeline for Kaspar. Only Caldwell acted disgruntled, muttering discontentedly to himself in an aside.

Nell felt a warm tingle course through her as, following their lovely afternoon and for the second dance in succession, the King held her close, smiling down at her fondly, or so she thought, close enough that she could feel his heart beating. Yet, when Kaspar and Moira passed them in an elegant sweeping arch, she caught sight of the bracelet and ring, a promise to be honoured.

Then, half an hour later, while she danced with Al, Nell watched Ed clasping Moira in his arms for yet another number and ogling the Princess with an intensity she felt he had not shown to her. All her joy suddenly evaporated.

"You look glum – is my dancing that bad?" asked Al teasingly.

"No, it wasn't you. I must apologise as my mind drifted for a second, but I promise I will now give you my full attention."

After the dance, however, Nell made her excuses and left.

"I'm still very tired – I need to retire early," she said. "You go and spend the evening with Rae. It's definitely her turn for a dance with you."

Al frowned a little, detecting the direction in which Nell's eyes continued to stray, and developed his own conclusions.

Also seeing her leave, Ed began to feel decidedly stuck. He smiled mechanically down at the girl in his arms, Moira, but felt nothing for her. As they had danced, he had slowly become aware that he had been gazing at her, not in pleasure at her face but preoccupied with the problem of the jewellery. He knew that if she pushed this idea of the trinkets being a promise, as she had already publicly suggested at court, he just might have to abide by it to preserve his honour. His ministers certainly seemed keen to press it. He would then be stuck with the woman he was growing to dislike rather than a woman he loved.

He swallowed hard. Buying the bangle and ring felt like yet another in a growing procession of mistakes. He had been meditating a lot all day about the errors he had made with Warwick, not spending time with him or hearing him out fully in the years previous to his treachery. Maybe all this trouble, all these deaths, could have been avoided. He again felt guilty for all that Nell had suffered at the hands of his brother; his battle scars were nothing compared to the death of her father. He understood that from the loss of his own. And now this Princess appeared determined to humiliate her.

Confused, exhausted and melancholic, Ed decided to make his own early exit, taking a large jug of wine with him.

An hour or so later, having busied herself in the kitchens and ensured that the soldiers' own feast was going well, Nell revisited the great hall. Stopping by the glass doors that led out to the courtyard, she heard Hope's voice. No more than a whisper, she could not hear what was said but realised her former maid lurked in the shadows with Marshall, Ed's squire. He was grasping her hands and talking earnestly in reply. Pleased at their growing involvement and moving slightly away to allow them privacy, Nell scanned about the vaulted room. Many people were still around but lots of others had gone, dispersed about the castle or retired for the night. She recognised Ralph amongst a group of young nobles still drinking, laughing and singing raucously by the fire. Nearby, Kaspar was busy conversing with, or rather being talked at, by the Princess, her arm firmly wrapped through his. Glancing up, he caught Nell's eye, grimaced and gesticulated behind Moira's back to indicate his boredom and need of rescue. Nell laughed and signalled back to suggest that it was his own tough luck, he had to untangle himself. She grinned a little smugly; the Princess certainly did not have an admirer there.

Peering into the gloom of the hall, Nell could just discern Pippa trying desperately to keep awake, her head nodding forwards occasionally before she jerked herself back upright, eyes staring wide open. Nell had left Wyn sneakily playing a game of dice with some soldiers. She would not tell on the children and spoil their fun tonight. She spotted their brother, Al, dancing with Rae in a distant corner, rather closer together than propriety allowed. Again, she smiled and decided to leave them alone.

She could not see Ed anywhere.

Nell reckoned it was time to go to bed. As she walked towards her own door, she heard a small crash from the balcony below. Creeping down the narrow spiral staircase, Nell came out on the King's landing. Surprised, she saw Ed, head laid forward in his arms, slumped over the table and snoring between occasional mutterings. An almost empty earthenware jug balanced beside him but an expensive glass goblet had rolled off the table and smashed into many pieces on the floor.

Nell sighed. Ed had definitely drunk too much wine. She knew this was unusual for him, wondered what thoughts had driven him to such measures. Tiptoeing over, she decided to try and move him, get him to bed, although that was not going to be easy with his weight and height.

Getting her shoulder under one of his arms, Nell was able to initiate lifting him. Fortunately, Ed awoke slightly, if very befuddled, but enough to steer himself by. Continuing to mutter incoherently, the King let Nell direct him into his room and help him to sit on the edge of the bed. Handling him as carefully as she could, she somehow managed to remove his tunic and shirt then lie him down in order to reapply the ointment to his wounds. As she did so, Ed twisted to and fro, but she did not know if it was because of the wine or the pain.

Suddenly, he opened his eyes, stared straight into Nell's face, making her jolt in surprise, and started to talk sporadically.

"Nell…" he said, grasping her hand, "Nell… love… Moira… love…" and for a minute Ed closed his eyes again.

Nell nearly choked. He was telling her he loved that Princess who belittled her and was only interested in his crown. Despite all they had shared – the friendship, the treatment of wounds, the battles with Warwick and the ecstasy of their physical intimacies – she meant nothing to him. Standing motionless for an instant, she felt a searing pain in her chest, could not breathe. Nell knew she had to leave, get away from the source of her agony: Ed. She needed to find somewhere to be by herself in order to gather her thoughts.

Quickly covering Ed up with a sheet and a blanket, trying to prevent the tears, Nell fled the room as quietly as she could.

When she did so, the clunk of the closing door as it shut roused Ed from his stupor and his eyes flew open again.

He spoke once more, loudly and clearly, but into an empty room and too late for Nell to hear him.

    "… I love you, Nell!"

Chapter 11

Nell had to abandon Erlwick. She needed to put distance and time between herself and Ed in order to think clearly. She could not face him again, not until she had gained complete control over her own emotions, enough to be able to see the man she loved with Princess Moira, who despised and wished to humiliate her, without letting her emotions show.

For a short while, Nell paced her room pondering where she might go. She had lost her father, her country and now the best friend she had grown to love. Then she had an idea. Packing speedily a few well-chosen garments in order to travel light, Nell set out for Stanholt on the northern border, one of Ed's castles currently being held by Lord Falkner, an old family friend and nobleman from Guthway. Taking just Hope and a couple of loyal Guthwayan soldiers, Nell did not even stop to speak to her sister, not wishing to be dissuaded from her journey, hoping instead to send her a message of explanation from a place of safety.

After a long three day trek north, Nell reached the large busy village of Stanholt and was welcomed with open arms into the castle by Lord Falkner and his wife, Eadlyn.

"Your Majesty," exclaimed Falkner, as many from Guthway still addressed her, "I don't know what has brought you to visit us, but it will be our great pleasure to have you dwell here as long as you wish."

"Thank you," Nell answered. "I need space to clarify my position in Torland, see my way forward, and I would appreciate the peace and tranquillity of a place like this."

"I'm not sure about peace with such a large brood as mine!" he laughed. "I'll try to shield you from them, although that may be difficult as we get few visitors, and they're bound to be curious about the erstwhile Queen of Guthway."

"Don't worry about that too much," said Nell, "a bit of family normality will go a long way to providing some levity for me."

Nell found she settled rapidly into the more mundane routines of a humbler castle. Much to everyone's surprise, she threw herself into daily chores, not afraid of physical work. Instead, she appreciated the overwhelming tiredness at the end of the day which ushered her swiftly to sleep, not allowing her time to deliberate when she was on her own at night.

She enjoyed spending time with Falkner's family, but as the weeks passed, she nervously waited, expecting to hear an official announcement of the impending marriage of the High King to Princess Moira of Frisged. Even in this modest community at the furthest reaches of the country where court gossip was rarely heard, news of that sort would surely arrive swiftly. But no such word came.

Part of Nell was content to stay and rest here, not face her uncertain future, and she was willing to let the months roll by until finally, with the Winter Solstice approaching, she knew it might be time to make decisions on her own, choose where she wanted to go in the new year and where she felt her future might lie.

Falkner and his wife had adopted the role of surrogate parents as Nell gradually opened up to them and they were happy to listen to her thoughts, feelings and fears, acting as a sounding board to her ideas, making considered suggestions but allowing her to come to her own conclusions.

One evening, as the women sat sewing by the light of a blazing fire, Eadlyn deciding on a few last minute preparations for the festive season, Nell overheard the older of Falkner's girls talking about Ed.

"Mama saw the King when she travelled all that way to market last week. She says he is still very handsome despite the battle scars. He'll have to marry soon – Torland needs an heir – and then, hopefully, we'll all be able to go to a fantastic wedding and the royal celebrations are sure to last for days. Mama will have to buy me a new dress for that, after making me fix up an old one for the Solstice feast!"

And then Nell realised tears were slowly rolling down her cheeks, dropping onto the red velvet gown she was sewing in her lap.

"What's the matter, my love?" asked Eadlyn gently, in a motherly fashion.

"It's just… just…" and suddenly the tears were falling faster in great big blobs, and through her rasping sobs, Nell finally poured out her story and her heart to someone.

Eadlyn sat and listened, her arm around Nell's shoulder and waited for Nell to finish her tale, the sobs to subside.

"And now I realise he loves another, has no room for me except as a friend. I don't know if I can bear it! I also understand that she will not tolerate my presence at court. So I will have to go away, find somewhere else to live quietly, hope to sort my future and my country's problems myself, without Ed in my life."

"It sounds as if you have already come to a decision," suggested Eadlyn. "You know what you must do, what feels right for you. And we will always support you, whether it is to persist here and help fight our enemies from Torland or whether we return with an army to try and regain Guthway ourselves."

Therefore, drying her eyes and determining to return to Erlwick, Nell decided to move on again soon, finding a temporary home on an estate of her own away from the royal court and the King. She would also try to determine the feasibility of building an army to return to Guthway.

Having finally made up her mind, she was then surprised to receive a letter from her sister the very next day.

"Rae's coming here to stay for the Solstice and through the Yuletide," said a delighted Nell. "She says it's a brief visit and she is bringing Al – the Earl of Langford – with her. I'm sorry that I'll be causing you more trouble with extra visitors at this hectic time of year."

"Oh, don't fret about it! We love a bit of excitement to energise our dull lives. And we're so busy anyway that a few more guests won't hurt, in fact – the more the merrier!" Eadlyn exclaimed laughingly. "We'll be delighted to host your sister and the Earl of Langford. Let's go and sort out rooms for them as they're bound to follow the letter quickly and may even be here tomorrow."

Eadlyn was right and, by mid-afternoon, Nell was running out to meet her sister, Rae, who immediately admonished Nell on her lonely flight from court. As they hugged, Al dismounted and came to join them, acting unusually nervous, almost sheepish. Something was afoot.

"Al wishes to have a discreet word with you," asked Rae hesitantly.

"Well, let's get you all inside the castle first and then we can talk. You can meet my gracious hosts too, Al."

They all went into the castle, leading a small entourage of soldiers, servants and horses across the drawbridge.

"Welcome to Stanholt, my lord," said Falkner, meeting them in the bailey. "We hope you will be comfortable for your visit. Perhaps tomorrow you would enjoy a hunting trip? There's some good sport in the surrounding forests, even reaching up into the mountains. And it's not bad for falconry, either."

"Thank you, Falkner," Al replied. "We don't intend to stay long – just for the festive period – but I would enjoy a ride out into the countryside. I would also like a confidential chat with you... perhaps in your solar before supper? I have letters and a message from the King – he would like me to report back on how things are doing here on the border. He knows it has been quiet since our enemies' last incursion. However, he is also aware that you retain scouts on patrol, watching for signs of trouble, and that it's never truly peaceful here."

"Certainly... We'll talk further later. I'll let you have all the news we've gathered to relay back to King Edward, and we can make arrangements for the week."

"Al, would you like to walk with me now, then, and you can ask whatever it is you need to ask of me?" suggested Nell, interrupting the conversation, feeling uneasy herself about what his enquiry, or news, might be.

Leaving the others, they proceeded out across the bailey, Nell guiding him through rows of low lavender bushes which were no longer flowering but still airing laundry, to a simple, secluded and fenced garden belonging to the lady of the castle.

"Now, Al, what is it you've travelled all this way to tell or ask me?" Nell inquired when they stopped just inside the gate, "I have a few suspicions."

Al grinned apprehensively back at her, coughed to clear his throat.

"You know that an attachment has developed between your sister and myself. I care for her a lot… In fact, I've grown to love her. I can envisage no better wife and companion for me. Please, as head of your family, would you consent to Rae marrying me?"

In answer, Nell just laughed and hugged him.

"Of course I give you my blessing! And I can imagine no one more suitable for my sister. Moreover, you are already like a brother to me. Let's go and share the good news."

They walked back arm-in-arm and smiling to the great hall where Rae lingered anxiously, twiddling a braid of hair and chewing her lower lip, anticipating the result.

"Was the answer ever in any doubt?" chuckled Nell, taking her sister's hand. "Then, in the presence of everyone here – nobles and citizens – I will formalise the betrothal between my sister Rae, Lady of Guthway, and my dear friend Albert, Earl of Langford."

She removed an old gold ring encrusted with a row of alternating amethysts and turquoise from her own hand and placed it on her sister's finger.

"Our mother's ring," Nell explained.

Then, taking a chain from around her neck, she detached a large jewelled gold ring from amongst several others and gave it to Al.

"And this was our father's. I know he would also have been pleased with Rae's choice. Here…" and she took one of Rae's hands and placed it in Al's. "And now the deal is sealed. I decree that my sister and this lord will both be married to one another at a date, time and place of their choosing, that no one should impede or thwart their union without punishment or recompense, unless it be by their own volition. Congratulations!"

Nell then kissed both Rae and Al on their foreheads before the couple themselves shared a quick kiss on the lips more shyly in front of the gathered crowd.

"Here! Here!" exclaimed Falkner. "Now that definitely calls for a celebration. More wine everyone?"

As the partying commenced, Al twisted the new ring on his finger, admiring the thick gold band etched with knots and loops and studded intermittently with emeralds. He looked thoughtful as he studied the ring before contemplating Nell.

"You know, Nell, Ed still wears your father's ring which you gave him in Guthway. What's more, he wears it with pride. He has always cared for you… a lot."

"But he doesn't love me! He loves… that… that Princess!" stuttered Nell, unable to mention her name. "I heard him say so!"

"You're wrong, Nell," stated Rae at Al's side. "Ed had an inkling of what had happened… a simple misunderstanding. He sent Moira home shortly after you left. I believe he tolerated her and her constant niggling for a couple more days, but then he could endure her comments – especially about you – no longer. In the middle of supper one day, and quite unforeseen, he stood up and declared that the jewellery he had given her were not a promise of marriage, just trinkets, an insignificant gift, and that in no way were he and she betrothed."

"In fact," broke in Al, grinning, "if my memory serves me right, I think he said something along the lines of not liking or being interested in anything she had to say, disapproving of the way she behaved towards others, and that he would not marry her if she was the last woman walking the earth, much to Caldwell's chagrin. I don't know what scared him more – the thought of Ed not planning to marry or the ensuing diplomatic incident. For us, though, it was quite a treat.

"Anyway, he continued by saying that the woman he really loves had travelled – no run – far away from him and that she was worth a dozen of Moira, whatever her current circumstances."

Nell felt the heat rising to her cheeks as she registered his meaning.

"But I surmise that, in truth, he may be a tiny bit scared of facing you, Nell, after all that has transpired, and that is why he's given you all the space you've needed."

"I think you should return home with us at the end of the week," suggested Rae, gently.

Nell nodded in agreement with her sister.

"Yes, I had already come to that conclusion myself – it's perhaps time I went home and made a fresh start for the new year."

At the end of a peaceful and enjoyable week with feasting, hunting and dancing, ostensibly to celebrate Rae and Al's betrothal as well as the winter festivities, Nell was packed and ready to return to Erlwick the next day. She went to bed with butterflies of anticipation in her stomach.

Chapter 12

Nell woke to urgent knocking on the door. Yet another rude awakening. As she squinted across the dark room towards the window, she realised it was still night but that the gloom was illuminated by a flickering orange glow. The hammering continued. Nell threw on a gown and opened the door. Falkner and Al materialised before her looking as if they had just flung on clothes too.

"I'm sorry to wake you, Your Majesty," apologised Falkner, unable to shake the habit of addressing her as Queen, "but you need to come and grasp the situation for yourself."

They led her up to the battlements, and surveying the village of Stanholt below, a horrifying scene lay before them. The houses were in flames, and a black mass seemed to be swarming across the burning buildings.

"We've been attacked, invaded once again by our enemies from the north," stated Falkner simply. "We had no idea they'd been massing troops – no idea how they kept them all hidden from our scouts! Sudden and unexpected, this has caught us completely off guard which is why they've managed to make so much progress so quickly. They're surrounding the castle – there's no way out. Our only hope is holding out until help comes.

"We have enough food to withstand a siege for several weeks if we're careful. We just need to keep secure."

Nell peered out in despair at the army before her. Then, circling towards the bailey, she saw the castle grounds were milling with the terrified villagers who had woken and managed to get inside the safety of the curtain wall in time.

"I suspect their timing was deliberate – they knew we would have been more relaxed over the festive season." Al shook his head then added, "We should go back to bed, try to get what sleep we can, because there's not a lot we can do until morning, as long as our sentries are alert to any changes. Lady Eadlyn is already sorting out the villagers."

Nell went back to her room to a fretful sleep. When she awoke again just a few hours later, their situation struck her as even bleaker. This time, she dressed for action.

"It'll take at least a week for help to come!" she moaned.

"Not quite that long. We just need to sit tight," reiterated Falkner confidently.

Yet, as the next couple of days passed, all their concerns grew.

"They're building siege machines!" gasped Nell when she understood that the enemy was felling and gathering trees from the nearby forests.

"We need to think quickly – do something to buy more time," suggested Al.

He and Falkner began to discuss the pros and cons of a foray into the surrounding army. They realised anything they could do to attack and delay the siege machines would help but that any incursion would be heavily outnumbered.

Having noted where the machines were being built, Falkner and Al, with as many men as they could muster from the castle, were ready for a raid as the sun began to sink in the sky and daylight failed. Without the usual resounding blast of horns, the portcullis was raised and the drawbridge lowered rapidly and noiselessly. The reinforced castle company rode out. Immediately, the small force of men was surrounded, and it was obvious that the skirmish attempt had failed; the soldiers had to battle fiercely just to manage a hasty retreat, having made no impact on the machine building process whatsoever.

Worse news followed. As the men withdrew back across the drawbridge under a protective hail of arrows and it was raised once again, it became clear many men were wounded. Al, bringing up the rear to safeguard the last of his men, had also been hurt, revealed by the blood dripping down his leg. Rae was chalk white as she ran to his side in the garrison, where they had set up an improvised hospital for injured villagers and soldiers alike. He smiled weakly at them as Rae started to tend to his cut, cleaning and stitching before binding it. His thigh was badly gashed but he had no intention of sitting idly by, only resting long enough to be treated.

Observing the many injured about her, lying on make-shift beds or propped up against the walls, Nell remembered the infusion and creams she had used on Ed. She immediately set about seeking the herbs and other ingredients required to brew and mix them, knowing that many people would need help to avoid any fever that might endanger their survival. Finding Lady Eadlyn in the kitchens, Nell gave her and the cook the recipes to make up the first batches before revisiting the garrison to give instructions for their use.

Then, leaving Rae to encourage Al into some heavy strapping for his leg and Hope, pale but rallying to organise many of the women to nurse the wounded, Nell wondered back out to the keep in search of Falkner. With night closing fast, there would be nothing much they could do until morning, except tend the wounded and maintain a vigilant watch.

They were still waiting for relief to come.

She was up early, though, and hurried to a tall tower above the gatehouse which gave them commanding views of what was left of the village and the planes below. Standing with the watch guards around a warming brazier, Nell was shocked to see that the siege towers and trebuchets were almost complete; it would only be a matter of time before the enemy began to use them. How could they gain more time until help came?

Then she suddenly saw it: the solution right in front of her. Calling for rags and oil, Nell pulled out some arrows from her quiver and prepared her bow for action. Since the siege was launched, she had kept it constantly by her side, had used it during the failed foray's retreat. Wrapping the arrow tips in rags and soaking them in the oil, she speedily scanned the area for the nearest siege machine. Spotting one directly in line with the drawbridge but still many yards away, Nell sprang to work. She positioned her arrow ready for flight, dipped it in the flaming brazier, and then, with just a fleeting pause for aim, rapidly shot it at the wooden tower. The arrow fell a few feet short but burnt and sizzled in the dewy grass around it.

Without hesitating, Nell loaded a second arrow, lit it in the flames before slightly adjusting her aim, and then sending it promptly arching through the sky. This time she found her target, repeating the process three more times until three arrows had found the dry wood and canvas and hungrily began to devour their prey.

259

With flames blazing into the sky from the burning timbers, Nell rapidly issued orders to the other archers circling the castle's battlements to follow suit before moving onto her own next target. It was not long before Nell and the archers had set alight any machine or tower in range, and many others were being hastily withdrawn to a safe distance. Al and Falkner, hearing the growing commotion, came out to see the morning sky glowing, while dark smoke billowed into huge rolling black clouds.

"Oh, well done, Nell… an excellent idea!" exclaimed Al. "That'll give us a few more days if we can keep the machines at bay, and that should be plenty of time now. I expect to see Ed here before the end of the day anyway."

Al was right. It was when they were preparing a hearty, warming stew from their dwindling supplies as supper for all the current inhabitants of the castle, that they finally heard good news.

Once again proceeding for a view from the tallest tower, Nell, Al and Falkner could see the Torlandian army gathering beyond the village, locking their northern enemy between themselves and the castle.

As Nell scanned the tiny figures closely, Al observed, "I have no doubt that Ed's there, Nell. After what happened to his mother and knowing how he feels about you, nothing would have kept him away."

"I shouldn't think they'll attack tonight, though," mused Falkner, "as it's getting too dark."

"No! And Ed's decent enough even with this rabble to give them the opportunity to leave. He might issue them an ultimatum soon," added Al.

"Well, I suggest we prepare every man who can fight or shoot an arrow and have them on standby," continued Falkner, "ready to join the battle at a moment's notice. It will help a lot if we can squeeze them between ourselves and the King's men."

Hence the men disappeared to survey and organise what troops they had, which guards they could afford to spare from their duties, and villagers willing and able to brandish a weapon. Nell was left with her thoughts. Soft padding on the stone told Nell that someone else had joined her vigil. Peeking over her shoulder, she saw Hope hovering closely behind her. She smiled comfortingly at the girl.

"The King is there and, if he is, so will be Marshall. Don't forget, they'll look out for one another. Two better knights – no, two better men – you couldn't find anywhere."

She clutched Hope's hand and for a few more minutes they both scrutinised the scene below them. Then Nell went to find her sister. Together they spent a nervous night, dozing fitfully or pacing the room fretfully, waiting for the growing light of day in expectation of developments outside.

As dawn broke, Nell was once more up and out early, walking on the battlements and carrying her bow with her to help defend the castle, leaving Hope and Rae to visit and assist in the hospital. Nell watched the Torlandian troops beginning to muster in a thick line before their enemy. Hugging her mantle around her against the early morning chill, Nell fancied she knew which one of the tiny figures must be Ed, and a strong, cold claw clutched her stomach with fear. Peering back into the bailey, she could see Al and Falkner gathering what was left of the castle guard and those villagers they could use, ready to cross the drawbridge.

When she revolved around, Nell could see the Torlandian army gradually creeping forward in a crescent, enveloping their enemy and pushing them back towards the castle walls. Their progress was smooth and steady until they reached the remains of Stanholt. Then the combat launched in earnest but quickly got bogged down as they had to search for the enemy and fight through every building and around each corner. Their advance became painfully sluggish to Nell viewing events on the parapet. She did what she could, shooting at any of the enemy who came within her range.

With the Torlandian army pressing hard and fighting fiercely, Falkner decided it was time to join the fray. He ordered the drawbridge to be lowered once more, and they galloped out to the accompaniment of a rallying horn blast. The enemy was trapped and progressively being squeezed. Nell monitored proceedings as the battle began to fragment and move away, the invaders slowly trying to return north in the direction from whence they came.

A small figure darted forwards, following Falkner's men. While Nell observed from the tower, Hope cowered in a corner of the gatehouse, staring into the swarming mass of fighting soldiers. She cried out as a man, the broken end of a lance piercing his body, staggered backwards across the drawbridge and crumpled in a heap at her feet, eyes glazing over. Terrified, stomach heaving, she was about to run back into the bailey when she gasped, spotting Marshall only a few feet away.

As she stood shocked, still as stone, an enemy sword slashed at Marshall's horse. Shadow reared, sending the squire careering to the ground, then vanished amongst the heaving crowds. While Marshall was raising himself off the ground, a knight all in black and on horseback speared him in the upper arm. Marshall grasped the spear, clenching his teeth as he painfully yanked it from his limb through the chinks in his armour. At the same time, the knight lifted his sword, ready to bring it crashing down on Marshall. Without reflecting,

Hope rushed forward into the melee, picked up a massive stone, and hurled it as hard as she could at the rump of the knight's horse. Screaming in pain, the horse bolted across the battlefield, following Shadow's escape, carrying it's rider away. Clutching his sword in his good arm, Marshall turned to thank his rescuer.

"Hope!" he yelled, horrified to see her there. "Get out of here! Get back into the castle. I want you – no, need you – safe."

Backing steadily, gazing at the fighting soldiers and gathering bodies around her, she was suddenly aware of the intense danger of her situation. Hope nodded, twisted about and ran into the bailey, tears flooding down her face.

Taking advantage of the battle action withdrawing from the castle walls and the drawbridge still down, a small company of the enemy broke free and, almost unnoticed, proceeded for the sanctuary of the castle. A few tenacious guards chased after them as the group advanced for the steps that led directly up to the battlements where Nell had positioned herself, tracking events below.

"Well, well, well… look who we have here! You'll be my ticket to safety."

Stunned, Nell wheeled around, coming face to face with Warwick. As he strode towards her, she shook her head in disbelief at his presence and gradually backed away. Around them, fierce hand-to-hand fighting broke out as the guards had caught up with the small band of the enemy, their own minor confrontation unheeded.

Hurriedly, Warwick grabbed Nell's arm and began wrenching her along the battlements as he briskly searched for a way out, peering from side-to-side. She desperately dragged her feet, trying to delay his bid for freedom, and frantically pawed at his hands where they grasped her wrist, digging her nails into his skin.

Suddenly, impatiently, he swung her out, bent backwards over the sheer drop from the castle wall to the floor of the bailey below, her feet teetering on the edge.

Petrified, she had to think fast.

"Do as I say and you just might live," threatened Warwick in a hiss.

Nell forced her muscles to relax, appearing to swoon, trying to lull Warwick into a false sense of security. Falling for her ruse, he began to draw her in. Abruptly, she pushed her body forwards, letting her weight shove Warwick away. Taken by surprise, he fell backwards, stumbling against the crenulations and dropping his sword with a clunk onto the stone surface.

Promptly, she darted forward, grabbed his sword from where it had landed, and began to inch away, ready to parry an attack from this man she detested.

"I have your sword! Go before I use it!" Nell yelled at him.

"I have your country!" Warwick sneered in petulant retaliation, lunging for her.

Instantly, she struck out, and the blade cut deep into his arm.

Yelping in pain, Warwick pressed his hand to his wound. For a moment he hesitated, deliberating whether it was worth continuing his attack.

Deciding instead to cut his losses, Warwick cried "This is not over yet!" before loping away across the battlements, the retreating villain dripping a trail of blood behind him as he once more abandoned the stage.

Still clutching the sword and panting heavily, rapidly, Nell realised her hands were shaking from her close encounter with Warwick now the urgency of her dilemma was over.

"Nell! Are you hurt?"

She exhaled a long gasp of relief. This time, the surprised voice was friendly. She turned gradually to meet Kaspar.

"No, I'm unharmed," she said, trying to sound convincing and smiling weakly at her friend. Then, seeing his eyes on the blood pooling at her feet from the dripping sword, she quickly continued to reassure him, "It's not mine… I'm not injured. And it's good to see you in one piece."

"We're just finishing up," explained Kaspar. "Most of what's left of the enemy is fleeing but I'd heard Warwick had come up here causing trouble."

"He was – you've just missed him – he went that way," and Nell's finger pointed Kaspar in the direction of the blood trail that continued along the battlements to the next tower.

Kaspar raised a questioning eyebrow at her.

"I cut him… It's… it's… his blood," stuttered Nell.

"Right. I'll try and catch up with him. If he's wounded, Warwick shouldn't be able to get far. See you later!"

Kaspar sped off in Warwick's footsteps, leaving Nell temporarily alone, shaken, on the battlements. Grasping the wall securely to steady herself, she surveyed the events below. Most soldiers had indeed departed, the Torlandians hunting down the retreating men of the North as they fled back across the border. A few troops persisted, though, to search the ruined buildings of the village in case any men were left in hiding.

Suddenly, Nell saw a tall figure she instantly recognised approaching the drawbridge on horseback. She caught her breath as her heart began to flutter. She scrutinised him hard. Reassured, she could not detect any great injuries on Ed this time. Swiftly, her feet barely touching the worn stonework, Nell ran across the walls and down the steps as Ed rode into the bailey. Kaspar was now waiting for him and, while the King dismounted, she caught some of Kaspar's words which floated across the yard towards her.

"I couldn't find him… definitely was here… in a tussle with Nell… vanished completely, like the snake he is… some hole or other then back to Guthway. I don't know how he does it!"

Then both men looked up as they became aware of Nell hurrying across the courtyard.

Without wavering or deliberating, Nell hurled herself at Ed, dropping Warwick's sword with a clatter and flinging her arms tightly about his neck, giving him little choice but to clasp her close in response, temporarily oblivious of the people around them.

"I was so worried about you!" she exclaimed, speaking rapidly in a stream of words directed into his chest, not daring to falter in case she would not have the courage to continue again. "I thought you might have been hurt again. I couldn't imagine not seeing you or speaking to you once more, especially after our last parting. I wanted the chance to say I was sorry, that I misjudged you – again – and that I can't bear to be… to live… without you. I thought you loved her, Princess Moira, and that I would have to leave court… leave you. But now she is gone and, even if you don't feel the same way about me, I must tell you… I love you!"

Only then, with her message complete, did she pause for breath and raise her eyes to his face.

Tired but amused, more than a little surprised and overwhelmed by Nell's sudden, emotional and overt show of affection, Ed lifted Nell slightly off her feet, bringing her up to his own height level and, unabashed by the watching assembly, leant forwards to kiss her on the lips.

Melting against him at his gentle touch, Nell, mesmerised, did not hear the cheers from the crowds around them.

"You never heard all that I had to say that night of the victory celebration," murmured Ed into her ear. "I was, like many, initially bewitched by Moira's beauty, but that did not last, especially once I witnessed her behaviour towards you. That's when I knew how much I cared for you, Nell. It's you I love, and whatever the state of your country, it's you I wish to marry. And it's what your old nurse read in our faces and predicted months ago."

They both laughed in delight, happy that they had finally been open with each other and admitted the truth of their emotions for one another. They kissed once more before Ed glanced up at their friends around them, witnesses to their confessions. He signalled for – and got – another cheer.

Spotting his squire standing close to Nell's lady-in-waiting, one arm hanging loose and wounded, the other with his fingers laced through Hope's, Ed grinned.

"Marshall, you are off duty tonight... you deserve it. Get your girlfriend to patch you up then return to the hall for something to eat. You come too, Hope."

Marshall chuckled with pleasure, but Hope blushed crimson, groaning at the King's words.

"Please don't tease me," she whispered.

"Oh, Hope, I'm laughing because I'm happy! I will do exactly as my lord has requested, and once my arm is fixed, I am going to escort you back to the hall where – wounded or not – I fully intend to dance with you all evening."

Without delaying for a reply, he coiled their fingers tighter and tugged her towards the hospital room.

Grinning after them, Ed turned back to address the crowd.

"We must secure the border quickly and settle extra men in this area to keep it so. Also, Falkner will need a lot of help to rebuild Stanholt. But, in the meantime, with another victory behind us, I want to hasten back to Erlwick, our home. After all, we have a wedding to announce and prepare for. And that's certainly worthy of extra celebrations tonight!"

Arms closely entwined, Nell and Ed proceeded into the castle, with Kaspar, Al, Rae and the others all jostling and joking behind them, full of congratulations despite the events of the day, excited and hopeful for their future and the new year ahead.

About the author

Annette V Hart is a retired primary school teacher who loves reading, drawing and history. Leaving Surrey where she grew up and lurked for many years, she is now living her dream, searching for elves, knights and dragons, from a cute cottage within her ancestral lands of Devon with several cats, some children and a husband.

Printed in Great Britain
by Amazon